SAME TIME, NEW PLAN

KP TURNER

Same Time, New Plan

Copyright © 2022 by Kerrie Turner

All rights reserved.

No part of this book may be reproduced in any form or by any electronic or mechanical means, including information storage and retrieval systems, without written permission from the author, except for the use of brief quotations in a book review or article.

This is a work of fiction. Names, characters, businesses, places, events, locales, and incidents are either the products of the authors imagination or used in a fictitious manner. Any resemblance to actual persons, living or dead, or actual events is purely coincidental.

Edited by Happily Editing Anns

Cover Design by Najla Qamber, Najla Qamber Designs

❀ Created with Vellum

For my best friend, Heidi, without you I never would have allowed myself to dream I could be a writer.

And for my Mom, who is my everything.

1

LAUREN

The backseat erupts in laughter as we pull into the dirt and gravel parking lot at the start of the trailhead. It's been years since the five of us were all together in one spot; nice to see not everything has changed. We used to be close friends, but it's been almost fourteen years since we graduated from college, and life has taken each of us down our own paths and time together has become less frequent.

I close my eyes as I exit my best friend, Eve's, Land Rover. The mid-morning light practically blinds me before I snap my sunglasses into place. I'm used to florescent light bulbs and diffused light through windows, not full-force summer sunlight.

I plaster a smile on my face. The first step in making amends for not meeting someone's or in this case four someones' expectations is to apologize, which I did several times last night when I arrived at the cabin late for our girls' weekend. Step two is to let them have their say, which they did last night, and without holding back. And step three, do whatever they ask without complaint, at least for this weekend.

So, here I am about to do one of my least favorite activities—hiking. Admittedly, the blue sky and white puffy clouds are beautiful. They look so perfect they could be from a painting in Eve's gallery, which is where I would prefer to see them, in a nice air-conditioned space, along with a glass of wine in my hand.

Positive attitude—I will have a positive attitude, I repeat to myself.

"Grab a water bottle," Eve announces in her cruise director voice. Her short blonde hair sticks out of a headband that matches her yoga pants and form fitting T-shirt. How can she be stylish even out in the middle of nowhere?

"On it!" Austin chimes and jogs to the back of the Land Rover and opens the hatch. Austin has her red hair pulled into a high ponytail and is sporting a Bobcats T-shirt. She owns more T-shirts than my husband owns ties, and he has a whole wall in our closet just for ties.

My other college friends Izzy and Gabby take their water bottles and walk toward the sign at the start of the trail. I read the words aloud as Austin and Eve join us. The plaque was originally bronze, but now it is a greenish grey and I have to get close to read the words.

Gods of the Waterfall
In years past villagers would bring offerings to the waterfall in hopes of eliciting the gods' guidance as to the path they should take.
Legend states that the gods of the waterfall
judge your heart and whisper in the ears of those found to be worthy.

"We didn't bring an offering. Now I'll never know if I'm worthy." Austin's laugh fills the air as she nudges my shoulder.

"Come on, let's get going. The light should be perfect," Eve's voice carries from the back of our little group.

I lead the pack. The sooner we get this over with the sooner I can take a shower.

The path starts with six makeshift stairs made out of dirt and railroad ties and a sharp right that widens into a flat dirt-covered area. In the corner sits an old woman selling jewelry and trinkets at a small folding table, like the ones my great grandparents used to pull out at parties for the kids to sit at.

Why would she pick this place? This location is terrible —no visibility from the road, low foot traffic, and hikers who don't always have cash.

Her whole face lights up as we approach; large brown eyes seem to dance with joy as she smiles at each of us. She stands, adjusts her long grey braid so it falls over her left shoulder, and runs her weathered hands down her white dress. The dress looks handmade and well-worn, but also beautiful with intricate red-and-yellow flowers at the bottom.

"Good morning," I greet her as we reach her table.

The woman claps her hands together in excitement. "Welcome, ladies. I'm glad to see you out enjoying this beautiful morning."

"We are," Eve says as she examines each piece. "Your jewelry's exquisite. Did you make these yourself?"

"Indeed, I did." The woman's voice is smooth and sweet like a spoonful of honey.

My fingers brush over several necklaces and rings, landing on a bracelet made of wire and stones. There are five almost identical bracelets with copper wire and five stones ranging from a dark blue sapphire color to a barely translucent pink.

A small token to remember our weekend by might help me be forgiven a little faster. "How much for all five?"

"Twenty dollars." The old woman's smile grows so large it's as big as a galaxy unto itself.

Obviously, sales have been slow if she's willing to take so little for the bracelets.

Location. Location. Location.

I never leave home without my driver's license, credit card, and some cash. You never know what's going to happen, even on a hike in a state park.

I hand her a fifty and wave off her offer of change. The bracelets are worth more than four dollars each.

I place the first bracelet in Austin's hand and receive an eye roll. She sees through my nice gesture.

"So we don't forget this trip." I keep my voice light while I glare at her. She examines the bracelet and gives me a wink. At least one person is on my side this weekend.

"And we take a little bit of this morning's beauty home with us," I say to the group as I hand out the rest of the bracelets and then pull mine on.

The light plays off of the copper and stone cuffs as we twirl them in the light.

"Thank you." I gaze at the woman's lined face.

She stands and practically bounces around the table. She is agile for such an old woman; I'll give her that. When she's next to me, she pulls my hand into hers, turning my palm up and placing something warm inside.

"Take this to the base of the falls and throw it in. The gods will appreciate the offering." Her smile is warm, and I'm not sure why, but I feel lighter once the stone is in my hands—like I can take a deep breath for the first time since I arrived at the cabin.

I shake off my thoughts and open my hand to find a dark grey river rock. My finger traces the images etched onto the otherwise smooth rock. On one side is carved two crossed arrows, and the other side shows a bear's pawprint. "What do the symbols mean?"

The girls turn to the woman, and we form a loose circle around her. She walks to Eve and places a similar stone in her hand. "The arrows represent the bond of friendship, and the bear paw shows your path."

"How do you find the right path?" Eve's voice cracks.

The woman turns and pats her hand but addresses the group. "Oh, the path is always there. It can be as easy as turning your head. Other times you have to find yourself first or be willing to look past the pain. Sometimes you have to take a chance or find a way to believe in yourself so others can too. And sometimes," she pauses and turns her gaze to Eve, "sometimes you have to free the ones you love to go down their own path and trust that it will lead back to you."

"What if it's too late for that?" Eve's words are barely more than a whisper.

What's Eve talking about? Her eyes stay focused on the woman as she holds her hand and closes the rock in her fingers.

"Oh, it's never too late," the woman croons.

She gives Eve's hand one more squeeze before releasing it and then walks to each of my friends, handing them a stone and speaking to them. Her words are too low for me to hear, but when she's done, they all nod and close their hands tightly around their stones.

"Take your offering and ask the gods for help."

Eve pulls her in for a hug. The old woman whispers something into her ear. Eve steps back and nods.

"Now, find your new path." She steps back off the trail.

I thank the woman one last time and turn to join my friends on the trail. She touches my arm as I walk by and whispers, "Or stay on the old one. It's your choice."

"What?" I turn back, but she has already turned back to the table. I must be hearing things.

No one speaks as we start the hike.

I don't need a new path. I have a great life. I'm happy, despite the concerns that Eve voiced last night that I'm not. I realize she was mad that I was late and felt the need to express her disappointment, but saying I was unhappy came out of left field. Of course, I'm happy. I have a steady job, a house, money in the bank, and Matthew. The path I chose has served me well. What else would I need to make me happy? I mean Matthew and I aren't one of those sappy true-love couples Gabby reads about in her favorite romance novels, but we're an unstoppable team, which is much better. When I get back, I'll start my new job as VP of Business Development, and I will have a whole new set of responsibilities that will increase my visibility to the executive team. And Matthew has been a supporter of all my goals, just like I am his. Eve's wrong. How could life be better than getting exactly what you planned?

My foot slips on a rock, and Eve grabs my arm to keep me from falling. Everyone stops and turns to look at me.

"So maybe instead of dwelling on paths not taken, we should pay attention to the one we're on," Austin chimes in, breaking the silence.

Laughter fills the air. And one by one I see everyone pull out of their own thoughts and back to the present. Austin pauses in front of me and gives me a small smile.

She is the best at breaking up an awkward silence.

I slow my pace and wait for Eve to catch up, allowing a little space between us and the rest of the group.

"I really am sorry I was late. It was unavoidable, but...I am sorry. Are we okay?" I ask.

She keeps her eyes straight ahead and her voice flat. "Let's get through this weekend and then we can talk."

Eve's always had a way of keeping things bottled up tight until she explodes like a volcano, spewing out all the words and feelings she's been pushing down. She hit me with what we call a Hard Truth ten minutes after walking in the door last night. Hard Truths started back in college as a way for us to be honest with each other without hurting someone's feelings. When one of us needs to tell the other something they may not want to hear, we call a Hard Truth and lay out the facts. The other person has to listen without comment and actually take time to think about it, not say "yeah" and move on. The point is to consider the possibility that you could be wrong and that maybe you have blinders on.

I do not have blinders on about my life, but I obeyed the rules and listened to all Eve's complaints about my being too busy for my friends, working too much, only caring about myself, and that all of my success at work has made me unhappy. Which is not true. I mean, yes, I do work ten-hour days and usually most weekends, but I love my job and I'm not selfish or unhappy. I'm so happy to be here I even paid for the cabin this weekend and worked late all week so that I could be here as requested—all for my friends. Now if Eve will stop scowling at me, I can have a good time, but even after the Hard Truth, she's still got something bubbling hot just under the surface.

"Eve, what's wrong?"

She shrugs. "I'm fine."

Clearly, she is not fine. Eve is the life of the party. She is the sun that we all revolve around, but right now she is more like poor demoted Pluto who can barely see the light from the sun.

I nudge her arm. "What's going on?"

"Nothing."

"You can't lie to me. What was all that about being too late?"

"It's a long story, and now isn't the time to discuss it." Eve's tone is meant to stop my questions, but it only spurs me on.

"Give me the Cliffs Notes version for now."

She looks down the path at the girls walking and chatting ahead of us. "Listen, just because you decided to show up this weekend doesn't mean you get to pretend to be my best friend again. You don't get to pick and choose when to care about what's going on in my life."

My chest tightens. "I'm not pretending. I heard you last night. Give me the opportunity to digest everything you said before you write me off. Let me at least try and be here for you. There's obviously something going on. I'm here now, and you know I care about you."

She looks straight ahead and says as emotionless as if she's telling me her coffee order. "Ollie and I are getting a divorce."

My feet stop moving.

My lungs stop expanding.

My heart stops beating.

"What?" I force my lungs to breathe out.

My mind spins like a tornado. Eve and Ollie are the true-love type, always with a kiss or a smile or a knowing glance. They have been inseparable since the moment they started dating back in college. I don't understand.

Eve pulls me forward, but my world's spinning.

"I didn't want to tell you like this, but things have been bad for a while." Her voice cracks at the end, confirming she isn't a robot.

"I don't know what to say. Are you okay?"

Is Ollie okay?

The world without Eve and Ollie is not okay.

"I don't know, but for now can we keep this between us? I'll tell the girls on the last night. I don't want to ruin the trip." Her back goes straight, and she marches us forward.

"It wouldn't ruin the trip. We all care about you. What happened?"

"I don't want to talk about it right now." Her words match her eyes—stern.

But in order to fix this I need to gather information. I need to know what happened. I need to understand the root cause.

Before I can say more, Eve drops my arm and runs to catch up with Austin and yells to the group, "Now to a topic more suited for walking down a steep hill. Should we or shouldn't we swim in the pond at the base of the waterfall?"

How can she tell me she's getting a divorce and then ask about going swimming? She's hiding her feelings too well. I guess she's had a lot of practice because I sure didn't see this coming.

"We didn't bring suits," Gabriella calls from the front of the pack, walking beside Izzy.

"Oh, it's only us girls. No suits needed," Eve says as she tips her head back and laughs.

The weight of all the lunches and dinners I canceled over the last few years makes my legs feel like lead. My heart sinks, but I can't fix this right now. I need to stay in the moment. I need to be here for my friend, and if she doesn't want to talk yet, then I will honor that.

But we will fix this.

"I'm not sure you're ready for all this," Gabriella calls, waving her hands over her ample body.

"Well, someone should see you naked at least once," Izzy teases.

"Thanks." Gabby scowls at her. The subject of Gabriella's sex life or lack thereof is not something she likes to joke about.

We all tense for a moment and then Austin pipes in with, "I think Eve really wants to know once and for all if I'm a natural redhead."

Izzy laughs so hard she snorts, which leads the rest of us to cackle. Austin always knows how to break the tension, which is why she is the glue that holds us together.

I watch as they walk toward the bend in the path and disappear around the corner.

"What are you smiling about?" Austin asks, having slowed down to let me catch up.

"I was just thinking about how much I've missed this—us all being together—and when we get home, I need to put together a plan to keep us in touch."

Groans echo against the rocks as we turn the corner.

"What?" Is everything I say wrong? I got a lecture last night about not prioritizing my relationships, and when I try just that I'm still in trouble.

"A plan? You can't plan everything," Eve says.

"Why not?"

"Friendship isn't something you plan. It should be organic, not scheduled visits that become obligations." Austin shakes her head like I've lost my mind.

Gabriella throws her arms out wide as if speaking to the

universe. "Sometimes you have to be spontaneous and go where life leads you."

Austin cocks her head to the side. "Who are you talking about, Ms. Never made a spontaneous decision in her life?"

"I have too. I...I took that job in marketing in Atlanta instead of staying in Nashville."

Austin refutes her claims. "How was that spontaneous? You were a marketing major, and your aunt lives in Atlanta,"

Gabby covers her heart with her hand, acting offended. "It was a job in creative when I was planning to work on the analytical side."

Izzy stops and looks at Gabby. "If you had taken the hot guy on the phone up on his offer to see his band play, that would have been spontaneous."

We all stop and watch as Gabby's face turns the color of hot embers in a roaring fire.

Eve's eyes open wide. "Um...When did I miss this?"

"It was a long time ago, and I didn't mention it cause it was nothing." Gabby's words are directed at Izzy. Oh, it must have been something, and Izzy should have kept that locked in the vault. They have been inseparable since they shared a dorm room freshman year, and some secrets are for best friends only.

Izzy keeps pushing Gabby's buttons, thinking she's funny. "Nothing, huh? You flirted with him on the phone every week for months."

"It was nothing!" Gabby's eyes flash at Izzy like Bruce Banner's before he becomes the Hulk.

"Girls...Girls..." I put myself directly between them. "We are—"

"Not now, Mama Hen." Izzy pulls Gabriella off to the side of the path, and the two exchange words while the rest of us continue our descent to the waterfall. I guess Eve and I aren't the only friends with some pent-up tension.

Best to give them a minute.

We turn a corner, and there is the waterfall.

Breathtaking.

Lush green leaves surround the falls on both sides, and the water plunges almost four stories into a small pond surrounded by rocks. The splashing into the pond sends waves of calm over me.

"Wow," Austin says, stepping beside me. "I see why the guidebook called this one of the seven wonders of Tennessee."

We stand in silence for a few minutes, watching the beauty of nature and turning to smile at each other. I catch Eve's eye and silently apologize for being a crappy friend. She gives me a slight nod and wipes a tear.

Austin pulls the carved rock from her pocket. "Well, shall we see if the gods are in today?"

We each pull out our smooth rock. I run my hands over the carving before raising it in the air. "To friendship and lives well lived. I love you girls."

"To friendship and lives well lived." We repeat the mantra and knock our rocks together.

"May the odds be on your side…or wait, what's the line?" Izzy chuckles.

"Are we going one at a time or all together?" Austin asks.

"Together," Eve declares. Eve has always been the most decisive of the bunch. "On the count of three. One. Two. Three."

I close my eyes and throw the stone. *Help me fix…*

The stone splashes into the water, and a searing white-hot pain invades my head. My hands go to my eyes, and I scream as images flash through my mind too fast for me to comprehend. I reach out to one of the girls, trying to steady myself, and instead I find something cold and hard. The pain subsides as fast as it started. My eyes flick open, and I stare at my hand pressed against a refrigerator.

What the hell?

2

BEN

I stand and stretch easing some of the pain in my neck. How do people put up with jobs that involve sitting all day? Don't they realize that our bodies are meant to move? Two hours of being stuck behind my uncle's desk—I mean my desk—and I've made little progress. There are piles of paper everywhere, and the filing cabinet's overflowing. Apparently, my uncle hoarded receipts and paperwork like some people hoard toilet paper.

Resuming my seat, I reach for an antacid. One month in and I've already started on an ulcer. At this rate I may not make it to thirty. Hell, Uncle Anthony only made it to fifty-three. My stomach clenches. He might have made it longer if Dad had been around to help him, but we'll never know.

I lean back and stretch, looking up at the wall of postcards. He kept them all. Every last one I sent, from everywhere I've lived over the past seven years. Tears well in my eyes.

No time for that. I need to figure out what to do. Keep

the place and be like my father and uncle—dying young having never seen or done anything outside this bar—or sell it and spend my life seeing the world while letting their dream die. My chest burns merely thinking it.

My phone rings, saving me from thinking more on my choices.

"What's up, Dex?" Dex was my uncle's right-hand man and is helping me keep this place going.

"Hey, Ollie's here. Can I send him up?"

"Sure."

Ollie's been in here before. He knows it's a mess. I stand and remove a pile of papers from the chair across from the desk. What's this pile? I went through it yesterday. Shit. Maybe I'm not any better at managing paperwork than Uncle Anthony was.

Ollie walks through the door in his usual well-worn jeans, black T-shirt and boots. His head swivels from side to side taking in the paper city I've created. "What the hell happened in here?"

"Turns out my uncle left me this lovely collection of paper. He was always so thoughtful."

"I'm sure he meant to color code it for you," Ollie laughs.

"Yeah, I'm sure he did. But I think he thought he had a few more years to do it. Which it might actually take to see the floor again."

"What can I do to help?" Ollie's a good guy. He and my uncle became friends over the years as Ollie and his band play here a few nights a month. We usually kick back and have a few beers after the bar closes when I'm in town.

"Did you happen to bring a lighter and a large trash bin to burn all this?" If only it was that easy, then I could be standing at the base of a mountain, nothing but my gear and wide-open space to explore instead of being surrounded by four walls and mountains of paper.

He pats his pants pocket. "Nope, must have left it in my other pants." We sit across the desk from each other. He props his foot on his opposite leg and taps his boot with his fingers. "Now, seriously, what's going on and how can I help?"

My thoughts bounce around my brain like lightning bugs caught in a jar. I need to clear my head, take a hike, and go somewhere where someone doesn't need me to solve their problems for five minutes.

"I'm serious. How can I help?" Ollie asks again.

Focus.

My fingers massage my temple. "I don't even know. I'm simply trying to get through this week and keep everyone paid."

"Cash flow problems?" He places both feet back on the floor and leans toward me.

I don't mean to dump my problems on him, but I have no one else to talk to. I can't tell the employees how bad it is, and truthfully, I don't have any friends left in town that would understand. "I think we can skate by, but…"

"But?"

My elbows hit the desk, and I lean forward and lower my voice, "But…from what I've seen so far, my uncle has had a few tough years. Sales seem to have slowed significantly since last summer. This place is off the beaten path, and with all the new bars opening on Broadway, I don't think he could compete."

"Business seemed steady but not packed on the Saturday nights we played here, but I didn't make it in much during the week. What's Dex say?"

Dex has been working here for the last four years. He

started out as a dishwasher and busboy because he was underage, but since he turned twenty-one, he's been running the bar.

I run my fingers through my hair. "He told me the weekday business has been slow for a while now."

Ollie's face falls. "Shit. So, what's your plan? Sell the place? Keep it going?"

The thought of selling my dad and uncle's baby makes me reach for another antacid. But damn if I know how to run a business.

"For now, I'm going to keep it going until I can figure out what the best option is."

Ollie looks around the room. "Does that mean you're staying in town for a while?"

"At least until I figure out this mess. Problem is, I have no idea what to do. I've worked as a bartender, ski instructor, hell, I could probably build you a house, but all this business crap...I'm learning as I go here." I lean back, letting my head hit the top of the leather chair.

"Hmmm." Ollie strums his fingers on the arm of the chair.

"You got an idea? If it's to burn the place down, I already had that one."

"I may know someone who can help."

"Is this person a magician? Can they make all of this"—I run my hand over the piles of paper on my desk—"disappear?"

He chuckles before standing. "I gotta run and get the rest of my gear before the gig tonight." He bolts out the door like a man on a mission.

I hope this someone is a lifeguard. I need one to keep me from drowning.

LAUREN

The pounding in my head fades, and I take in my surroundings. I'm in a kitchen, but not my kitchen. My kitchen has marble countertops and beautiful black cabinets and a herringbone pattern floor that took three weeks to install.

"Wait?" I turn in a circle and pick up a blue juice glass with a chip at the bottom. "What the hell?" I turn in a circle. I'm standing in the middle of my old house. How is this possible?

There's a ringing sound I can't seem to pinpoint.

Are my ears ringing? I put my hands over them, and the ringing is muted but doesn't stop.

I shuffle through a stack of papers and find an old cell phone. It feels heavy in my hand, and the cover is blue. My cover is white, and my phone is much thinner and... Whose phone is this?

Eve's name is on the screen, and relief washes over me like a kid running through a sprinkler on a hot day. Whatever this is, Eve is here too. We can figure this out.

"Eve, I'm so—"

"Why didn't you answer?" Eve's voice is loud and demanding. She must still be pissed at me.

"What?"

"Why didn't you answer your phone? I called you three times."

"Are you yelling at me?" Moments ago, I showed up in my kitchen. Why is she yelling at me?

"Not unless you aren't dressed."

I look down. I'm dressed—dark jeans, silver tank, and my favorite black boots. I lift my heel. Wait. I threw these away three years ago when I broke the heel walking up the front steps at my new house.

I must be dreaming. Did I fall and hit my head?

"Lauren. Are. You. Dressed?" Eve demands.

"Dressed for what?" I answer automatically. Why is Eve asking what I'm wearing? Shouldn't she be asking how we got here? Unless...unless she doesn't remember.

"Ollie's band is playing, remember? You promised you would go. Don't tell me you have to back out for work."

"Well...I'm dressed for that." I glance down at my outfit. Eve doesn't pick up on the confusion in my voice.

"Good, I'll pick you up in ten."

"But..." The line goes dead. What is going on? This is my old house, the cute little two-bedroom on Twelfth. I sold it, like, seven years ago after Matthew and I got married. And Ollie isn't in a band anymore, and if they're getting a divorce why would Eve want me to go and see his band play? I run my hands over my temple; at least the pounding is gone.

This has to be a dream. Maybe I'll wake up soon.

I steady myself on the island and stare at my hands. There's no wedding ring, not even an indentation of where it should be. My knees buckle and I sink onto the barstool.

Maybe I fell at the waterfall, and I'm in a coma.

But everything feels so real.

This is definitely my old house. My purse is hanging on the back of the chair where I always put it, and my laptop and piles of files are on the table. I obviously live here. Maybe I'm asking the wrong question. Maybe the question is...when am I?

An open cable bill sits in front of me. I take a deep breath before picking it up to check the date.

That can't be right. "Ten years?" I can't actually be ten years in the past. Can I? Maybe I need to go to sleep. Once I wake up it will be fine. It's just a dream. Or maybe I'm having a psychotic breakdown.

On autopilot, I walk to the mirror in the hall. The same face stares back at me, except now I have on my smoky eye makeup, a few less wrinkles, and bangs. I haven't had bangs in years. I sweep them to the side.

"Maybe I should do bangs again. I look...younger."

The knocking at the door pulls me out of my examination. Eve is standing on the other side when I open it. Her hair is longer than it was just...a minute ago...or will be in ten years...And the pain in her face is gone.

She gives my outfit the once-over and nods her approval. My heart contracts. It's been too long since I've seen that look in her eyes.

"We have to leave now. Grab your purse. We're already late, and Ollie is gonna be pissed if he doesn't get a chance to talk to you. He needs a favor."

Ollie? Eve is still with Ollie. Maybe I like this dream. Maybe I can take a moment to enjoy it. I'll analyze it tomorrow when I wake up.

We arrive at Grayson Brothers' Bar without much of a chance to talk. Eve's phone rang the moment we got in the car, and she spent the entire drive talking to one of the buyers at the art gallery she manages. The conversation feels familiar; some guy bought a painting and wants to return it because the color scheme doesn't match his living room like he thought it would. Maybe this is part dream and part memory, or maybe I really am in a coma.

We park in the lot across from the bar. I've been here a few times before. I remember Ollie's band used to play here every once in a while. Oh wait...my eyes scan the building. This place closed years ago after the owner died.

"Ollie is very excited about tonight." Eve interrupts my thoughts.

I glance around the bar looking for signs of a special event. "What's special about tonight?"

"I thought I told you one of the record execs from Argon is supposed to stop by."

I've heard this one before. They usually don't actually stop by, or else aren't interested, or are plain unprofessional.

"He says this one is for real." We exchange a glance and tip our heads back laughing.

"Maybe tonight is his lucky night," I say, feeling a sense of déjà vu. If this is a memory, the guy shows, listens to one song, and leaves, never to be heard from again.

My eyes adjust to the dim light as we make our way into the bar and toward the stage. This place is like the magic tent in Harry Potter, larger on the inside than it looks. There are enormous floor-to-ceiling windows on the front corner and down one side, while the rest of the walls showcase the original brick. The music from the band bounces off the high wood ceilings like a physical assault.

Ollie and his band, Rusted Heart, are onstage performing one of his band's original songs. I know all the words and know more about country music than most fans. Ollie and I became instant friends in college after I knocked him down and spilt his coffee. His coffee order was exactly like mine then, black two sugars, so I knew we would be friends. He's a walking encyclopedia of knowledge, which means I know things whether I like it or not. Through him I've met my fair share of up-and-coming artists, some of whom even went on to make it big. I used to think that one day Ollie might make it, but he never set clear goals. Somewhere along the way he changed his mind and now he's still managing the motorcycle shop, but at least the money is steady.

Eve grabs my arm and pulls me toward the stage. The place is somewhat busy, but there are still a lot of open tables scattered around. We stop at the wives and girlfriends table to the right of the stage. I'm neither. I could never date a musician. It would make me crazy never knowing where they will be each week or how much money they would make. I don't know how Eve stands it. Oh, maybe that's what caused the riff between them?

The band announces they are taking a short break, and they filter down to the table. Ollie gives Eve a big kiss.

She pushes his hug away. "You are so sweaty."

"I thought you liked when I was sweaty?" He winks and runs his hands through his short dirty-blond hair, causing it to stick up at all angles.

"Not when I'm wearing silk." She laughs.

He releases Eve and turns to me. "You wearing silk or can I hug you, stranger?" His eyes narrow, daring me to answer yes.

A shiver of familiarity runs down my spine. I remember this exact conversation. My voice is thick as I respond. "A hug would be great."

Eve didn't lie about him being sweaty, but I pull him close, his arms wrapping me up tight. It's been too long since I've seen him, let alone hugged him.

This is a good dream- or maybe it's a memory?

He releases me and pauses to study my face. He gives me a questioning look, and I deflect his question with a smile.

"Good to see you," he says.

It's good to see him too. I haven't seen him this excited in years, certainly not since he quit performing. How do I look him in the eye knowing he and Eve are getting a divorce?

Forget that this is a dream and I should enjoy seeing him this happy.

"You too. The band sounds fantastic," I say, keeping the conversation on his music.

He leans in close. "Good, there's a guy from a major label coming tonight. I haven't told the guys. I don't want them to get nervous."

"Good idea," I whisper.

"Hey, I need you to do me a favor."

"Anything for you, Ollie." And I mean it. I would do anything for him. Especially if it helps him and Eve find a better solution than divorce.

"Great, my friend Anthony who owned this bar passed away a few weeks ago, and his nephew is taking over."

Oh, this really is a memory. My gut clenches remembering his face when he found out I didn't help this guy out.

"He's a good guy, but I think he's in over his head. Anthony knew how to run the front of the house, but I'm not sure he understood any of the actual business stuff. I think his brother handled that part, but he died a few years back in a car accident. Can you help? Maybe have a look at the books? Give him some advice?"

I promised last time I would call the guy but then I got a new client and got buried at work and never got around to it. Ollie never let me forget it. Every time we drove past this place and saw the sub shop that replaced it, he would remind me it was my fault Grayson Brothers' was gone. Ollie never got over it.

Maybe I should have met with the guy and given him some other options, but unlike my dad, I didn't deviate from my goals and that is how I have manifested the life I always planned. Sometimes that meant I couldn't help out a friend of a friend, but this is a dream, after all, so I can have it all.

I smile brightly. "Sure. I can give him a call next week."

"Really? That easy?" Ollie's face contorts in confusion like I asked him to list pi out to ten digits.

"Of course," I reassure him.

He hugs me again. We chat for a while, in which I agree to meet with the owner on Wednesday. Apparently, today is Friday and Ollie wanted to give me a day or two to arrange my schedule. I agree to everything he asks. Why not? Tonight, I get to fix an old wound between the two of us. Even if it's only in my head.

"Anyone need a drink? I'm going to the bar." The waitress came by once but hasn't been seen for a while, and I need a drink to get me through the rest of this dream.

Eve tilts her glass. Vodka tonic it is.

It's ten p.m. and I easily find a seat at the bar. No wonder this guy needs my help.

A baby-faced boy who looks barely old enough to drive let alone serve drinks walks my way.

"What can I get you, ma'am?"

Really? Ma'am? This is my dream and I'm only...what...twenty-five? Shouldn't he be calling me miss or honey or babe? I hold in my chuckle at the thought of this kid calling me babe.

"Do you have any Glenlivet?" I ask, resisting the urge to smirk as he looks me over, the confusion that I didn't order a Cosmo written all over his face.

"All we have is the twenty-five-year-old, and it's fifty dollars a glass." His skeptical tone makes me smile. I love that people always underestimate me, even bartenders. My boss is an Ivy League snob, so I've had to work harder than everyone else at my firm to prove myself. Surprising her is my favorite thing.

"Fine." I reach in my purse and pull out my emergency hundred and set it on the table in front of him.

His eyes grow wide. "Coming up. Give me a minute; it's in the back."

"That's fine." My attention shifts to the other patrons. The few that remain are either up front watching the band or huddled in groups at the tables. Where did everyone go?

I turn my head to see the bartender pouring drinks and flirting with my missing waitress at the opposite end of the bar. What about my whiskey? I catch his eye, and he motions toward the swinging door. Oh, maybe he's too young to handle the good stuff.

The door doesn't move. It doesn't even swing a little in the breeze. Come on. I could use a drink right now. This feels too real.

What if I really was pulled back in time? I shake my head and laugh a little at myself. It's not possible, but I suppose it's fun to think about.

What would I do different? I would totally invest in all those stocks Matthew's always talking up at parties. I could be rich quick with my stock knowledge. I could even go to Vegas and make a few sports bets. I probably know the winner of every major sporting event for the last seven if not ten years. I could…

A glass of amber liquid slides next to my hand, pulling me from my thoughts. "One Glenlivet for the lady." A warm, deep voice vibrates along my spine. I pause. Definitely not the voice of the boy bartender. Nor is the large, tanned hand resting on the bar close to me. My gaze makes its way up the long muscular forearm to a dark grey-and-red flannel shirt covering strong shoulders and then lands on a pair of blue-grey eyes that remind me of the sky before a storm. A smile forms on my lips as I take in the rest of the man standing before me.

Well, hello. Where did this guy come from?

As if I'm hit by a solar flare, my whole body heats in an instant. "Thanks." My voice trembles.

He smiles back and places his other hand on the bar, giving me his full attention. Damn, I need a drink to put out the fire in my veins, but as I reach for my glass, he slides it back his way.

"I'll need to see some ID first." His face is unreadable.

Seriously? I ordered a twenty-five-year-old whiskey, and he thinks I'm underage. I cock my head to the side. "Really?"

His eyes narrow on me, and he leans a hair closer. "It's the law."

"Fine." I roll my eyes, but he doesn't move a muscle, not even a blink. Easing back in my chair to avoid contact, I pull out my license and present it to him with what my brother always called "the stink eye." He takes it from my hand and looks at the picture and then at me. This guy is too much; does he think I'm using a fake ID too?

I reach over his arm and pick up the glass and salute him with it as I let the smell of the whiskey hit my nose before I tip it back. The amber liquid slides down my throat. A slight smell of citrus mixed with the taste of a sweet caramel apple relaxes me. My eyes close as the whiskey warms my chest. I can almost feel Matthew's arms wrapped around me, laughing and handing me his glass so I could have a sip of his favorite drink. One he only had on special occasions, and one he always shared with me—at least until we had enough money to get two. I sigh. It's been a long time since we shared a drink alone, or a long lingering kiss, or a night of celebration in bed. Ugh. This is my dream, and I will not ruin it with reality.

I set the drink down and see the bartender hasn't moved. His eyes flicker over my ID one last time before he hands it back.

"Good?" His deep-set eyes fix on mine.

"As always."

"Anything else I can get you?" His voice is professional, the heat in his eyes not so much.

My eyes lock with his, and for a moment I feel like I've seen that look before, that those eyes have locked with mine. More memories?

Before I can think about where I might have met him, my attention shifts to the sound of a familiar laugh.

Matthew?

My head swivels toward the sound, and I lean back in my chair. It is Matthew. He's next to a pillar about two tables over with his back to me, but I would know him anywhere.

This memory is getting weirder by the minute. My mouth goes dry, and my back straightens as I strain to see him. His head turns, giving me a view of his profile. Well, now I know this is a dream. Matthew wasn't here last time, and neither was the hot bartender.

Matthew's waving his hands, probably telling a story about how he helped someone double their money in a matter of months or how he saw the sharp decline in the market coming before anyone else. I've heard them all, more than once. I'm pretty sure I could tell them myself.

His hair is longer than I remember ever seeing it. He turns to the girl next to him and gives her an easy smile as she sets her hand on his thigh. Why is she putting her hands on my husband? I start to slide off the barstool when I remember that this is a dream. A weird one where I've magically traveled back in time and I'm not currently married, nor have I even met Matthew.

I shake my head and take a breath, letting my heart resume its normal rhythm. I must have really hit my head hard.

"You know the birthday boy over there?"

"Who?" I turn back to see the bartender nodding in Matthew's direction.

"The guy you were staring at."

It's Matthew's birthday? That means we meet only a few months from now. He did have a girlfriend before we met. When did he break up with her? I can't remember. He always said we met at exactly the right moment. That he had to make some big life decisions and that my coming along when I did was like fate giving him a nudge on which path to take.

I concentrate on the drink in my hand and not that Matthew is twenty feet away. I can't deal with him right now. The last time I saw him, he waved to me as he ran out of the house, late for a breakfast meeting with a new client. He didn't even have time to kiss me or thank me for going to the party with him, but he did have time to remind me to be home on Sunday before five to go to his parents' for dinner. He hates going to his parents' house and especially hates going alone.

Ugh. No more thoughts of the real world. Reality can wait until I wake up.

It's been a long time since a bartender flirted with me. I'm going to enjoy this while it lasts.

"Old friend," I offer as an answer. The bartender's smile fades a bit, no doubt sensing my lie.

"Too bad," he says, more to himself than to me.

"Too bad?" I push gently.

"I was thinking it's too bad you have friends to hang out with tonight." Oh, I like his honesty. I take a moment to fully take in the man standing in front of me. He's tall, with a long, lean torso, a dark brown beard to match a thick head of hair, and his hair is long enough to get your fingers tangled in. His face looks to be chiseled from stone with a perfect jaw line. And those eyes—eyes that draw you closer in hopes you might see how many colors there truly are. Hmmm.

"Oh really, and why is that?" I say, sheepishly daring him to say it, but he's on to my game and gives me a sexy smile. Then he leans in close, close enough I can smell tequila and sweat and a hint of aftershave. I take a slow deep breath, both to smell him deeper and because if I move an inch we would touch.

"Because I would like to spend some time alone with you when I'm done here." He pulls back, but his lips graze my ear. A shiver runs down my body and my breath hitches. Damn, this is a good dream—a hot guy with perfect comebacks, and I'm showing no signs of wrinkles or sagging.

I mean if one whisper of a touch does that, what would kissing him be like or... A river of lava flows through me. Matthew is literally twenty feet away, and even in this probable coma-induced dream, that feels a bit much.

"Too bad I can't stay that long or I might be tempted by your offer," I say, trying to sound casual.

He laughs, not what I expected. A smooth comeback, yes. A laugh, no. I raise my eyebrow in confusion.

"Sorry, but you don't act twenty-five." He chuckles, sending a jolt down my body. And his million-watt smile might be better than his sexy smolder.

"And what would a twenty-five-year-old say?" I bait him.

"Probably something about my being too direct."

I beckon him closer again with my finger. He leans his tall frame over the bar with ease.

"Physical age and maturity are not the same. My body may be twenty-five, but my mind is that of a girl who's lived a long life and knows what she likes. Plus," I add as I get within a breath of his lips, "I'm a girl who knows what she wants and goes after it. No games needed." His body stiffens, and he takes his time straightening back to full height. I surprised him again. I forgot how much fun flirting is.

His heavy brow furrows tighter as if trying to figure out some insane math equation before allowing his lips to form a sexy grin.

"Tell me one thing," I say.

"Anything." He cocks his head to the side and lifts his eyes to mine. Boy, he looks good when he does that.

"Are you wearing skinny jeans?" The question may be silly, but after all these years I still can't take a man seriously who wears skinny jeans, has a man bun, or is into Ultimate Frisbee. Those are my deal breakers.

The confused look on his face answers my question. "What?"

"You know, skinny jeans. Men try and squeeze into very tight jeans that show off their package and taper down at the leg." I pause to shake the thought out of my mind. "Skinny jeans are often paired with beards and flannel shirts. The trend won't last much longer, so I'm glad you only have two of the three."

His smile lights up his face as he shakes his head. "So, you're saying I need to change my shirt and shave my beard?"

I reach my hand to his beard, which is neatly trimmed and full, not like the usual wannabe beards that are all patchy like a Scottish field of moss. The coarseness of the hairs scratches my hand and feels so real that I force my hand away from his face and back to the bar.

"Nope, you have a nice beard, and that shirt fits you just fine." The admiration I feel reflects in my voice.

"Who the hell are you?" Each word comes out like its own question.

I laugh. The question is more on the mark than he knows. I'm twenty-five-year-old Lauren mixed with thirty-five-year-old Lauren, mixed with flirty dream Lauren. But I don't think trying to explain that now would be possible. Instead I say, "Must be the whiskey."

"Somehow I doubt that."

Time to leave. This is getting out of control, and while sexy time with this man looks to be delightful, I think it's time to go home. I need to end this dream and get back to reality.

"I need to run, but first I need two vodka tonics for my friends. And how about a round of drinks for that table over there," I request as I nod to Matthew's table. "And one of these"—I lift my glass—"for the birthday boy."

I hand him my credit card, and he pauses for a moment as if trying to decide what to say. Instead he gives me one last smile and walks to the boy bartender, giving him the drink orders and my credit card before heading into the back to get the whiskey.

Once boy bartender hands me back my credit card and my drinks, I head back to my table. I need to get away before the hottie comes back with the other drinks and I change my mind about finding out what he's thinking.

3

LAUREN

I circle my small house for the fourteenth time today. I'm still here.
   I slept.
I woke up.
I'm still here.
This can't be possible.
What the hell!?!?
My legs wobble and I make my way to the desk as I twist the bracelet on my wrist. I didn't have this bracelet ten years ago. How did it get here? The others made a wish too. How can I be the only one here? I called all the girls this morning, and they didn't act like they knew anything. I didn't want to come right out and ask if they had time traveled last night, so I'll have to assume it's just me.

Ugh. Should I tell Eve? Would she know what to do?

No, I saw her last night and she has no idea that...that I'm not me or that I'm the future me. I'm going to have to figure this out on my own. If I tell her, she is going to think I've gone crazy. Hell, I think I've gone crazy.

This can't be real.

I cannot be here.

But I am.

What do I do now? What's the last thing I remember before Eve called me last night?

The old woman.

The waterfall.

The wish.

The wish? What did I wish for? I don't remember... something about fixing things. I glance out the window. The sun is shining through the leaves that are beginning to change colors. It was July when we made the hike. Now it's the start of fall? My eyes sting with frustration.

No time for tears. Think. How do I figure this out?

What's the name of the waterfall? I can see the sign in my head, but there wasn't a name. I type in the address of the cabin into my computer, and with a quick search of the area, I find the name and location.

To figure out a problem, you need to start by gathering data, and there is no better way than to go to the source. A field trip back to the waterfall.

An hour and a dozen websites on the waterfall later I'm in my car headed east. Thank goodness it's Saturday, and the traffic out of Nashville is light. Maybe I can find some answers there.

The eighty miles feels like three hundred. When I finally find my way to the parking lot, nothing looks familiar. It's just trees, trees, and more trees.

The air is cool and crisp. I pull my jacket tighter and walk to the sign. I take a picture and read the words slowly.

Gods of the Waterfall
In years past villagers would bring offerings to the waterfall in hopes of eliciting the gods' guidance as to the path they should take.
Legend states that the gods of the waterfall judge your heart and whisper in the ears of those found to be worthy.

That sounds the same. Maybe the old woman can give me some answers. She seemed to know more than she let on.

Rounding the first corner, I find the place empty. No table, no woman, no answers.

"Dammit," I mutter as I make my way down the path.

If it weren't for the fact that I hate bugs, I'm alone in the woods, and I've traveled back in time, I might say it was a nice day to be outside.

Splashing water confirms my arrival at the falls. They look exactly the same. I guess some things don't change in the next decade. I stop in my tracks to watch the water cascade down from the ridge into the basin at the bottom. How do you confront gods who live in a waterfall? At work I would schedule a meeting and lay out the facts, but these gods are ruining my life, unlike the idiot guy in accounting who just likes to ruin my day.

"Why me?" I demand. "What am I supposed to do? Am I cursed? I'm not a bad person. I had a good life going. I worked hard for it. And now I have to do it all over again." Fear fills me like I've fallen into a frozen lake, and I start to cry. I rarely allow myself to cry—it doesn't accomplish anything—but today I can't stop. Maybe if I sit here long enough, I can create my own waterfall that will carry me home.

The words spill out between the tears. "What do I do now? What's the point of this? Do I have to do everything again the same way? Do I need to change something? I want my promotion back. I want Matthew back. I want my house back. I want my friends...to be fair, maybe you have a point with them, but I really will make an effort when I get home. I don't need to relive ten years to be a better friend."

Or do I? How absent have I really been? Eve's getting a divorce; I failed both her and Ollie. I let Izzy flounder in that dead-end job and left Gabby to isolate herself with her books and work. I brush the tears away with my sleeve. And Austin...that girl needs friends in her life that will care for her. And I should have been one instead of assuming the others were checking in on her. Still, I can fix these things.

"But I haven't been all bad. Matthew and my job were good. I did something right."

Or did I? Eve said I was unhappy. No. She's wrong; she was just mad at me for being absent this last year. My life is exactly what I wanted—a career, a husband, a home.

I jump to my feet and yell at the cascade of water. "I was happy. And you ruined it. You got this one wrong. I just want to go home."

"You can go back." I almost tumble into the pond at the sound of the old woman speaking behind me. She looks exactly the same as when I saw her yesterday or will see her...never mind. I turn and face her, pointing my finger in her direction.

"You. You did this to me."

"No one did anything to you." Her calm voice causes my blood pressure to rise.

"Really? I beg to differ."

She tilts her head and waves toward the water. "They did it for you."

"How is having to repeat ten years of my life something FOR me? I had everything I wanted."

She steps toward the water and places her hand in the mist, and the droplets swirl around her hand. "Did you?"

"Yes." Of course I did.

"That's not what your heart believes."

This woman is crazy. My hands wave wide. "My heart? You dropped me here all alone. My husband doesn't know who I am. The thought of not being able to talk to him breaks my heart."

"Hmmm." She turns her attention to me. "He's a good man, but is your heart broken for him or for what he represented in a scared little girl's idea of a perfect life?"

"What does that mean?" Why is she talking in riddles? I speak in facts.

"That's for you to figure out."

I take a deep breath. "No, I don't want to figure anything out. I want it back—all of it." My voice is strong and confident.

"Well, if you really feel that way." She turns back to the waterfall and looks to the top. "Drop the bracelet in the water and you can go back."

"What? As easy as that? I can go home." My heart sinks a bit. What? No, I want to go home. Right?

"Yes, but you can't really go home again. You will remember this, and things will be...different. Or..." She pauses, pulling my hand into hers and turning it over the same way she did the day I first met her. This time she traces a line on my palm that splits and curves to the left. "You can follow your heart and find out why you are here."

"Do I have to decide now?" I swallow hard. How did I go from wanting to go home to not sure? I want to go home, but knowing the future wouldn't all be bad.

"No, you have until the second full moon. Throw the bracelet in and go back or don't and stay."

The bracelet on my arm twists in my fingers as I take a step toward the water. Home now or wait a few days and decide? The wind shifts and the mist from the water hits my face. My arm automatically retreats into my jacket. I guess part of me wants to stay. What's the harm? I have a few weeks; I might as well explore and see what I missed the first time.

"What about my friends? Why aren't they..." Where did she go? Looks like that's all the information I'm getting today. I guess it's just me. Time to go home and see what it is my heart thinks I need to know.

My mind whirls all the way home. The last ten years were the best years of my life. I met Matthew, got married, built my career. I might have spent a little too much time working according to Eve. I guess this time I could breeze through some of that. Hmmm...I could start our nest egg early. I paid attention when Matthew spoke about what companies to invest in. Especially since many of those were the same companies I would push my firm to go after. But where do I get the money for investing? I make decent money now, but not enough for that. I don't remember any lottery numbers.

A smile fills my face.

But I do know who wins all the major sporting events for the next ten years. Thanks, Matthew. I guess I shouldn't have complained about all those games we had to attend with clients or watching *Rewind* every night. Now how does one find a bookie?

BEN

"Ten, Eleven, Twelve...Shit." Images of the girl from this weekend flash in my mind—the sexy look of her eyes peeking out under her dark bangs, her comebacks, her fingers caressing my beard. That last one kept me up last night thinking of other places I would like her fingers to caress.

Shit. Enough. She was beautiful, smart, and sexy, but not likely to walk back into my bar anytime soon. And besides, she didn't look like a girl who'd be into a casual relationship. She's the kind of girl you build a life with, and that's not in my plans.

Back to work—get the inventory done, pay the bills, sling a few drinks, and then you can go home and dream of those caresses. My phone vibrates.

OLLIE: You busy at 3 today?

BEN: No. What's up?

OLLIE: The business consultant friend I mentioned has time at 3 to come see you. That work?

Not really, but Ollie said his friend was a wiz at helping businesses turn things around, and I'm in no position to refuse free advice.

BEN: I'll be here. I'm always here.

Ollie didn't provide any other details, and it's not like this guy could make it worse. Maybe he'll tell me to sell and then I won't have to feel guilty that it's my fault Grayson Brothers' went under. Then I could take my buddy Ethan up on his offer to work at his cattle ranch in Texas for a few months. Wide open spaces are exactly what I need.

. . .

"Hello." I hear a female voice call out as I stack cups under the bar. I rise up from my crouched position to find a brunette woman in a black pencil skirt and blue shirt standing ten feet away, her back to me. She turns and my breath catches.

It's her.

I must have stood up too fast. I shake my head a bit and she's still there. It's the Glenlivet girl.

"Hello," I respond, before she catches me staring like an idiot.

Her eyes widen just a bit as they make contact with mine, and she takes a long blink. She remembers me too.

"Hi, I'm looking for the owner. Is he around?"

Play it cool. Don't scare her away. "He is."

Why is she looking for me? Wait. She can't be.

"Could you tell me where to find him?" She pulls the computer bag up on her shoulder and adjusts her jacket.

"Yeah."

It is. She's the business consultant. My stomach as well as my pride plummet to the floor. Fate can't help but punch me in the gut again; set a smart and sexy woman in my path and then make me tell her I'm a failure.

I round the corner of the bar and walk her way, taking my time in order to pull myself together.

I reach my hand out to her. "Ben Grayson. Nice to meet you."

"I believe we've already met." Her eyes narrow as she shakes my hand.

Damn, I love that she didn't pretend not to remember me.

"Not formally, but it's hard to forget someone who buys two hundred dollars' worth of drinks and then disappears." And looks the way you do with that clever mind of yours.

"I'm Lauren Mitchel. I'm a friend of Ollie's. He says you need some..."—she looks around the bar, at the few employees who are starting to set up for the evening—"advice."

All business today I see. I motion toward the door on the other side of the room. "Yes, how about we go to my office."

"Lead the way."

She follows me up the stairs keeping a noticeable distance between us. Maybe she feels it too. The pull to be closer, to finish the verbal dance we started last weekend. The smile on my face dies when I open the office door and see the stacks of papers littering the floor. Shit.

"Mr. Grayson, I see you have an impressive amount of data for us to work with."

I'm impressed that she manages to utter the words without laughing.

I chuckle. "That's one way of putting it. Ben, please call me Ben."

She dips her head a bit, and her eyes hide behind her bangs.

"Ben, call me Lauren." My name on her lips causes me to swallow hard. Damn, I wish she would say that again. And in my ear like the words she whispered the other night. My heart beats faster as my thoughts go to other things I wish she would say.

She obviously senses the direction of my thoughts and her lips tighten. "I'm not sure this is going to be a good fit."

"Why not?" Oh, hell no. I'm not giving up that easy.

She tilts her head to the side. "Well, we..."

"Flirted? You can't help me figure out this mess because we flirted for like ten minutes? I'm pretty sure we can both be more professional than that." At least until you agree to work with me and then there will be nonstop flirting.

Her hand goes to her mouth and she bites her nail. When she catches my gaze, she swiftly moves it back to her side.

"You're right. We're adults. I was only trying to avoid this being awkward for you," she says.

"Not awkward at all." Definitely not awkward.

"Fine." She opens up her folder and pulls out some papers, looking around the desk for a place to set her things. I pick up a pile and set it on the floor beside me.

She nods in appreciation. "Let's start at the beginning. What do you see as the current problem?"

I take a deep breath. Might as well lay it all out. She's going to figure it out soon enough. "Well, to tell you the truth, my uncle wasn't much of a businessman. I didn't realize this until he died last month. When he passed, I took over the bar and found out he'd taken out a second mortgage on the building and that he was behind on a few bills. I've been juggling money around to keep this place running, but...we're losing money each week, and I can't keep it going much longer."

"I see. Are you thinking of selling, or do you want to increase revenue enough to keep it open?"

My heart constricts at her words. All the postcards on the wall mock me as I say, "Keep it open."

I should say sell it so I can get the hell out of here and not get trapped like all the other men in my family, but the thought of saying those words makes me want to vomit.

There is no chance Lauren doesn't see my doubt, but she doesn't call me on it. Instead, she gives me a nod of understanding and goes back to business.

"All right then." She pauses and makes some notes. Pulls out a separate notebook and flips open a calendar. "I'll be doing this on the side, which means I'll need your cooperation to work some odd hours and meet me when I can free up time. I'm not exactly sure what we're looking at yet, so I'll need to see your books, interview your staff, do some research, and then put together a plan for changes." She sets her notebook down and leans forward, focusing all of her attention on me.

I fight the urge to lean back, away from whatever she is about to say.

"Are you willing to make changes?"

"Yes." Obviously, I'm sitting here, aren't I? I've upended my whole life so I can sit in this uncomfortable chair. I should be in Hawaii surfing or Alaska whale watching, or anywhere experiencing life, but instead I'm here. In this bar. Where I promised I'd never end up.

"Really?" She wrinkles her brows as if she doesn't believe me.

"Yeah, otherwise I wouldn't have agreed to Ollie calling you in." Why is she asking me this? Why else would she be here?

"I need you to be sure. Small businesses are personal, and people have certain ideas that they're not always willing to change. If there is something you don't want to change, please tell me during the process and then we can design the plan around that or"—she pauses and tilts her head to the side, and damn she looks cute doing that—"discuss it more."

I will discuss anything you want, anytime you want. But I don't say that. Instead I say, "I'm in."

"Based on what you've said, it sounds like this needs to happen fast, so I'll be taking more of a hands-on approach until we get the plan in place. Any questions for me before we get started?"

I have a million questions, but not work-related. I sit up straight in my chair. Today is about business. "How long have you been in this line of work?"

"I've been doing this for more than fifteen years. I've—"

I stop her midsentence. "Fifteen? I thought you went to college with Ollie." The color in her face drains. She straightens in her chair.

"Sorry, it's been a long day. Let me clarify. I've been with McNeil Consulting for over three years, but I have successfully helped more than fifteen businesses while there."

"Any references I can call?"

She leans back in her chair.

"Normally, I would offer you a list of CEOs to call, but since I'm doing this as a favor, you will just have to trust that I can do the job." The corner of her mouth ticks up a fraction of an inch in satisfaction at her subtle call of my BS. She knows I wasn't planning to call any references.

I hold in my growl. What I wouldn't give to see that look with her under me and touching me. I shake the thoughts away.

"When do we start?" As in now.

"This process won't be easy. It's going to require some hard decisions and even more of your time and probably some additional money." The concern in her eyes is real.

Ripping off the Band-Aid fast is always better, and I don't have any time to waste. "Yes. And I'm looking forward to your hands-on approach."

She shakes her head at my words. Oops, I may have emphasized "hands" a little too much.

"Listen. This is business. You're going to need to keep your flirty remarks to yourself." What she doesn't realize is her scold only makes me like her more.

"I'll do my best." I raise my eyes to hers and cock my head. But no promises.

She laughs. "I have a feeling that might be difficult." I love this girl. Not love. Like. I like her honesty.

"I promise, I won't mind any flirty comments you choose to throw my way."

"Well, I'll try to keep them to myself." She shakes her head.

I would rather she didn't, but this isn't the time to discuss that. "If you must. Now. When can we get started?"

"How's Saturday? I need to do a little research on my end and then I'll come by the bar around two and we can get started." She scans the room. "Can you get your taxes and records in order for me to review by then, or do you need more time?"

"I can make that work."

"Great. I look forward to working with you, Ben."

Man, I love when she says my name, so much so that I can't stop the smile that forms on my face as she says it. I reach my hand out, and she gives me a firm handshake like before. I release her hand and hold eye contact for a moment more. Waiting until Saturday might kill me. "And I look forward to working with you, Lauren."

LAUREN

I DROP into a red upholstered chair and listen as the clip-clop of heels echoes off of the gallery's hardwood floors, notifying me of Eve's arrival. She's in the middle of setting up for a new artist opening next week, and even though there're no customers, I'm sure she is in full fashion mode, four-inch heels and all.

"You look like crap. What's wrong?" she says, as she walks past me, dropping a pile of papers on her desk. One of Eve's superpowers is perception. Somehow, she always knows what I'm feeling.

"It's nice to see you too." I was right. Eve's long flowing white dress with black piping looks like it belongs on the walls. I glance down at my outfit and adjust my shirt.

"What has you all twisted up?" she asks.

"Nothing."

"I thought we were meeting at Izzy's?" By nature, she's suspicious. I'm going to need to tread carefully around her until I figure this out.

I cross my arms and I lean back nonchalantly. "Oh, I thought I would swing by, and we could go over together."

She stops and turns to me. "But that means you left work early."

Oh yeah, I forgot about that. "I took the week off."

Eve sits in the chair behind her desk and looks me over. "Are you sick?"

"No." And I have the MRI to prove it. I had to lie to my doctor about some sudden headache issues, but finally got her to agree it was best to check it out since it was so sudden. So, now I know it's not a brain tumor, though I almost wish it had been so I could understand all this.

"What's wrong?" she asks, not giving up.

I roll my eyes and put on my everything-is-fine face. Her question could only be answered with a long list. The fact that I'm now a junior account manager when last week I was promoted to Vice President. That I'm afraid to go and see my husband whom I haven't even met yet. That I should go back to the waterfall and throw this damn bracelet into the water now. Or that Ollie's favor is going to be trickier than I thought. Oh, and the fact that I've somehow time traveled and I'm not sure how to tell anyone without ending up in a loony bin.

"Nothing, I needed a little vacation, and Ollie asked me to help out his friend, so I thought I would take a little time off before I got started."

Eve picks up her mail and starts sorting it. A few moments of silence feel like a year when she finally asks, "What has you biting your nails again?"

I sit on my hands to avoid looking at the chewed-off corners. Dammit, I thought I had stopped that for good.

I sigh. I can't tell her about Matthew or the job. "Do you remember when I said I flirted with a cute bartender while I waited for drinks last week?" She raises her eyes and lowers the piece of mail in her hand.

"I do remember you making some off-hand comment before you headed home, but you said you only spoke to him for a few minutes."

"And that was true."

"But?" The gears in her head are almost visible.

"He wasn't just the bartender. He's Ben Grayson, the guy Ollie wants me to help."

"Why is that a problem? I've met him. He's a nice guy and handsome. Him being cute should be a bonus. Maybe he'll like your work so much he'll give you a bonus." She wiggles her eyebrows at me.

I shake my head. "Not helping."

"What's the problem?" She shrugs as if dating a guy I'm working with is no problem.

Not to mention I'm married...well, not really, but still. I rub my bare ring finger. And then glare at her. "He's a client now."

"Fine. Then flirt a little and have some fun while you work."

Absolutely no help.

I stand up. "Get your purse. We're late, and you know how Izzy is about being on time. Being late for her birthday dinner could get us killed."

"FINALLY," Izzy says, as she opens the door. Izzy's apartment is what a real-estate agent would call cozy. The rent in downtown is ridiculous, but Izzy likes being close to work and not having a house or yard to take care of. She's a city girl who likes being able to go out without having to drive.

"Happy Birthday!" Eve and I yell in unison. Izzy crosses her arms and kicks out her hip all the while giving us the stink eye. We are late.

"What? We're only fifteen minutes late which means we are fifteen minutes early for me." Eve laughs and Izzy gives in and joins her. She knows it's true. Eve is the queen of fashionably late.

"Get in here. Izzy made some pre-dinner drinks," Austin yells from the kitchen.

Izzy gives Eve a quick hug as she goes through the door, and when it's my turn I hug her tight. I don't know why, but seeing Izzy looking younger and happier brings up emotions I don't normally allow. I forgot what we looked like before life started to weigh us down. "You look amazing," I say, giving her a long hug before joining Eve and Austin in the kitchen area.

Austin steps in front of me. "Hey, stranger."

She always looks gorgeous. Her long red hair frames her face while the simple navy blue shift dress shows off her long legs.

"Hey, yourself. You look gorgeous. When did you get in?"

Her smile shifts slightly before answering. "Last night.

I'm in for a conference tomorrow and fly out late tomorrow night."

She gives me a brief hug and then turns back to Izzy. Izzy grimaces and shakes her head, warning me I've screwed something up.

"What?" I mouth as Austin walks into the kitchen.

Izzy whispers, "I thought you picked Austin up at the airport last night."

I freeze. Was I supposed to? It was not on my calendar. Was this new? Did I forget last time too?

"Oh no, Austin, I'm so sorry. It wasn't on my calendar. Did you call me?"

She shakes her head. "It's no problem. I called for a ride."

"I'm so sorry." Tears fill my eyes. Where is all this coming from? I don't cry. I will not cry. I swore I would be a better friend, that I wouldn't repeat my past mistakes, but here I am failing already.

"It's fine. I had a backup plan." Austin shrugs, and I feel like this is not the first time she has had to use her backup plan when it comes to me. How many things did I promise and not follow through on?

Eve nudges my arm and gives me a side glance that tells me to move on.

"Set me up, bartender," I say to lighten the mood. Eve chuckles at my comment. Oh hell, I guess I have bartender on the brain.

"What's that look?" Izzy cuts her eyes from Eve to me as she slides two dark red drinks with blackberry skewers to us. I ignore the question and reach for the drink. It looks like a glass of black cherry Kool-Aid. The sweetness hits my tongue first and then the whiskey. Izzy loves anything whiskey and regularly comes up with her own recipes. I could drink ten of these.

"This is delicious." I take another long drink. I need a drink after today. Ben's stormy-blue eyes and dark lashes fill my vision, sending a chill down my spine.

"Yes, it is. Now spill; you've been weird all week," Izzy says.

"Aren't we calling Gabriella?" I ask, deflecting the grilling I am about to receive.

Eve reaches for her phone. "Fine. We can call her and then you can tell us all at once."

"There's nothing to tell." I cross my arms and shake my head to keep from laughing. What would they say if I told them the truth? *"Oh, hey girls, you won't believe my week. I got pulled back in time, met a hot bartender whose business I'm now in charge of saving, spent the week filling a notebook up with all the things I remember about the future, and last night placed my first bet with a bookie so I can make some money to start my nest egg early. So yeah. It's been a weird week."*

Gabby appears on the phone.

"Wait. Before we get to boy drama, what the hell are you wearing?" Austin asks Gabby.

"Um...a T-shirt." Gabriella looks down at her shirt and pulls at the bottom of it to straighten it out.

"Are you in your pajamas?" Izzy screeches.

Gabby nods, indicating she doesn't see the problem. "Yeah."

Izzy shakes her head. "What the hell? It's only seven thirty,"

"It's eight thirty here, thank you very much, and it's Wednesday night so this is appropriate attire," Gabby defends.

"Speaking of things to wear..." I chime in, "Gabby, do not

try and wear that black maxi dress with the white polka dots next weekend." Last time she wore it, she kept tripping on it while dancing and almost landed face first in a guy's lap. She was mortified and wouldn't dance the rest of the night.

"How did you know I was planning to wear that dress? I just bought it last week," Gabby replies.

Oh, shit. Ummmm. "You told me about it when you bought it. Just pick something shorter because we're going dancing."

"And show more cleavage," Eve adds.

Gabby grimaces. "I'll see what I can do."

"Where are we going anyway?" Izzy asks.

"Actually, if you guys don't mind, I was thinking we could check out Grayson Brothers'. Ollie has talked me into helping out the new owner, and I could use some expert eyes. We could grab a drink and then go dancing at the place down the street."

"We're in," says Eve. "Apparently, the owner has Lauren a little hot and bothered. I've met him before but I feel we need a little extra recon"

"I'm not hot and bothered." I'm also not blind. He's attractive if you like the tall, dark, and handsome type. But this is business and I'm...married. Kinda.

"Your face disagrees with you. It's like three shades redder than my hair," pipes in Austin.

I cross my arms. "Forget it. We don't need to go."

"Oh, hell no. We're definitely going now," Izzy says, her face lighting up like she won a year's supply of whiskey.

"Fine, but this is professional, not personal." I look around at each of my friends, conveying the importance of what I'm saying.

Austin interrupts my staredown, "We'll have to discuss

the cute bar owner more later. Right now we need to finish our drinks. Our reservation is in twenty minutes."

"Have a good birthday dinner. We'll do birthday drinks next weekend," Gabriella says and then her face disappears.

"Well, I guess she was done with us," I say, as Izzy and Eve burst out laughing.

I tap my empty drink and smile brightly at Izzy. She gives me a refill and drops in another blackberry. I stab it with the wooden spear and eat it. "This drink is one of your best ever."

"New recipe—Blackberry Bourbon Lemonade."

"I love it. Maybe we should just stay here and drink these all night."

"Maybe another night. Tonight, we have trouble to find." Izzy's smirk leaves me worried.

LUCKILY, we don't run into any trouble at dinner. Eve directs us to this cute little Mediterranean restaurant on the West End. With all her artsy friends, she always knows the best places to eat. We drink and laugh and share a few dishes while rehashing all of Izzy's wild antics, of which I only slip twice and mention something that hasn't happened yet. I cover nicely with "seems like something you would do" which makes them laugh even harder.

Izzy finishes off her dessert, and she and Eve head to the bathroom to fix their makeup. I chuckle to myself as I think of the impression Izzy does of her coworker and how I about fell out of my chair when I leaned over to fix the strap on my shoe. Why is she still stuck dead end jobs for the next ten years? How does this company not see her potential? I need to pay her a visit at work, take her to lunch. I need her to introduce me to these people and figure out a strategy to get her the job she deserves.

"What's wrong?" Austin says, pulling me out of my thoughts.

"Huh?"

"You're chewing your nails. You always do that when something's wrong."

She knows me too well. I remove my finger from my mouth and wrap it around my napkin. "Nothing."

Austin crosses her arms over her chest. "Fine, don't tell me."

Eve chimes in behind me, "But we'll just assume you are thinking about the cute bartender."

I check to be sure Eve came back by herself before I answer. "Fine...I was thinking about how to help Izzy get a promotion at work."

Austin uncrosses her arms and leans back in her chair. "Oh, well...she's only been there a few years, and she's not quite as career obsessed as you. So, maybe give her a minute before you try to fix a situation that may not need fixing."

Oh, but it does. Current time Austin and Eve have no idea. "She needs to fix it now, or it's just going to get worse."

Eve shakes her head and sighs. "But she needs to figure it out. Not you. Stop trying to make life perfect. It's never perfect."

Why can't it be? And now that I know the future, I should use this knowledge to fix things. "I can help."

I'm saved from a lecture on how I'm not responsible for everyone's happiness when Izzy returns. "Okay. Let's get out of here. I need a birthday drink, and I want to see this cute bartender."

"Oh no. We aren't going there." No way.

"It's my birthday, and on my birthday, you have to do what I want." Izzy's eyebrow lifts, daring me to question her.

Austin looks a little smug. I feel like this is her payback for me not picking her up. I nod in defeat and apology. She gives me a chin lift, and I know my I've paid my penance.

There is no point in fighting it anyway. I know this is a battle I can't win. "Fine. But I can't guarantee he's working. And one drink. One drink only."

There is no sign of Ben as we walk in the door. I let out a slow breath. I really don't need the girls making things more awkward between us by mentioning how attractive I find him and hinting about my single status.

The young bartender from the other night is working.

"Glenlivet?" he asks.

Good memory.

"Not tonight," I say, "but we will take a round of whiskey sours."

"You got it. Ben said you were going to be helping out around here. Doing a little recon?"

I chuckle. "Not really, but it doesn't hurt to get first-hand knowledge."

The girls proceed to politely grill him for thirty minutes about himself and Ben. They are about as subtle as a politician asking for money as they ascertain Ben's single status as well as his nomadic lifestyle and that he's genuinely a nice guy.

Izzy and Eve head to get the car while I pay the tab and Austin washes her hands. The bartender, whose name I now know is Dex, hands me the receipt.

"Listen, Ben's a good guy; you should give him a chance."

My eyebrows furrow in confusion. "I am. I'm going to help him any way I can."

"Good, 'cause he needs this place. He may think he

doesn't want to be tied down, but his uncle did everything he could to keep this place because he knew Ben needed a home base."

Dex turns and walks to the other end of the bar before I can utter a response.

Great! Now I'm in charge of his happiness not just saving his business. No pressure.

4

LAUREN

My heels click on the sidewalk as I near the front door. I settle my messenger bag on my shoulder and make a few notes in my notebook.

*** Corner lot - clothing store attached to the right.**
*** Parking lot across the street - selling point ***
* Most buildings nearby are occupied.

The road has some steady foot and car traffic. The neighborhood looks in decent shape, but I need to do a little more research into the demographics and upcoming zoning permits. The white paint on the brick is fading which in some ways is charming, but is charming what we want this bar to say? Hmm...I'm not sure yet. As I reach the door, I take a deep breath and pull on the handle, ready to take on my new client.

Seated at the far end of the bar are three gentlemen—maybe in their early sixties—with beers in their hands. They give me a wave as I walk in, and I hear one of them yell

Ben's name. The light coming in from the large windows at the front and sides bounces off of the white wooden tables and columns. The room feels too quiet and empty without customers. The last time I was in here, the noise level was high compared to the number of patrons. I glance up at the wood ceiling.

* Sound board on ceiling? - Call Dillon?

Would sound boards ruin the acoustics? Dillon would know. His sound installation business doubled in size due to the advice I gave him, so I'm sure he would give us some guidance on what we should do.

"Lauren," a deep voice calls from behind the bar. I turn to find Ben in a blue dress shirt, sleeves rolled up to the elbows, smiling at me. My heart speeds up a bit as I recall that same smile and him leaning in and whispering in my ear. I smile back, willing myself to calm down.

What has gotten into me? I've never been this affected by someone before. All this time travel has my emotions on overdrive. I should remove myself from this situation, but I already promised, and I'm not going back on my promises this time.

"Mr...."—his jaw starts to clench—"I mean, Ben. Nice to see you."

"You too." The smile on his face returns and I step closer, setting my bag down on a barstool.

"I didn't think you were open yet," I say, inclining my head toward the end of the bar.

"Oh, we're not. Those are my uncle's buddies." Ben raises his voice a bit and says, "They come in early cause they're old and have to get home before curfew." He chuckles and turns his head their way, no doubt waiting on a smart-ass comeback.

"Make fun if you want, but when you find a good

woman, you keep her happy, and me being home for dinner makes her happy."

Ben's eyes narrow on the man in the green shirt like a warning. The man laughs and goes back to his beer, though I can tell they are all watching our every move.

"I might as well introduce you. Then maybe we can get some peace," Ben says.

I fight a smile, not wanting to admit how sweet it is they are keeping an eye on him for his uncle. "Sounds good."

Ben walks to the end of the bar and I follow.

"Hi, I'm Lauren." I extend my hand to the salt-and-pepper-haired gentleman who spoke a moment ago.

"I'm Wayne. Nice to finally meet you. This is Eddie and that's Junior over there." His hands wave to a man with silver hair and a beard to match, and then to a bald, super fit-looking man on the end. I walk over to each and shake their hands. The man on the end holds my hand a little longer than the others and studies my face. Looking out for Ben. I like these guys.

Ben glares through the exchange. He must have told them to be on their best behavior, but I can see from the light in their eyes it's hard to contain all the questions they have. I stop myself from laughing at the sight. "It's nice to meet all of you."

"And what're you doing here, Miss Lauren? Taking this poor chap out to lunch?" Eddie, the bearded one, says.

"Like I told you earlier. Lauren is here to help me find a way to keep the business going. Be nice to her. She may say I need to cut you three off and solve all my problems."

I laugh at that one. The men do too.

"Without us you would be lost, boy," Junior says.

"How about you take me on a tour?" I suggest.

Ben glares at the men and points his hand toward the

back of the building. "Let's start back here."

"Let me grab my notebook."

Ben walks a few steps behind me as we weave our way through the tables.

"The light in here is really nice. I guess it was overcast the last time I was in here. It's very bright and inviting on a sunny day," I say, turning my head back his way.

"Are you saying it's normally dark and scary?"

A small chuckle escapes me. "No, I just assumed bars were always dark and only lit by neon signs during the day."

"You don't do a lot of day drinking. Good to know."

His sarcastic tone makes it too tempting to continue our banter, but it's time to get down to business. "How many seats do you have?"

"We have seventy-five tables and around three hundred seats."

I make a note.

"What's the weekly lineup like?"

"We're closed on Monday and Tuesday. Wednesday and Friday, we usually have live bands, but sometimes a DJ. Thursday and Sunday we use a playlist, and Saturday we have a DJ."

* How do we pull people in?
* Thurs and Sun need a hook

This is a tourist town, and we need a reason people choose this place over the other bars in the area.

As we reach the dance floor, Ben makes his way past me and a hint of cologne finds me. It reminds me of the outdoors—must have some kind of wood scent as the base note. My eyes follow his back as he walks to the stage. Strong back, confident walk, and nice ass. I look down at my paper and make an unnecessary note about the type of flooring.

Ben jumps up on the stage and walks the length of it. "This is the stage; it's not big, but it's able to hold a decent-sized band."

There are large speakers located on each side of the stage. "How old is the sound equipment?"

"No idea, but it might be in the records upstairs." Ben tips his head toward the ceiling.

"That's fine. I can have someone check it out." Well, now I have two things for Dillon to check out.

* Sound system? Upgrade?- Call Dillon

Ben's voice betrays his concern. "It works fine."

"I know. I've heard it, but I want someone to check it out and tell me about the acoustics. If you have bands, you want them to sound good. Um. What's behind there?" I ask as I spy a set of doors to the right of the stage.

"A kitchen. This place was a restaurant before my father and uncle took it over, and they served food until about five years ago."

"Can I see it?"

"Sure." He pushes the door open to a decent-size kitchen with a large stove, giant prep island, and even a fryer.

"Wow. Does it still work?" I ask. This could be a game changer. Food can be high margin if done properly.

"I think so. We use the oven once in a while," Ben answers, obviously having no idea.

I walk around the kitchen and take a quick inventory of the equipment. "Why did they stop serving food?"

Ben shrugs. "My uncle didn't want to run a restaurant. He wanted to run a bar. After the chef moved to Chicago, he decided to close it."

* Kitchen - what is needed to open?

"And what do you think?" I ask. If the equipment is in good shape and we could find someone willing to run the kitchen for a reasonable salary, this would really help the bottom line.

"What do I think about what?" Ben says, his voice trailing off at the end.

He doesn't see the potential I see. "This is your bar now; do you want to serve food in order to make more money?"

The color on Ben's face pales. "I didn't set out to own a bar, let alone a restaurant too."

He's still not sure what he wants even though he says he wants to keep the place. We need to keep things simple and move forward slowly. "For now, how about I get someone to look at it and see if we have any potential?"

He looks around the room, and I see even more color drain from his face. Change is scary. I place my hand on his forearm. The heat from his arm radiates up mine as he turns his head to me and smiles. "Change is difficult. Trust me. I'll be gentle with you."

He lets out a chuckle and sets my arm into the crook of his elbow.

"Shall we continue the tour?" I should pull my arm away, but the gesture is...well, sweet, and instead I follow him through the doors. "Ben, I should have asked this earlier, but what did you do before you took over the bar?"

"It's not important," he says, guiding me away from the kitchen and all the things he doesn't want to talk about.

"Actually, it is," I say.

"It's in the past. I run a bar now." Ben's tone suggests I should let it go, but I can't.

My arm falls from his as I stop and turn to him. "But you don't have to. If this isn't what you want, I can help you get the place ready to sell."

He looks back toward the stage. "Right now, all that matters is saving the bar."

"Why?" I know it's none of my business. I should focus on the bar, but the why is always important.

He pauses, his lips pursing together. "The truth is...it's all I have left of my family. And it was important to them."

My heart sinks. What happened to his family? He said his uncle left him the bar and Ollie said something about his dad dying in an accident. His mom must be gone too. I may not talk to my dad, but I have my mom and grandparents to rely on.

"I didn't mean to pry. I...I'm trying to understand why you're doing this."

"It's fine." He pulls my arm back to the crook of his elbow and restarts the tour.

As we exit the dance floor, I see the entrances to the bathrooms and a long empty wall with a few tables.

"Do you ever set up another bar on this side or closer to the dance floor?" I say, changing the focus back to work.

"No." He glances back at the bar, a bit of confusion on his face.

I pull my right hand out of his arm in order to add a note to my list, noticing immediately the loss of his warmth.

* 2nd bar - what would be involved?

"Bathrooms," he says gesturing at the entrances, not stopping to offer me a personal tour. No problem, I used them the other night.

* **Bathrooms - need paint and minor repairs**

"And in there is the storage area and the stairs up to my office."

He unlocks the door and holds it open. We walk into a small room with stairs going up to the second-floor office we were in last time. The stairs are metal and wide with a landing halfway up.

"No elevator, huh?" I give him a smile.

"No, It's good exercise."

I look down at my three-inch heels. I should really dress down for this job. I take a deep breath. I can do this.

"Ladies first." His hand waves up the stairs. As my foot hits the first step I look back to ask who has keys to the office and see his eyes have landed on my ass. I stop and turn around.

"Really? Are you being a gentleman by letting me go first or did you just want to look at my ass?"

Ben's head tips back, and a loud laugh comes roaring out, bouncing off of the concrete and metal.

"There she is." He takes a step closer, putting us eye to eye. "You've been a little uptight since you got here. Glad to see the woman I met last week is still in there. I like her. She's feisty and says what she's thinking."

"I normally reserve that side of me for after-work hours."

"Well, technically you're doing me a favor after hours, so feel free to always be yourself with me." His voice lowers a bit and his eyes are sincere. I hold his gaze for a moment longer than I should before snapping back to reality.

"Thanks." I turn back and walk up the steps, concentrating on my feet and not swaying my hips.

The office is tidier than the last time, with a stack of boxes in the corner. Ben's been busy. There is a long leather couch against the wall that I hadn't noticed last time, a few filing cabinets, and two leather chairs in front of a large wooden desk. I walk around for a moment, and my hand skims the surface of the desk.

"You're surprised it's this clean, aren't you?" Ben leans against the door frame.

"A little," I admit with a smirk in his direction.

"You said you needed the info, and I thought it only fair I organize it... Somewhat." He motions to the boxes.

"I'm impressed. That was a lot of work. Can we sit?"

Ben nods and I slide into one of the leather chairs. Ben sinks into the chair next to me instead of going behind the desk.

I set my notebook on my lap. "From our previous discussion I know that the business is losing money. The question is how long has it been losing money?"

He swallows and sits up straight in his chair. "A while from what I can tell. I found the tax records, and sales have been declining the last five years."

"Then I think I should start by going over your financials for the last five to ten years and your bills for the last two years. This will allow me to analyze your sales and purchases and find out exactly where you're losing money and where best to put our efforts."

"Okay."

"Do you trust me?" I ask.

"Yeah."

"Yeah, but you have no reason to. I understand." I turn toward him. "Listen, I know what I'm doing. I've saved big companies millions of dollars, and I've helped small companies come back from the brink of bankruptcy. We can fix this."

"That's a lot in only a few short years." He stands and walks to the filing cabinet.

Dammit. He's right. I've only technically been out of school a few years.

"True, but in those few years I've worked very hard and with some of the best business minds in the world. I can help you."

He nods his head so slowly I'm not sure it's actually

moving.

Without thinking, I stand and walk toward him. He watches me approach, a look of apprehension in his eyes. My hands go to his arms and lock on. "I promised Ollie I would help you. So we are going to figure this out and get you in the black." He nods his head but I continue. "I can tell this is important to you. And now it's important to me. And if you know anything about me, you need to know that I love figuring out how to fix a problem, putting a plan together, and watching it be executed to perfection."

This gets me a weak smile.

It's a start.

"Now, can we sit back down? I have a few more questions."

An hour later I have my questions answered, and I even got Ben to crack a smile and loosen up when I made a semi-lewd joke. Girl's gotta do what she's gotta do, and it worked.

"Can we meet again next Sunday around three? I want to spend a few days going over these." I pat the boxes stacked in the corner. And I have to deal with work next week and the girls coming in Friday and decide what to do about Matthew. Should I check on him? Should I leave him alone until the day we meet? What if I see him before that and mess everything up?

"That works," Ben says, pulling me from my thoughts.

"Great, I'd also like to meet with some of your staff."

His dark eyebrows squish together. "My staff?"

"Yeah, I want to get their opinions on what works and what doesn't."

"Okay," he draws out.

"I promise it will be mostly painless. Unless you're actually a total ass and they all hate it here."

His laugh fills the room. "No, I don't think that's the

problem. Hell, I probably need to be more of an ass."

"Well, give them a heads-up. I would like to talk to them individually. Could they come in fifteen minutes early one day before their shift to answer a few questions?"

"Sure."

I place my messenger bag around my torso and pick up the box, overflowing with paper. Ben grabs three boxes and nods toward the door. Fine, if he wants to carry the heavy boxes, I'm not going to complain. I'm the one that has to look through it all, and walking down the stairs in heels with one box at a time is probably enough.

I sure as hell hope it's better news in these than he thinks. I may have gotten him to laugh, but with each question, his posture stiffened and the light in his eyes dimmed. I hope I can keep my promise.

BEN

"That woman gonna help you save this place?" Wayne calls from the end of the bar as I return from walking Lauren out.

"I see you're the last man standing...I mean sitting tonight."

"Yep, now answer the question."

"That's the plan," I say, making my way back behind the bar. The work is never done when you own a bar. Prep, clean up, serve the customers, pay the bills, make the schedules, clean up some more, and do it all again the next day.

"Thought you didn't want to own a bar?"

"I don't."

"Then why save it? Why not simply sell and go back to finding yourself or whatever it is you have been doing traveling around the country?"

I grab a clean rag and walk to the sink, ignoring his usual rant about my lack of ambition and inability to grow up. Because apparently if you don't settle down and get a nine-to-five job, you're wasting your life. When it's really the opposite. The monotonous repetition of a normal job leaves no room to really live.

"Life is short, Wayne. Some of us are trying to experience as much as possible before it's over."

Wayne leans forward. "I know you haven't had the best of luck in your family, kid, but that doesn't mean you're gonna die early too."

My jaw tightens as I wash another glass and avoid his gaze. "It doesn't mean I'm not, and I'm not taking any chances. I refuse to spend my life cooped up in this place like my father and uncle."

"But—" Wayne starts in again.

"No buts." They wasted their lives here and I won't do the same. I've seen more of this country in the last seven years than my dad saw in his whole life.

"Then why are you trying to save this place? Let it go and move on," Wayne's voice rises as if I didn't hear him the first time.

My head turns his direction, but I don't just see Wayne. I see the memory of my dad and uncle laughing and chatting up their friends as they pour drinks. "I wish it were that simple."

"It can be," he says quietly, and I choose to ignore him.

I remove the plastic caps from the soda spray and wipe everything down one item at a time. All I can do is one thing at a time. Losing this place on top of losing Uncle Anthony... I'm not sure I'm ready for that.

My family memories are here. The corner by the front window where my mom threw my sixth birthday party. Dad throwing me the keys to my new truck over the bar as congratulations for getting into UT the summer before he died. My uncle telling me for the ten millionth time that the next trip I took he would go with me. But he never did.

All here.

They're here.

"What?" I ask, not remembering Wayne's last dig.

"What're you gonna do?"

"I'm going to try and save the place. If I don't then you and your merry band of men will get soft and start drinking coffee over at the Denny's all weekend long."

"We can take care of ourselves. Now about that woman you hired to help you?"

"Lauren." Damn, just saying her name makes my body tense up.

I chance a glance at Wayne who doesn't miss a thing. He has his head tilted, questioning me.

"She seems legit," I say.

"That's not what I meant."

"I know." She's different—smart, funny, obviously gorgeous, but there is something about her I can't quite put my finger on. But I would like to find out what that is. The smile forms on my face before I can clamp it down. Wayne gives me a head nod, as if he can read my thoughts. Lord, I hope not.

"You falling for this girl?"

"I've met her, like, three times, and I don't do falling in love. Love is complicated and messy and usually results in being stuck in the same place doing the same thing for the rest of your life. No, thanks. That's not going to happen."

Wayne's laughter fills the bar.

"What?"

"As if you have a choice in who you love."

5

LAUREN

I feel like there should be a joke about five girls in short skirts and high heels climbing out of a minivan in front of a bar, but I can't think of one. Our rideshare driver, Sharon, is the best. She cranked up ABBA and sang with us the whole way, telling us all her best stories from other fares. She says she enjoys taking people to the clubs on Friday and Saturday nights. Everyone is all dressed up and excited.

She does not, however, pick them up at the end of the night.

I don't blame her.

"Thanks, Sharon," Gabriella says from the passenger seat.

"Best ride EVER!" Austin exclaims as she opens the door and sets her heels on the ground.

I open the door and put my hand out to help Izzy and Eve exit the vehicle. The night does not need to start off with anyone face-planting on the ground.

"Night, girls, don't have too much fun," Sharon says as she pulls away.

We stop in front of the building and look up.

"Well?" I address the group as I look up at the Grayson Brothers' sign hanging above the door.

"Cute building. I love the giant windows, but it needs a paint job and a little curb appeal. Maybe some etched glass or vinyl letters that look etched. And it needs a better sign. I like the painted sign, but something that sticks out would be better for those driving by to see it as well. But lots of potential," Gabriella says, taking a photo with her phone. "I'll work on some mockups."

I could kiss her. I knew she would have great marketing ideas. Asking the girls to make a quick stop was the right idea. They all have something to bring to the table. Gabby knows what sells, Eve has an eye for aesthetics, Izzy loves going out and knows what makes a business valuable, and Austin knows more about how guys think than most, having two brothers and working for a professional baseball team.

"The location's not bad. There are several other bars a few blocks down, and the fact that they have a place to park is a plus. But my bet is not everyone who's parked here is at Grayson's. You may need to fence it in or do something to keep others out," Izzy adds.

"Sounds good. Let's get inside," I say.

The place is busy, but not enough for a Friday night. It should be wall-to-wall people and maybe even a short wait at the door—at least that's my goal.

My eyes scan the bar. No Ben. Dex, however, is working again tonight. He sees me and gives me a nod to several open stools at the opposite end of the bar.

"Do you want to get a table or order at the bar?" I ask the group.

"Bar. I need a shot, pronto!" Izzy declares.

Fine. My eyes scan the room to check out the crowd. Just the crowd. I'm not looking for Ben. Eve slaps my hand out of my mouth.

We make our way over to Dex, and I ask him for five Hot Damn shots.

"You girls are starting the night out right." He smiles bright in approval.

"Hey, Dex. We're celebrating my birthday," Izzy says, raising her hands in the air and doing a little twirl. I shake my head as I laugh. This girl—what am I going to do with her?

"You mean again," he says, giving her a big smile and showing off the dimple in his left cheek.

"Yep, I couldn't make it on the actual date so we're celebrating again," Gabriella adds, turning around to the bar, where Dex is given a glimpse of the best cleavage this group has to offer. She wasn't happy we didn't let her wear a camisole under that top and has forgotten that when she leans over, her girls are on display. I look down at my own chest. Being twenty-five has its upsides. My breasts may still be perky, but my decent size B in a push-up bra does not compare to Gabby's DD in any bra.

Gabriella doesn't notice his look as she turns back to talk to Eve, while Dex swallows hard and says, "I'll be back."

"He can come back anytime. He's a little cutie. Did you see his dimple?" Austin says in my ear, making no attempt to hide she's looking at his butt.

"You're dating a professional athlete; how does that young man's butt even compare?"

"Young man? He can't be more than a year or two younger than we are." She smacks my arm and adds, "When did you turn into an old lady?"

"I think I have an old soul." And ten more years of experiences.

She rolls her eyes at me. "And Tommy does have a nice ass, but a girl can look."

We both laugh and turn toward the crowd. Speaking of nice asses, Ben has one too. Those jeans he wore Saturday...oh my.

Stop.

Here for work, not to think about Ben.

The girls survey the place, and I tell them about the weekly lineup and lack of food. Eve demands the first thing we do is ditch the DJ—his playlist is garbage—and Austin suggests some seating areas off to the side with comfortable chairs and couches.

"Drinks," Gabriella announces as her eyes go wide.

I turn to find Ben setting up our drinks.

Busted. And damn if he doesn't look even better than last time. "Hi," I say as I look him straight in the eye, hoping he can't see my heart beating through my top.

"Hi." His eyes take their time traveling down my torso and back up.

I can't help but chuckle as his eyes meet mine. It's been a while since a man looked at me like I was good enough to eat, and usually they had the decency to look a little ashamed for having been caught, but not Ben. I can tell he likes what he sees, and I simply respond. "Thanks."

I'm rewarded with a bright smile that has me mesmerized as if I'm watching a starry night sky in the middle of the desert sparkle back at me. Someone knocks my shoulder, and I realize I've missed what he said. Pre-drinks at Eve's... bad idea.

"You gonna introduce everyone to your new friend?" Eve

says, poking me in the side, all while giving Ben her best innocent smile.

"Um. Yeah. Ben Grayson, these are my friends. You already know Eve. And this is Gabriella, Austin, and Izzy."

"The birthday girl," Izzy adds. I try not to laugh. Two drinks and she goes from wallflower to Venus flytrap.

"Well, happy birthday. This round's on me, Birthday Girl."

My hand lands on his. It's warm and stiffens a bit when we touch. I've seen this man's financial records, and he does not need to give out free drinks. "You don't have to do that."

"No, but I did." His eyes are tight, a silent warning that he will do what he wants.

"Then, thank you." I lean in closer and whisper, "But as your new business advisor...don't do it often."

He gives me a nod of understanding as his eyes go to the counter. Dammit, I didn't mean to make him feel like he's failing, but he needs to be responsible, which means he can't give things away for free.

Izzy laughs, and I realize that I still have my hand on his. I squeeze his hand briefly and smile to get his attention. He smiles back and pushes the shots in my direction.

Everyone pauses, glasses raised, waiting for our usual salutation. My heart races and my palms become sweaty. The last time I said this was two weeks ago or ten years from now, the night before I ended up here. I swallow hard and join the group.

"To friendship and lives well lived," we yell over the music.

I close my eyes. Lives well lived...who knew I would get more than one chance to get my life right? I gulp a little as I force a smile back on my face and down the drink. The liquid is like a sweet burn flowing down my throat. Ben watches me as I set my glass on the bar. I give him a little wink.

What the hell?

Stop flirting with your client.

I reach in my purse and set my credit card on the counter. "We're gonna need a tab for the rest of the drinks."

He takes it and looks around the group. "Hope their tastes aren't as expensive as your other friends."

Austin hears him and gives me a "who the hell is he talking about" look. I wave her off and glare at Ben. He catches my warning and shuts up like any good bartender would do.

Austin bellies up to the bar. "Bartender Ben, we're going to need more drinks. I'm thinking another round of shots, a whiskey straight up,"—Izzy gives a whoop—"two whiskey sours, a vodka martini with three olives, and a margarita."

She's testing his bartending skills. I hold in my laugh.

"Yes, ma'am." He gives me a wink and walks to the middle of the bar to work his magic. The sleeves on his flannel shirt are pushed up. When he reaches in for ice, his shirt pulls tight around his broad shoulders, showcasing them very nicely. He doesn't throw bottles around or anything, but he does make the drinks while still watching our group.

I feel a bit hot from the shot. Maybe I should've ordered water instead of another drink.

Austin whispers in my ear. "That is one fine-looking man, and you better not wuss out on this one. He likes you."

"He's my client," I remind her.

Austin leans down next to me. "And he owns this business, right?"

"Yes."

"And you aren't getting paid, right?" She raises her

shoulders as if her line of questioning is innocent.

"Right," I answer, unsure of what she's trying to imply.

Austin smiles. "Well then, there isn't a written rule forbidding you from working and playing together, is there? So go for it."

"I guess you would know all about forbidden romances," I say.

Her mouth opens in fake shock. "We notified Human Resources. We are in compliance with the team rules, thank you very much."

I almost laugh. "How many times have you had to say that statement?"

Austin rolls her eyes. "You have no idea. People are horrible." She leans in close. "But that boy over there looks like he would be worth the trouble."

So much trouble.

I don't have time for trouble.

"After the next round of shots, we need to dance," I say, ignoring Austin's Cheshire-cat grin. My thumb rubs my empty ring finger. What am I doing? Admiring his many assets is one thing, but physical contact is quite another. I don't want to disrupt his life. Maybe he's destined to meet the woman of his dreams in the next few weeks, and I wouldn't want to mess that up. That doesn't seem fair.

"Or we could stay right here and watch the hottie behind the bar stare at you," Eve says.

I roll my eyes. He's not…Oh, he is. Damn.

"I think he's picturing you naked," Eve suggests over my shoulder, "and in some kinky position."

"He is not. Do I need to cut you off already?" I warn.

I look over at Ben, and he looks like he wants to laugh, but instead he breaks out a sexy as hell grin. Oh, he might be. I wonder what…no, I do not wonder what.

Ben picks up the tray of drinks and walks back our way. I should back away from the bar, let Eve interact with him, but I hold my ground, not wanting him to think he's getting to me. He slides the shots toward me and leans in close. "You here for work or pleasure?"

My heart races as he draws out the word pleasure. "A bit of both, I guess," I breathe out, tipping my head up and purposely meeting his eyes.

"Well, let me know if you need any assistance with either." His voice is deep and gravelly, and I love the way it vibrates off my skin. Smooth.

A smile fills my face as I laugh. "Did you really say that?"

"Yep." His smile is bright, and I feel like it's shining just for me. Damn, he's cute. Damn his flirty lines. I can't get enough of them.

Izzy spots the drinks, and her hand goes between us. I look down, breaking eye contact.

As the drinks are passed out, we wave goodbye to Ben and make our way to the dance floor. I'm thankful it's far enough away I can't see him.

We spend the next hour dancing or trying to, as Eve is right—the DJ is a disaster. As soon as he plays a good song, he follows it up with some obscure beat that clears the floor.

I make my way to the bar while the girls gather up Izzy who has been dancing with some guy for the last two songs. Ben is not behind the bar, causing a wave of adrenaline to roll over me—relief or sadness, I'm not sure. I flag down Dex to pay the tab and tell him to thank Ben for us. He gives me a nod and then is off to make more drinks.

We decide to walk the four blocks to the next bar where Ollie and his band are playing.

My purse vibrates. Who's texting me this late?

UNKNOWN: Was it so bad you couldn't face me to say goodbye?

Ben. I did give him a business card. I save his number as a contact, and his beautiful eyes flash in my mind.

LAUREN: No. A friend's band is playing down the street at End Zone.

"Keep up," Eve yells from the front of the pack.

"I'm coming." I pick up the pace and attempt to text and walk, but a few drinks and heels cause me to slow back down to avoid dropping my phone or tripping and falling.

"Who are you texting? All your friends are here." Izzy grabs my phone. "Ohhh. It's Bartender Ben," she announces to the group and a few other partygoers walking by who yell back, "Hell, Yeah."

She leans toward me like she's going to whisper and instead yells, "If he offers to take you home, I approve."

"Shut up. I'm not going home with him; he's my client."

"He's only your client for a few weeks, but he will be seriously gorgeous for a lot longer. And the way he looked at you. Girl...." Gabby pulls Izzy toward the front of the group, and Austin shakes her head and pulls my arm into hers as we walk down the street.

"We aren't talking about Ben anymore tonight. New subject," I announce.

"Fine. You finish text flirting while we walk, and we won't mention him again." Austin exaggerates her nod and squishes her face.

Liar.

I try and remove her arm from hers. "Go away."

She doesn't let my arm go; instead she keeps me on a straight line while I look back down at my phone.

BEN: Friend?

Jealous? I almost laugh.

LAUREN: Ollie—you remember him right? The one making me help you
BEN: Yeah I remember him
BEN: My friend Nick is a bartender there. I'll tell him to look out for you
LAUREN: Don't go to any trouble
BEN: No trouble
Thanks for coming in
And your dress was beautiful
LAUREN: Thanks
BEN: Be safe
LAUREN: You too
BEN: Me? Well you might be right. A group of college girls are here. You know how they get

Eve pulls the phone from my hand. "These are the most boring texts ever. Oh wait, he's jealous and trying to make you jealous. I like him."

"Give it back."

"He said you looked beautiful and you said thanks? You suck at flirting. Tell him—"

I hip check her to get her off balance and take my phone back.

"I don't need you to tell me what to say." The girls all laugh along with me. We are always telling each other what to do, not that we always listen.

LAUREN: Tough job
BEN: Giggly girls. Ugh
LAUREN: Night. See you Sunday

I smile. He's not into giggly girls. He seems nice, but I'm not sure how long I'm going to be here. I have a few weeks to figure out if I want to stay. There are so many things I need to think about before my time runs out. I really should check on Matthew, but how do I check on him without actually speaking to him?

Eve grabs my hand, pulling me out of my head. Concentrate on the now. I'll deal with the rest tomorrow.

The girls weave down the sidewalk in front of me, laughing and pushing each other. My heart feels full. I could go home, back to my life, but then I couldn't keep us from drifting apart.

We stay until Ollie's band starts its last set and then move on to phase two of girls' night—late-night breakfast and deciding the winner of who got the worst pickup line of the night. Austin wins this round with some line about her red hair and reminding him of the cherry on top of a hot fudge sundae.

I HAVE the next day to myself. Old me told the girls I had to finish a project and wouldn't be available, so they are planning a sushi lunch—my least favorite food on the planet—and shopping, my second least favorite activity. This leaves new me with free time. Good thing I have plenty of work to do on Lauren's Life 2.0. By noon I've already gone to the gym, had breakfast, and figured out what teams to bet on this week.

Since I still have a few hours before I meet the girls at Eve's for dinner and movie night, I sit on the couch and finish my initial proposal for Ben. I made it through all six boxes of Ben's records, made some notes, did some analysis, and even found time for a little market research all while sitting at my desk at work this week. I feel a little guilty, but I did finish the project I was assigned in less than three hours. It helps that I remember most of the details from last time, and Mr. Holt loved my proposal which led to him opening a third and fourth store within the year. And it's not like I can tell my boss I got it done that quickly. She will think I can do all the projects that quickly when I can't. I'll meet my deadline and that's what counts. And with the work on Grayson Brothers', I looked busy all week instead of like one of my lazy teammates who scrolls the Internet most of the day.

Being reminded of Ben's financials has me heading for the ice cream. These are some seriously depressing numbers.

"How have you stayed afloat this long?" I stare down at his latest numbers.

My phone buzzes.

Ben.

The smile forms on my face before my brain remembers this is a bad idea.

BEN: How's the head?

LAUREN: Not bad. The girls said to tell you thanks for the drinks

BEN: No problem

LAUREN: Good night? Any coed trouble?

BEN: Nothing I couldn't handle

BEN: What's the expert prognosis?

LAUREN: I won't lie, the place needs some work. But nothing we can't fix

BEN: Good to hear

LAUREN: I'll have some preliminary ideas for you tomorrow. You working tonight?

Why did I ask that? I shouldn't have asked that.

BEN: Yeah. Headed for a quick hike over at Radnor Lake. The day is too beautiful to not be outside

I look out the window. Clear blue skies. Maybe I should sit outside and finish my proposal.

LAUREN: Have a good time soaking up some vitamin D

I set the phone down and pull out the next file.

The phone chimes.

BEN: Wanna come?

Me and Ben hanging out? Not a good idea.

LAUREN: I think I'll stick to reviewing your financials and coming up with some fabulous ideas to put GB's on the map

BEN: Do you need my help?

LAUREN: Not today. You need to get some rest and relaxation before I get my hands on you

That didn't come out professional. Why did I hit send before rereading that?

BEN: That sounds fun. How about you let me buy you brunch before we get started tomorrow?

I roll my eyes. He can't let me get away with anything.

LAUREN: Not necessary

BEN: It will ease my guilty conscience now that I know you're spending the weekend thinking about my problems

LAUREN: Fine. If it makes you feel better

BEN: 11 Nashville Eggschange

LAUREN: OK

LAUREN: Don't get eaten by a bear

BEN: Will do. I would hate to miss out on you getting ahold of me

This flirting has to stop. It's fun, but it can't go anywhere, and I don't want to lead him on. I have a plan. No deviations. Especially ones of the stormy-blue eye variety.

6

BEN

My head lifts for the hundredth time as the door opens. False alarm. I take another sip of my water when I hear the chime again and look up to see Lauren enter and scan the room. A smile spreads on my face as she spots me and waves. How does this woman look more beautiful every time I see her? I look down and adjust my shirt, trying not to stare, but the light grey sweater she's wearing pulls tight in all the right places and dips a little in front, and I can't help taking all of her in.

Dammit.

Keep your cool.

She's only here to help with the bar. This is not a date. Sure, she's smart, witty, beautiful, and easy to be around, but girls like that want more than some short-term fun. I may be here now, but I can't stay in this town forever. Once the bar is sorted, I need to resume my life.

Today is about the bar. A professional, working lunch. Nothing more.

As she reaches the table, I lean in for a hug before realizing we might not be friendly enough for hugs. Too late to turn back now, idiot. She reaches her arm around me and squeezes gently. A whiff of her soft floral perfume surrounds me, and I take in a deep breath as I release her and ease into my chair.

"Thanks for getting us a table," she says, her voice a little wobbly. The hug must have surprised her too.

"No problem."

"How was the hike?" She unloads a pile of papers from her bag onto the table.

"Good. You should've come. It was a beautiful day, and the leaves are just starting to change." I pick up my phone and find the picture before handing it to her. "Here, I took a few shots you can look through."

She takes my phone and scrolls through the pictures, stopping on one of a big oak tree with one red leaf.

"It's beautiful. Did you go hiking alone?"

"Yeah. I usually go alone."

"That doesn't sound safe. Alone in the woods." Her brows furrow as she looks up from the pictures at me.

"I stay on the trail; it's fine."

"Do you normally do day hikes or are you into camping also?" Her face scrunches at the word camp.

I chuckle. "I'm guessing you didn't spend a lot of time in the outdoors as a child?"

Her laugh is light and almost musical. The sound goes straight through me, lighting up all my nerve endings.

New mission.

Make Lauren laugh.

"No, I happened to be more of a bookworm and straight-A student. Playing outside in the backyard satisfied my need for nature. I'm guessing that's not true for you." She hands me back the phone, and I let my hand linger on hers for a moment before setting it on the table.

"No, it's the one thing my dad and I did, just the two of us. We would go out into the woods and forget everything else. Those are some of my favorite memories." My voice betrays me a little. Memories of my dad are always a double-edged sword, happy and painful. Dad would have loved the hike yesterday.

"That sounds nice. Father-son bonding." She pushes her sweater sleeves up and gives me a sweet smile.

"Yeah, so, no father-daughter bonding in the woods for you?"

"There wasn't much father-daughter anything. We didn't see eye to eye on much. He's a bit...never mind. We should get started." She pats the pile in front of her. "As you see we have a lot to go through."

"A bit what?" My curiosity is piqued.

She pauses. "You're not going to get to work until I tell you, are you?"

I shake my head.

"Fine. Selfish. Which is the opposite of what a parent should be."

I lean forward. "How so?"

Her hand rises and she bites her cuticle for a moment until she realizes what she's doing and puts her hands in her lap. "Truth?" She seems unsure I would actually want to know this.

"Always."

She takes a deep breath before speaking. "He bought a hardware store before I was born, but business started to decline, and he ended up losing it. He tried several times to start a new business. When they didn't turn a profit immediately, he would shut the doors. After that he had countless jobs—always trying to find the perfect one—but he would quit or get fired and always blame his failure on someone else. It was all about him."

"That doesn't make for a stable childhood."

"Lots of people have it worse, but I can't say it would be anyone's ideal childhood."

"And now you save other families from having to go through what you did. He must be proud."

"I never really thought of it that way, but I guess you're right. I do want to save others from going through what we did." Her voice is quiet like she is talking to herself. She recovers quickly and adds, "Anyway, I don't know what my dad thinks. We don't talk. He and my mom got a divorce when I was a freshman in high school, and we moved to Tennessee...and he stayed in Ohio."

"I'm sorry."

"It's fine. I'm over it now; it's been twenty years." She waves a hand to try and convince me she's indifferent.

Wait...what did she say? "Twenty years? I thought you said you were in high school."

"What? Oh yeah, it just feels like twenty. I mean...yeah." Her eyes lower to her hands and she rearranges the pages and pens in front of her. Why do I feel there is more to that story?

LAUREN

An hour and a half of being within a hair's breadth of Ben has me biting my nails again. How did he get me talking about my dad? I haven't spoken about him in years. He caught me off guard with his questions, and he looked so good when I got here that I about tripped over the tables on my way to greet him. The boy knows how to wear a button-up shirt and jeans. And the hug when he greeted me should have been awkward, but he smelled so good and felt so nice that the thoughts of it being awkward left me. Now he's being quiet. Not even a flirty line. Which should be a relief, but I'm not sure I like Ben being quiet.

I look down at my growing list. Once we started and I laid out some initial ideas, his mood changed.

* **Serve food - limited menu to start**

* **Additional staff**

* **Add bands to Thurs. Night - new bands - draw crowds**

* **Upgrade decor - inside and out**

* **Marketing**

* **New DJ**

His face became unreadable. He didn't make any comments—not a word. I did ask him to let me finish before he commented, but I didn't expect him to sit perfectly still and not utter a word.

I hate to spring all this on him at once, but we have a limited amount of time to save Grayson's and I need him on board as soon as possible, and that means he needs to start the change cycle. Change is no different than grief, and you have to work your way through it.

And I know about change. I'm in my own change cycle now and not sure which way to go. Less than six weeks to decide if I should stay or go back is not enough time to decide.

While I wait for Ben to return from the bathroom, I pull out my journal and to-do list, with Matthew and my looming timeline at the top of my list.

* **Countdown to Matthew**

I don't think there is any coincidence that the date of

meeting Matthew is the same as my last chance to return to the future. But I'm not sure what that means. I haven't seen him since my first night back. What if I meet him too early and mismanage this time travel thing? I wish I could talk this problem through with him. We could figure out a logical conclusion. But not yet. I need to wait until the time is right to see him. My finger runs down my list, and I cross off this weekend's birthday bash. I add a note to send Gabby a card next week to congratulate her on her latest ad campaign success and send some flowers to Austin to make up for not picking her up at the airport.

Ben taps my shoulder as he returns. I close my journal and tuck it back in my bag. He resumes his seat next to me and takes a deep breath and sits up straight. His hands cross over his chest, his jaw is set tight, and his brows are knitted so tight they look like one. That's not good. Change is hard. And even harder when it's personal.

I lean forward and rest my hand on his crossed arms. "I know it's a lot. But I'm here to help you. We're a team." A team. That's what Matthew and I were, not what Ben and I are. "Well, maybe not a team. I meant to say I'm here to guide you through these changes. You're not in this alone."

His eyes go to my hand. His arm is warm, and my cold fingers are soaking in all the warmth they can after sitting under the air conditioning all this time. He uncrosses his arms, and I start to move my hand away when he wraps it between his two large hands. His eyes find mine, and I see the crinkles in the corners from his smile. He seriously has the most beautiful eyes ever.

"Your hand is freezing." He runs his hands back and forth over mine. I swallow hard and hope he can't hear my my blood rushing through my body as fast as race car goes around the track. "So, you hate my DJ that much?" His lip curls on one end as I slide my hand out of his and reach for my pen.

"Yes, he's a disaster."

Ben chuckles. He has a great chuckle, deep and musical and filled with amusement as if he's remembered an inside joke and you are in on it.

"Adding food sounds expensive."

"I know, but I think it's where you can really make some money. I'm thinking limited menu, limited hours—say, only four to nine."

"Booking bands is time-consuming, and I like music, but I'm not an expert."

"I have a music connection, and I know a few up-and-coming bands that I think will help put you on the map."

If we can get a few future superstars on the lineup, they will make Grayson Brothers' the place to see the best new bands. Good thing Ollie made Eve and I listen to all his favorite musicians and watch the Country Music Awards every year. Who knew that would come in handy?

"And a new DJ—got one of those in your arsenal?"

"I have a lead on that."

He shakes his head. "Of course you do. I'm..." His phone chimes for the tenth time since we sat down. Each time he ignores it.

"I have an idea. Instead of just looking at all of this on paper, let me show you what I'm talking about. Can you get someone to cover for you on Wednesday?"

His look is suspicious but curious. "Yeah…"

"Good, then we're going on a little field trip."

He squints his eyes and cocks his head as if trying to figure out my plan. "Okay."

"I'll meet you at Grayson's at eight on Wednesday."

"We haven't discussed the cost of all this yet."

"Let's decide what you like first and then we'll figure out the costs. I can't scare you all at once."

"Gee, thanks." His face stays neutral, but his jaw is locked. I know inside he's screaming. I want to give him a hug—not a friendly hello hug but a hug that says it will all be all right. That I'm here for him, but that could cross a line, and after already opening up about my dad, I don't think that's a good idea.

"I promise, it's all going to work out. It might even be fun."

His phone chimes again, and he pauses to read it then sighs before giving me a weak smile. "You know I'm going to hold you to that, right?"

"I don't break promises." Not anymore.

Izzy's office is not what I expected. The building is from the forties, but the inside is all glass and metal and marble. They had to have gutted the entire building, removing all of the charm one brick at a time.

I ask the front desk where to find Izzy and head up the elevator to the sixth floor.

"Not much privacy in this place," I say to Izzy, as I walk into her office.

"I thought we were meeting downstairs," she says, jumping from her desk to greet me with a hug.

"Well, I thought I would check out your workspace. I realized I've never been up here."

"What do you think?" she asks.

"It's bright. Like how I imagine the sun shines on Mercury."

She laughs. "Yeah, they went a little overboard with the glass, but you get used to it."

"Do they not allow personal items?" I ask. Her office is sparse. There is a large framed photo of a rowing team and something about teamwork, but other than that nothing besides office supplies and electronics.

"No, they do." Izzy looks around, obviously not understanding what I'm saying.

"Then where's your stuff?"

She picks up a picture of the five of us girls that is tucked behind her monitor. "Right here."

"That's it? What about a plant or a photo of something you actually like to do?" I gesture to the rowing picture and try not to laugh.

"I don't need all that at work. It would be distracting."

Distracting? She spends at least nine hours a day here. She should have a few things to make it feel like her space. I'll have a plant delivered next week to fill up part of the large wall of glass that overlooks a park.

"Let me grab my purse and we can go. I blocked off my calendar for a long lunch. Never know when you'll have time for another one."

"What? We've had lunch before."

"You are correct. Once. My first week here. But that was almost three years ago." She ushers me toward the door.

"Oh." She's right. But I'm fixing that, starting today.

"Let's go." She nods toward the stairs.

"No tour?"

"You want a tour? You can basically see everything from here." She sweeps her hand around the open hallway.

"I still want a tour."

"Fine, I'll give you the two-cent tour on our way out."

I turn around and look toward the wall of offices across the small foyer, all similar with large glass windows and wooden doors. Seriously, there is no privacy in this place.

The man across the hall steps out of his doorway while pulling on his dark blue suit jacket around his nicely toned...well, everything.

"Well, the view from your office isn't half bad," I whisper.

"What?" Izzy asks, coming to stand next to me. "Oh, that's the new guy. He stole my job," she whispers back.

"Stole?"

"I told you. The acquisition manager position should have been mine. I've worked here for almost three years, and I'm the best analyst here. That should have been my job."

I don't remember this. I can't remember her mentioning applying for anything. "What happened? The interview didn't go well?"

"Interview? Why should I have to interview? They should know my worth and promote me."

I turn and face her head-on, my mouth gaping open. "You never asked for the job, did you?"

"No. Why would I?" The perplexed look on her face says it all.

"I don't know—so they actually know you're interested. Iz, they don't usually hand people promotions. People have to actively participate in their careers."

"My work should stand for itself," she mutters and takes off down the hall.

She gives me the quick tour, and we head down the stairs. I can't help but compare the charmless building to Izzy's attire. Her suit is tan and lifeless. Her usually long curly hair is in a tight bun at the base of her neck, and her makeup is...well, I'm not sure she's wearing any. Where is Izzy? Big hair, bold colors, overbearing personality Izzy.

As we reach the street, I can't stop myself from asking.

"Izzy, what's up with this outfit? Were you running late this morning?"

She looks down at herself. "What? I wear this every Tuesday."

I stumble at her words. "Seriously?"

"What's wrong with it?" she asks, as if looking like you got dressed in the dark in someone else's apartment is normal.

"It's tan, which is not good for your skin tone, it's too big, and well…it's not you at all."

"It's not that bad. I'm at work to work, not to be a fashion icon. I have five outfits for five days of the week. That way I don't have to think about what I'm wearing. No one cares anyway. I'm in my office, like, ninety percent of the time."

Is she kidding me?

"Are all your clothes like this?" I demand.

She shrugs her shoulders. "I guess."

"Change of plans." I pull her to the street and hail a cab.

SIXTY-FIVE MINUTES, two stores, and five new suits later, Izzy and I sit down for a quick lunch. Glad she penciled in a long lunch today. Izzy fought me about buying her new clothes, but I refused to listen. There is no way she is ever going to get promoted when she looks like she doesn't care about herself. If she doesn't care about herself, how is she going to care about the client?

We settle at a table outside along the sidewalk with our salads and iced teas. The day is beautiful, and I could use some sunlight.

"I can't believe I let you talk me into all these." Izzy pats the garment bag on the empty seat next to her.

"I can't believe you wouldn't wear one back to the office." I shake my head and reach for my drink.

She looks at me as if I have grown a third eye. "How would it look if I showed up back at work in different clothes?"

"According to you, no one would see you. So, who cares?" I remind her.

She grabs her glass of tea and takes a drink, ignoring my comment.

"Izzy, I'm not trying to be rude. But I'm confused. This" —I swipe my hand up and down toward her—"isn't you? Who is this?"

"It's me. Work me is a little less..."

"Fun? Beautiful? Interesting?"

She crosses her arms and her tone becomes serious. "No one cares about my personality at work, only how I do my job."

She's so wrong. They need to see her fierceness. Her never-give-up attitude.

"That's not true. They care..." My words fall short as I see Matthew walking up the street with a gorgeous blonde woman in a red coat. She looks like the same one from the bar that had her hand on his leg. Her arm is wrapped around his and they are laughing. His smile is so bright, and his wide shoulders seem so relaxed, I barely recognize him. What is he doing out at lunch? He usually works through lunch unless he's meeting a client.

Well...maybe that's later. Maybe this Matthew takes leggy blondes out for lunch. They stop about twenty feet from us as Matthew pulls out his phone, reads, and then types out a message. Her gaze sweeps around, and I lower my eyes.

"You alright?" Izzy asks.

"Fine. Just thought I saw someone I knew."

She glances behind her, obviously not recognizing anyone.

I chance another glance at them. Matthew places his phone back in his pocket, and they turn to walk toward us. My back stiffens, and the woman catches me watching. I give her a smile and a small head nod as if it's an accident I was staring at them, as if I didn't want to stand up and take her hands off my husband and have him smile at me the way he's smiling at her.

"Are you sure you're okay?" Izzy asks.

"I'm fine. Let's finish lunch. I need to get back to work."

And not think about how Matthew never smiles at me that way.

7

LAUREN

The light from the fading sun drifts into my bedroom, causing the usual cotton-white walls to shift from orange to pink. The fabric wrapped over the king-size four-poster bed flaps in the breeze from the open window allowing me to enjoy one of the few truly nice fall days.

I pull on my third outfit, looking for the right mix of night on the town and business. Ben and I are going to three bars tonight to see how they've incorporated ideas similar to what I have in mind for Grayson Brothers' or GB's if I have my way. That suggestion will wait until later. I think I dropped enough on him already. He tried to hide the "are you insane?" look from me, but I could see it in his eyes. Seeing things tonight will help.

My arms go to my side as I examine my outfit—black jeans and a shiny silver tank top that will look great under my short black leather jacket. Too sexy? I mean I don't want to look like I just left work, but I don't want to look like I'm hoping to take someone home with me tonight. My mind flashes to thoughts of Ben in my bed, his rough beard kissing my neck.

Dammit. No. No. NO. This is professional, not personal.

Working on this project is keeping me from hunting down Matthew and from overthinking everything about this blasted time travel business. Though at some point before my full moon deadline, I need to sit down and make a decision.

But not tonight.

Tonight, I have work to do. My deep plum, crossbody purse holds the three things I need— small notebook, phone, and wallet.

Time to go.

Ben's leaning against his truck when I arrive. I park next to him and take a second to appreciate his outfit through my tinted windows. Dark wash jeans that fit perfectly and a dark grey denim shirt covering a white tee. Damn. It's going to be a long night. This is work. Not a date. Work, I remind myself.

I open the door, and Ben's hand extends down to help me out.

"Thanks. Sorry I'm late." His grip is firm as he pulls me to my feet. Standing this close has my nerve endings begging for more contact. Maybe this is a bad idea.

"You aren't late. We said seven thirty. It's..."—he looks at his watch—"7:31." He chuckles.

"I consider being five minutes early, late," I tell him, adding my own chuckle to his.

"Shall we?" He opens the passenger door of his truck to let me in. I can't keep the smile off my face at the sweet gesture. Not all men are gentlemen anymore, but Ben is.

Once I'm settled, he shuts the door and walks to the driver's side.

"So, where's our first stop?" He buckles his seatbelt and turns on the ignition before moving his eyes to meet mine. I pull out my notebook and see him bite his lip before asking, "How did you fit a notebook in that purse?"

I shrug. "It's small."

"Answer me one question."

"Okay." This sounds serious.

"You seem to have a pretty good memory, so why do you need to make so many lists?"

Is he serious?

"Lists keep you on track, help you stay on plan and achieve your goals. Lists are the best." My enthusiasm earns me a head-shaking laugh.

"If you say so. To me they are more like lists of never-ending tasks that eat up your life."

"Yeah, but you're ten times more likely to achieve your goals if you write them down. Like tonight. We have three places to go and three different reasons. We need to make sure to pay attention to those things at each place and not get caught up in the night and forget. So, I made a list."

"Where to?" he asks again without further comment, obviously knowing I won this battle.

"Methos on Church. The food there is similar to what I think you should offer. A few specials, but mostly staples with a slight twist."

"A slight twist?" Skepticism oozes from his pores.

"Don't look scared; it will be fine."

I admit the place is a dive bar, nothing special. The furniture is older than the old me, but the food is fantastic, and the company isn't bad either. Ben is easy to be with. I don't have to put on a show or be on the lookout for a client.

Dammit, I'm comparing again. Ugh…stop comparing him to Matthew. Though Matthew would never eat here. Even when we were first dating, we ate at places to be seen and to network. Well, when we actually took the time to have dinner together. Those first years were so busy, so full of…work.

"Hey,"—Ben nudges my arm—"you alright?"

"Sorry, random thought. I'm good. So, how long have you lived in Nashville?" I ask.

He lets me change the subject. "Born and raised. I've even lived in the same house my whole life."

"Wow. That doesn't happen often. Did your parents leave you the house?" I cringe. I shouldn't have brought up his parents; that's too personal.

Ben doesn't seem to notice my dismay as he answers. "Yeah, my mom died when I was young, and my dad died when I was seventeen. They left it to me. I rent it out when I'm out of town."

"I'm sorry," I say quietly.

He shrugs but doesn't look my way. "No need to be sorry. It was a long time ago."

"That doesn't mean it still doesn't hurt." I reach out to touch him, reassure him, but pull back before making any contact. Stay out of his personal space.

"Did your dad ever remarry?" I ask quickly, trying to deflect the awkwardness of my gesture.

Ben's head tips back as he laughs. "No, he most certainly did not get remarried. My parents had one of those soulmate kind of marriages. They were…perfect, and when she passed, he never gave anyone a chance to get close to him. He became the king of the one-night stands. There were so many I gave up trying to learn their names." The laughter drains away as he speaks.

"That..."

"Sucked. Yeah. But that was him. Not me." His voice is stern, and he catches my eye as if trying to convey the truth in his words.

"So, you don't take a new lady home from the bar every night?" I give him a wink.

"No, I'm not a one-night stand kinda guy." He doesn't wink. He doesn't smile. He's serious.

"I didn't...mean to imply that." The food arrives. I dig in and burn my tongue.

"What do you do besides save small businesses in a single bound?"

I barely avoid choking at his joke. "What do you mean?"

"You have any hobbies?"

"Not really. Umm...I used to enjoy taking photos." I start laughing.

He tilts his head.

"Sorry, I just remembered I begged for a camera for Christmas one year and never even took it out of the box." That thing has been in my closet forever. Maybe I need to dig it out and donate it before it becomes an antique this time.

"What do you do at night when you go home from work?"

"Well, I have dinner and then usually make notes on my current projects or review spreadsheets. Sometimes I read."

"Basically, you're saying your hobby is more work?"

Is he right? Do I relax by doing more work? Since I've been back, I haven't spent time on work, but I have been using my nights to work on Grayson's and also building up my portfolio and making notes for what and when to buy stocks in the future and what teams I need to bet on.

Hmmm. Is he right? "Umm...no. I hang out with my friends."

"That's not a hobby." He grimaces and places his hand on mine. "We need to find you a hobby."

"No, I'm fine." I remove my hand and pick up my drink.

"No, you're not. You're gonna burn out before you're thirty if you don't find something else to do besides work. Do you like to work out?"

"I do a few days a week, but I don't want that to be my hobby." My words come out quickly, and Ben nods his head as he sets down his drink.

"Got it, no running."

"What? Are you making a list?" That will be the day.

"Maybe."

We spend the rest of the time eating and Ben coming up with the craziest hobby suggestions. My sides hurt from laughing.

"I'm officially a lost cause. How about we refocus on Grayson's? What's your opinion on the chopped steak?"

"You should know; you ate half of it," he scolds me with his deep velvet voice.

It's true. Even though this isn't a date, he has been sweet all night, even sharing his dinner when he caught me checking out the chopped steak and mashed potatoes he ordered. My chicken wrap had everything I was looking for —good presentation, quality ingredients, and tasted great. It was on par with what I think would work at GB's. Simple food, amazing quality, and taste.

"So, what do you think? Could you serve something like this at GB's?"

His eyes cut to me. "GB's? Are we calling it that now?"

I tilt my head to the side and shrug my shoulders. "Just trying it on."

"Let's not." He shakes his head, not buying my attempt to be coy.

"Fine. More on that later. Back to the food."

He lets out a long breath. "It was good. Nothing fancy. Seems pretty straightforward, but we would need to hire more staff, not only in the kitchen but on the floor."

"True. But right now, we're only talking about the food. If money were no object, would you want Grayson's to serve this kind of food?"

He looks at his plate and picks up the menu, flipping it over. "Yeah."

"Excellent."

"But..."

"No buts, that is all we need to know for now. Come on; we have two more stops."

BEN

Stop two is only a few blocks south so we walk. I deserve a medal for resisting the urge to wrap my arm around her shoulders. She looks so good in those jeans and little jacket. I think she's trying to kill me. All dinner long I wanted to touch her, move her closer to me. It took every ounce of control not to reach over and push her bangs off to the side so I could see her eyes better—see if all these feelings I'm having are one-sided—but now isn't the time for that. This is just business for her, and I need to try and respect that, even if it kills me.

Our next stop is darker inside than Grayson's. The tables are metal, and there are more low-top tables than high tops and even some booths on a far wall. The ceiling exposes all the heating and plumbing. I stop to look around, and

Lauren nudges my hand, nodding to a booth in the corner with a view of the whole bar.

Before we can sit down, she starts with the questions. "Well?"

"Well what?" I can't help giving her a hard time. She looks adorable when she rolls her eyes at me.

"What do you think of the decor?"

"What decor? It looks like an abandoned building that they filled with tables and chairs."

She laughs as we slide into the booth. Her laugh is like catnip. I can't stop wanting more. She needs to lighten up. How can she not have a hobby? How can she be this smart and beautiful and sweet and waste her life in an office?

Her laughter dies down, and I fight to keep my focus on her words and not her red lips.

"Good, I wasn't sure if you were into the industrial look. Grayson's is a little of both, but I think we should go more toward a modern feel while showcasing the wood beams and feed store history. Kinda mix it up a bit."

"That I like." And her ideas too.

She leans down to reach into her purse, and her shirt falls forward, exposing the tops of her perfectly round breasts and a pink bra.

"Ben?" I'm startled by her calling my name. It sounds so good when she says it. It would sound even better if she said it while under... Shit, she's talking to me. I take a long blink.

"Yes," I answer, no idea what she just asked. My head tips up, and I'm looking into her deep green eyes. Today they seem a little darker than last time due to the heavy lining of her eyes, making her look a little dangerous. It would be worth the risk to find out what's...

"What where you just thinking?" I've been caught. Her voice is a warning, but her lips are turning up.

My eyes and mouth both squish together as I think of an answer. "Baseball?" That's not much of an answer. I give her my best innocent grin.

She raises an eyebrow and tips her head to the side. "Sure. Listen, maybe we need to talk again about boundaries and mixing business and pleasure."

"I'm all for mixing business and pleasure," I add with a bit of a Tennessee drawl for effect.

Her face turns a slight shade of pink, and she sighs but doesn't look angry.

"Ben."

"What? I like you. Why should I pretend I don't? Do you have a boyfriend?" She hasn't mentioned one, but she seemed pretty interested in Birthday Boy the night we met.

"What? No."

Is that a *no, I shouldn't pretend* or *no, I don't have a boyfriend*?

"Are you seriously always this straightforward?" she continues.

"Usually. Does it bother you?" I lean back in the booth and cross my arms over my chest.

"No." Her answer is swift and sure.

"Good, cause it's actually one of the things I like best about you too."

She pauses. Is she unsure of her next words or unsure she wants to say them? Maybe both.

"Ben, I like you too, and I appreciate you being honest, but I can't." Her stern words are meant to get me back in line. I know this, but the rest of me would not mind her using that voice to tell me exactly what she wants. Damn, she's going to kill me.

I keep my eyes locked on hers. She's probably right.

Getting involved is not a good idea, but I can't get her out of my head.

"Why?" I ask.

"Why?" she asks back to me like my question makes no sense.

I square my shoulders toward her. "Yes, why? You don't have a boyfriend. You don't have any hobbies filling up your time. Am I not your type?"

Lauren looks me up and down. "I don't date my clients."

Oh, that's not the reason. There's something else. "We've been over this, and I thought we agreed I was technically not your client."

"I think that was your conclusion, not mine," she states matter-of-factly.

She leans back, and I follow her lead and push my back to the cold faux-leather booth. "You should make an exception for me." I smile and chuckle trying to lighten the mood. "It's not like I'm actually paying you."

She doesn't answer. She shakes her head and then takes a deep breath. "I can't. I don't have a boyfriend, but there is…someone."

Birthday Boy. I knew it. Time to defuse the situation. "Fine,"—for now, I amend silently— "I'll keep my appreciation focused on your business talents. What's next on the list?"

Lauren meets my gaze for a moment then reaches for her purse.

I'll let her think on my proposal for a while. We have time. Time to get to know each other. Time to get her to make an exception to her rule. Time for me to convince her I'm better than Birthday Boy.

. . .

Stop number three is much more what Grayson's should be —live music, people mingling and dancing. The decor is a little too modern with its clear plastic tables and concrete bar, but the patrons are enjoying themselves.

We've only been here a few minutes when a fourth green-shirted employee walks by. How many people work here? I'll have to double the staff on the weekends if we have this many people.

Not that it would be a bad thing, I guess. But short term, how am I going to afford more employees? My stomach clenches as tight as my bank account feels. Hopefully, Lauren has something in her bag of tricks to help with cash flow.

Lauren walks a few steps in front of me. My hand keeps reaching up to touch the small of her back as we weave around the tables. So far, I've managed to pull it back before making contact. She's been clear she's not interested in starting anything, even though she keeps flirting with me before she remembers to shut it down.

The sway of her hips, the curve of her breasts in that shirt, those red heels—I force my eyes forward and to the top of her head away from all the lovely things that are Lauren. She checks her phone and makes a left turn in the sea of people. I follow along and glance toward the band. I see Ollie and give him a wave, and he nods in return. They have a good country-rock sound, and people are filling the dance floor.

Lauren stops at a table near the edge of the stage and hugs Eve. Eve is dressed in a beautiful white dress that reminds me of a toga with one shoulder bare. She's an art dealer or something like that. I can see it; she's petite, a little too thin for my taste, and her short hair is going in all directions. She looks a little out of place in this bar but doesn't seem to notice.

"Eve, you remember Ben," Lauren shouts.

"Oh yes, I remember." She gives me a wicked smile and I extend my hand.

What exactly have these girls been saying about me behind my back?

"Nice to see you again."

"You two been having fun?" She raises her eyebrow at Lauren who is giving her a "shut up" stare. I turn my head to the band to keep from commenting.

"Yes, it's been very productive," Lauren says through her teeth.

"How about I get some drinks? You okay here?" I ask, as Lauren's attention turns to the band. She nods her head and smiles. Damn, she's pretty when she smiles.

The line for the drinks is two deep, but I recognize an old Grayson's bartender behind the bar. Mateo left about a year ago, and I can't blame him; tips are low when there's no one to serve. He gives me a nod, and I mouth for a vodka martini, a whiskey sour, and a beer.

The guy next in line glares at me, no doubt wondering why I am being served before him. It pays to know people behind the bar. I make my way to the waitress station as Mateo sets down the two drinks I ordered and my favorite beer. If Lauren is able to help me save Grayson's, maybe I can steal him back.

"On the house," he says. I nod and drop a twenty on the bar.

This place on a Wednesday is busier than any Saturday I've seen at Grayson's. The energy from all the people runs through me. I miss Grayson's being this way. Could Lauren's ideas really get it back?

Eve is standing alone watching the band when I arrive at the table. I set the drinks down, and she looks my way before nodding to her right. Lauren is about twenty feet away talking to a man dressed in jeans and a long-sleeved t-shirt shirt. Who the hell is that guy? My protective instincts go into high alert.

I pick up Lauren's drink and walk straight up to them. The music is blaring, and the stage lights aren't bright enough to make out what they're saying. I slide my arm around Lauren's back and place the drink between her and the man. Sure, it's a dick move staking my claim, but I don't like the looks of this guy.

Her back straightens as she turns to look at me, her eyes growing wide. I can't read this situation, but I don't like it—not that she's talking to another man, but this one in particular. Something is not on the up-and-up with him, and years of being around a bar have taught me to read people, so I don't doubt my instincts.

"Who's your friend here, Lani?" the man says.

I turn my head toward Lauren who shakes her head ever so slightly as her eyes bore into me. Be quiet. I get it. Why is the man calling her Lani?

"This is my boyfriend, Billy. I told you he doesn't like my betting, so I had to give it up."

"You cost me a new customer." He pokes me in the chest. "You're crazy not to let her bet. She was doing pretty good for a newbie."

"You flatter me," Lauren says, laying it on a bit thick.

Betting? Oh, shit. This guy is a bookie. Why is Lauren on a first-name basis with a bookie?

"We better get back to my friend." Lauren motions back toward the bar.

"You know where to find me," he says, before he turns and walks to the back of the club.

I lock my hand in hers and pull her to the table. She drops my hand the moment we stop.

"What the hell, Lani?" I ask loud enough for her to hear as I lean in.

"Long story."

"I bet it is, but that guy is not someone to screw around with. How do you know him?"

Eve dips her head down and looks away. Her chest is shaking.

I turn my attention to Eve. "I don't think this is funny. I doubt your husband would be all too happy to hear who you two are hanging out with."

Lauren turns to me. "Ollie knows all about it and... happy isn't the word I would use. But I'm a grown woman, and I can do whatever I want."

"You're still placing bets?"

"Yes, but not directly. I have someone place them for me."

I close my eyes and let the music roar into my ears. Calm down. She's fine. She isn't going to see him again. But she's still gambling? Who the hell is this girl? She drinks twenty-five-year-old whiskey, is a workaholic, helps clueless people like me for free, and apparently has a bookie. What... the...hell?

Her hand reaches for mine and squeezes.

"Let's forget that happened and dance. Ollie's band is on fire tonight." I turn my attention to the stage and let her lead me to the middle of the dance floor. The music slows and I twirl her around once and enjoy the surprise on her face when she stops in front of me. My hand wraps around her waist and I pull her close, close enough to smell her coconut shampoo and feel the heat from her body. Her lips part slightly, and she slings her arm over my shoulder before falling into step with me.

"Where did you learn to dance?" she asks.

"My mom taught me. I grew up in a bar, remember, and girls like to dance, so I paid attention to that lesson."

I twirl her again, causing her to laugh and give me a bright smile.

"Well, nice moves, cowboy."

"Not really much of a cowboy."

"Keep your mouth shut. It's not every day a girl finds a boy who actually knows how to dance."

"Yes, ma'am." I do a little two step and then twirl her again. Her laugh fills my ears like a sweet symphony. Later she can try and blame it on having too much to drink, but she's only had two drinks all night. For once she's actually having fun.

Fun with me.

If she meant to distract me from the bookie incident, she nailed it. The only things I can think of are how her hand fits perfectly in mine and how touching even the edge of her hip is causing my body to hum. My mouth goes dry as her eyes search mine, asking questions I don't know the answers to. I reach my hand up and touch her face, causing a shiver to run down her body. I lean toward her and she pulls pack.

"We should check on Eve." Her voice is shaky, her body stiff, the laughter from a moment ago gone. She drops my hand and makes her getaway.

"Yeah," I say even though she's too far away to hear. Eve is waiting at the table with a shit-eating grin on her face. Guess she didn't miss the show.

"Done dancing already?" she asks as I arrive back at the table.

"We need to head out," Lauren informs Eve.

"Oh, really?" her voice sings.

"Yeah, I have to be up early tomorrow. I need to get home." Lauren is faced away from me, but I'm sure Eve is getting the stare down.

I know it's too much too fast, but having her in my arms for even a minute is worth whatever cold treatment she's going to give me now.

"Seems like a waste of a perfectly good night to me. It was nice to see you again, Ben. See you soon," Eve says.

"You too, Eve. Tell Ollie to swing by when he gets time this week."

"Will do. Have fun."

The ride back to her car is silent. I keep my thoughts to myself as I can tell she is having some internal debate on her side of the truck. Her door opens before I can turn off the engine.

I round the truck and find her standing between our cars with her eyes set on me.

"I hope tonight proved useful. I feel like we got to see what we needed to. What do you think?" she asks in her professional voice—back to business I see.

The need to ask questions and understand what she is thinking pushes against my better judgment, but I hold it back and answer, "I think you're right."

"Great, so I'll make some notes and come up with some recommendations that we can review next week."

"Sounds good." It takes everything I have to lean back on the side of the truck and not reach for her.

She pauses and then takes a deep breath. "I know that got a little weird. I'm sorry."

I chuckle. Here I thought she would run away and not mention it again, but instead she lays it all out there. "Yeah, the bookie threw me for a loop. Ready to tell me how that happened?"

"No."

"Hmmm. Well, how about you tell me why you pulled me on the dance floor and couldn't bear to dance with me for a whole song? Do I smell?" I lift my shirt to my nose.

She shuffles her feet and lifts her eyes to mine. "You know why."

"No, I really don't. You keep telling me we need to be professional, but every time you look at me, I see something else. We're two single adults who obviously have a connection, so what's the real problem?" I watch her tense, but I don't move.

"Ben, listen, I...can't start a relationship with you. And I don't think us hooking up would be a good idea." She may be shooting straight, but I don't like it.

"Or does it have something to do with Birthday Boy?" My instincts say it's him. I saw how she looked at him. There is something between them; even in the lights of the parking lot I can see her face turn white. Bingo.

"Who?" Her voice is barely a whisper.

"The old friend you bought a fifty-dollar glass of whiskey for on his birthday." My voice comes out a little harsher than before. Her answers tonight about another man have all been BS, and she and I both know it.

Her mouth opens and then shuts. I see her mind working.

"Don't start lying to me now. Who's the guy?"

She pauses before clenching her jaw and crossing her arms. "His name is Matthew."

"That's it? His name is Matthew. You obviously know him, but you didn't even talk to him. You bought him a drink and left. When I asked him, he didn't know who you were."

"It's a long story, and if I told you, you'd never believe me." Her voice trails off as she looks to the sky.

I cross my hands over my chest. "I have time."

Lauren's posture changes as the words leave my mouth. Her back straightens, and the wistfulness of a moment ago is gone. It's like a metal rod was shoved down her back, and her words come out like cold steel. "But I don't. And no offense, but who I buy drinks for is none of your business."

She's right of course. Who am I to demand answers? I'm just some bartender she flirted with, some guy she's doing a favor for, some guy who won't be around long enough to have a relationship with.

"You're right. I'm nothing to you." And I guess I never will be.

8

LAUREN

The smell of fresh paint and grease greets me as I enter the motorcycle shop.

Music maker by night, auto mechanic by day—building a music career takes time, and life takes money hence Ollie's day job. He majored in business to make his parents happy and got a minor in music for himself, but working a corporate job didn't last more than a year. I chuckle to myself. He's not the shirt-and-tie type.

I sidestep past a pair of bikes in various states of being dismantled or re-assembled and see one of the mechanics off to the side. He gives me a nod toward the office.

Ollie is standing with his back to me with a pair of navy coveralls hanging around his waist. As usual he's rocking a T-shirt that's pulling tight against his lean back and showcasing the tattoos on the hard-earned muscles of his arms. He turns the moment I enter the door.

"Hey, Lauren. What are you doing here?" He twists the

leather straps on his watch. "I'm about to head home and get cleaned up before the opening."

"I know. I just wanted to catch up with you for a minute."

Like the girls, I've made an effort to make sure Ollie and I stay connected. He's not only Eve's husband, he's my friend and has been since college.

He leans against the corner of the desk and studies me.

"What kind of trouble you in?" He eyes me trying to assess my mental status. He's been watching me closely since I got back. He knows something's up but hasn't said it outright yet. If anyone would believe me, he would, but then he'd ask questions about his future and him and Eve...and I can't.

"Why do you assume I'm in trouble?" I mock surprise.

"Cause I've known you for more than a minute and last time..." I wave his next comment off.

"I'm not in trouble. I need a favor." I give him my best innocent-girl look.

He runs his hands through his hair. I guess grease won't make his dirty-blond locks look any darker. "Oh, that's worse."

I punch him in the shoulder, causing him to laugh. I met Ollie sophomore year of college and we became instant friends, which didn't make sense since we are opposites. His interests tended toward music and riding his motorcycle, while I stuck to studying and finding suitable internships. But somehow it worked, and I made sure he didn't fail out of school while he made sure I didn't spend all my nights studying.

"Can you help me with the Grayson project? I think having you at our next meeting would be a big help."

His face contorts in an exaggerated thinking face. "You need me to chaperone your meeting?"

"No, I need your input. Like the stage. It seems small to me. When you play there do you have enough room? Need more outlets? A place to store equipment?"

"And I need to come to your meeting to answer those questions? Cause I can answer them now and save us both some time. I would love it if the stage was double the current size, had three or four more outlets, preferably in the floor, and yes, a place to store some equipment off to the side would be ideal."

"Thanks. I'd still like you to come to the meeting. I think you can offer other insights since you've played at bars all over town." I use my business voice to convey the serious nature of my request, because this is not about needing a chaperone, it's about his insight. Though it wouldn't hurt having someone else in the room to keep things from getting more complicated between Ben and me.

"This isn't about him trying to kiss you on the dance floor and you running away?" A smirk forms on his lips as he speaks.

A huff escapes me. "That woman of yours has a big mouth."

"Yes, she does." He smiles, giving me the impression he's not talking about her gossiping.

I shake my head. Men.

"Seriously, what's the problem? Ben's a good guy."

"When did you become a girl?" I pipe back.

He glares at me like a teenage girl who is over her mama telling her what to do.

Moving closer to him, I lower my voice back to normal. "You know it's not that easy. There are too many things going on in my life right now, and I don't need any additional complications."

Ollie turns to get something off his desk.

"Sex doesn't have to be a complication. It could be about having fun. You remember having fun, right?"

"I remember." My eyes sting with all the things I remember. There are too many memories battling in my head, along with a giant load of what-ifs.

"Then, what's the problem?" If I didn't know better, I would think he was trying to read my mind.

"You know I don't do casual," I say, batting away his questions and the memories flapping around in my brain.

"Maybe you should try it." He crosses his arms and leans back on the desk.

"You're not being helpful." I can't start anything with Ben. I can't. Casual or not, it feels...weird.

"Oh I am." He drawls out the words. "The last few weeks you have been...different. What's really going on?"

"Just busy. Work and Grayson's," I lie. I wish I could tell him what was going on. I wish I could tell anyone, but I'm still having trouble believing it myself some days.

"That's what's different. You haven't mentioned work in a while." Ollie nods his head up and down like he's a bobblehead.

"Work is work. Why would I mention it?" I think I did a total of two hours of actual work this week. I spent most of my time on Grayson's and updating my stock portfolio.

He chuckles. "Because normally you bail on us because you have to 'work.'"

Now he's making air quotes. What the hell? "No, I don't."

"Yes, and you usually talk nonstop about your latest project, but you haven't mentioned even one. So maybe work isn't your number one priority now and Ben is." His eyebrow and lips rise on one side in a sinister grin. Jackass.

"Work is my number-one priority. But Grayson's has been taking up a good bit of my time also. Which is why I need to finish up the project and get back to focusing on my career and future."

He rolls his eyes. "There's the old Lauren."

What was so wrong with old Lauren? Nothing. Except maybe missing out on a few things with her friends here and there. But telling him I'm Lauren version 2.0 probably won't fly right now.

"I assume that was a no to being at my next meeting."

"That's a no."

I should smack the smirk off his face. But I know when to kill a project.

"I better get going. I'll see you at the opening."

Well, this was a waste of time, and now he will hold this over me at Eve's art opening tonight. Great.

"Oh, it's going to be a good one." His tone is close to a laugh. I don't dare turn around.

He's up to something or his wife is.

Double great.

Eve is easy to spot as I enter the gallery. She's standing in front of a sculpture that looks like a bull standing on his hind legs trying to throw a ball but is probably something super sophisticated about the state of the rainforests and mankind's impact. Eve says I can't let go enough to see the true meaning behind art. She says I need to learn to enjoy the moment and not look to understand everything. What I understand is people spend thousands of dollars on ridiculous things.

Eve on the other hand sees all the colors. She is and has always been able to live in the moment. She's surrounded by a group of men hanging on her every word, all vying for her attention. Poor bastards don't stand a chance of leaving without a significant reduction in their bank accounts. Eve's short blonde hair is in light waves framing her face and she has on a fabulous red strapless dress that flows out at the waist. She turns toward me as I make my way around the room. She may not be manning the door, but she's keeping an eye on who's coming and going. Her brow lift acknowledges that my late arrival did not go unnoticed.

I'm purposely an hour late; I deserve the eyebrow of shame.

Izzy had to have dinner at her mother's tonight, leaving me on my own for this, and as much as I love Eve, I don't care for the art scene. Without Izzy I'll be forced to talk about art and how that blue painting with a smidge of purple in the middle makes me feel. And I can't tell them the truth. I can't tell them that it makes me feel sad that this was the best the artist could come up with.

With my look of concentration and slight disdain firmly in place, I venture into the gallery and toward the bar. Maybe I can find Ollie at the bar. The bar is on the opposite end of the room, surrounded by men and women dressed in everything from haute couture to ripped jeans and T-shirts —buyers and artists in a delicate dance vying for each other's attention.

I order a white wine and turn around the room looking for Ollie. I spy him near a piece of metal that has been welded into the shape of an arrow. Maybe?

He's talking to a tall man with broad shoulders and dark hair. The man has on a dark blue suit that looks custom-fit to his body. Ollie's talking up a buyer? That's a new one. Ollie looks more like one of the artists in his dark jeans and V-neck black T-shirt.

Before I take a step, a pair of arms wraps me up, and the smell of gardenia perfume wafts around me. Eve.

"Well, look who finally made it."

She releases me and steps in front of me.

"I thought it was called being fashionably late." I give her a smile so bright I should be in a toothpaste commercial. She rolls her eyes.

"It's only fashionably late when you want to make an entrance, not when you are trying to avoid the party."

Busted. I cock my head to my shoulder and attempt an innocent wide-eyed look. It never seems to work. She shakes her head at me.

"I'll forgive you since you made an effort to look nice." She looks me up and down and gives a nod of approval. "I love this dress." Her hands skim the cap sleeves on my navy blue knee-length dress. It fits tight around my torso with ribbed accents and then flows away at the waist. It makes my calves look fabulous and goes with my favorite nude Jimmy Choos. I knew she would forgive me if I dressed to impress.

"Thanks. I'm headed over to talk to Ollie."

"Oh good." The excitement in her voice sets off an alarm in my head. I glance back to Ollie, and he and the man have turned our way. Oh shit. His stormy-blue eyes meet mine and my breath catches. Ben.

"You're welcome," Eve whispers as she turns and waves at Ollie.

I nod to Ollie and Ben and grab Eve's arm and turn her toward me, smiling all the while so I don't cause a scene.

"Hey!" she says, as she delicately removes her arm from my hand.

"Hey, yourself. Why is Ben here?" My face hardens as fast as my blood is racing. Eve doesn't even hide her smile. She's happy with herself.

"I invited him."

"Why?" The words come through my gritted teeth and big smile.

"Cause I'm your best friend and I know what's good for you, even when you don't. And that boy is good for you." She steps to my side and gives the boys a smile.

She doesn't know anything. Maybe old me could have used a fling with a handsome bartender, but new me...new me knows things and can't think about such things. Plus, Ben is better off not getting involved in my mess any more than he already is.

"I'm surprised he came," I admit.

"What did you do?" Eve face turns serious.

"Why do you assume it's me?"

"Cause you overthink everything and well...I know it was you."

"Fine. It was me. Ben said we have a connection and should stop fighting it, and I told him I didn't think it was a good idea." And it's not.

"And?" Her eyes lock on me like an eagle latching onto its prey.

"And nothing. I said now wasn't a good time."

"And?"

"And that I didn't think hooking up would be a good idea."

She throws up her arms. "Why not?"

I clamp down on her arms, and I see Ben and Ollie watching our every move.

"It's for his own good. Ben's a great guy, and I don't want to mess something in his life up." I'm already uneasy about helping him. What if he was supposed to lose the bar and keep up his travels and now I've ruined it?

"Ben's a great guy?" Her face is smug, and I want to slap her.

"Shut up."

"Why can't you just sleep with him?"

"That's what Ollie said."

"When did you discuss this with Ollie?" Her eyes narrow.

"This afternoon. Calm down. I didn't go to Ollie for advice on men instead of you. I went to ask him some questions about the stage and he mentioned last night, and he basically said, 'what guy would turn down sex with no strings.'"

"He's right."

"Maybe." I glance over at Ben in his button-down striped shirt with no tie and sigh. He gives me a closed-mouth smile and keeps his eyes on me while talking to Ollie.

"Well, we better get over there or they will think we're talking about them." Eve smiles and grabs my hand.

BEN

The more time I spend with Ollie, the more I see why my uncle liked him. Honest and hardworking, he'll do anything to help his friends, even ones no longer with us. His invitation to this art opening came out of left field, but he said his wife insisted I come, and that Lauren would be here.

This might not have been a good idea. Saying she was pissed last night is an understatement. Hell, so was I, but she's right. I don't have a right to be jealous or pissed off. What do I have to offer but a few weeks of fun? I'd have to be willing to stick around to earn the right to be angry. I can admit I'm not that guy.

Time to apologize.

My heart races as I scan the room, and I spot her

walking our way. Her mouth opens slightly before forming a smile. Not a big, bright, I'm-excited-to-see-you smile, but a smile, nonetheless. I can work with that. Her dress highlights her curves. I swallow hard and nod my head toward her with a tight smile on my face. Damn. Why does she have to tempt me with all that is Lauren? Why can't she be hateful and ugly and make it easy on me?

I turn my attention back to Ollie as best I can with my eyes still on Lauren.

"I see Lauren's finally arrived."

"Yeah," I mumble.

He taps my arm with the back of his hand. "Fashionably late is Eve's thing, not normally Lauren's, but she's not a huge fan of these things."

"And you are?" I chuckle, knowing these can't be something he enjoys.

"Not really but seeing Eve in her element is worth it." His head turns as he zeroes in on Eve standing next to Lauren. I can't blame him. From what I know of Eve she's intelligent, sophisticated, and fun all wrapped into one. And the fact that she's beautiful doesn't hurt. She seems to own this room. I've seen her talking to all different types of people. Her face lights up when she talks and so do the faces of the people she's talking to. He's a lucky man.

"So how long have you known Lauren? She said something about college?"

"Yeah, we met sophomore year. She knocked me down on her way into the Union. Lucky for me the only thing I lost was my coffee."

I chuckle, only half hearing what Ollie says as I watch the exchange between Lauren and Eve. They are obviously talking about me. My name has passed Lauren's lips several times. The lower half of my body rouses at the thought of her saying my name in my ear.

I force my full attention back to Ollie; thoughts like those are going to make this a long night.

"It was pretty funny," Ollie adds.

"She does tend to blow in like a storm and knock things down."

"That what happened to you?"

No point in pretending. Ollie's very perceptive, and I'm sure tonight's invite was a setup. "Pretty much."

"Listen, Ben." Ollie's smile fades. "Be careful. She's got a lot on her plate right now and has a lot of preconceived ideas of exactly how her life should be."

Shouldn't he be using that big brother tone to warn me not to hurt her? Odd. He must know who this Matthew guy is. Actually, I don't need to know him, I know his type. That night at the bar he kept telling stories to his buddies about all the money he made some investor of his and how it made him a shoo-in for some promotion. He was decent looking. Polite when I dropped off the birthday drinks, but his eyes scanned the room looking for her when I handed him the napkin. When I told him she left, he didn't seem to give it much thought.

Maybe Ollie can fill in some blanks. "And why is that?"

"It's a long story, and not my tale to tell. But she's pretty great."

"I've noticed." I want to push more, but now isn't the time as Eve and Lauren walk our way. I'll figure it out eventually. "I appreciate the heads-up."

Eve settles into Ollie's side before giving him a kiss on the cheek. Lauren stands next to them in front of me and fidgets with her skirt.

"Can I talk to you for a second?" I ask. Might as well get my apology out of the way.

Her lips purse tight and she nods. "Sure."

"Don't be long," Ollie says. "I have some embarrassing Lauren stories to share."

Lauren glares at Ollie and points her finger in warning. Ollie laughs.

We step beside a statue, both waiting for the other to speak. Screw it. "I'm sorry."

"No, I'm sorry." Her shoulders loosen and her gaze travels from the floor to meet mine.

"Listen, I had a really nice time last night, and I didn't mean to overstep. It's none of my business."

Lauren gives me a half smile. "Thanks."

"Friends?" I extend my hand; she pauses and then puts her hand in mine. It's warm and soft and I let it go before the temptation to pull her closer wins out. "We good now?"

"Yeah."

"Good. Now, let's get back to Ollie. I want to hear some stories."

Her eyes open wide and she shakes her head. "There will be no embarrassing stories."

"Oh, but there will be." I grab her hand and tug her back toward Ollie, releasing her hand the moment we stop. Don't want to push my luck. "Now about those stories."

LAUREN

Twenty minutes and an empty glass of wine later, I smack Ollie on the head as Eve rejoins the group. "You are not telling that story. Ben has been entertained enough."

"One last one—I missed most of them," Eve urges Ollie.

I roll my eyes. "Fine." There is no point trying to stop them and at this point no dignity left to be saved.

Ben taps my shoulder with his and gives me a wink as Ollie starts his story. At least someone is enjoying this.

"So, I told you Lauren and I met when she ran me over and spilled my coffee. Well, the next day I asked her out." Eve starts laughing as she sees Ben's confused look.

"Wait. It gets better." Her body is shaking as she tries to contain her laugh.

Ollie's hands move as he continues. "We go out, have some dinner, see a band, get along great, and at the end of the night I lean in for a kiss."

Ben tucks his hands into his pockets, and his back straightens.

"And it's horrible." Ollie scrunches up his face and pauses for effect. "I mean from the moment our lips touched it was…bad. I mean it was like kissing your mom, sister, and grandma at the same time. It was the worst kiss in history. Like kissing a brick wall."

My hand goes to my hip, and I glare at Ollie. "No one else has ever complained."

Ben's laughing along with Eve and Ollie. I can't stop myself from joining in.

It was horrible. His mouth was too small, his tongue was too much, and it made me want to spit afterward like I ate a sour grape.

"Well, they were just being polite." Ollie raises one eyebrow, giving me a dare you grin.

Lucky for the boy I love him, or I would kick him in his happy parts right now.

I poke Ollie in the chest. "Maybe you're the bad kisser?"

"Not him," Eve says, pulling Ollie close and kissing him

long enough that Ben and I look at each other and then to the ceiling. Awkward.

"Umm. We're going to get some drinks." My hand slides into the crook of Ben's arm, and I jerk him toward the bar.

"Well, that was interesting," Ben says.

"Indeed. The college years certainly were more entertaining than I remember."

"They always are." His head bends to my ear. "And for the record, I don't doubt your kissing ability."

I swallow hard. Kissing Ben sounds so tempting, and I know with everything I am that it would be amazing, but I can't.

"Thanks," I whisper.

"Anytime." His voice is thick, and his breath caresses my neck.

Is it hot in here? I excuse myself to the bathroom and take a few deep breaths before rejoining the group.

We mingle and chat for another hour, then Ollie has to leave for a late set at some bar downtown. Ben heads to the bathroom and Eve grabs my arm.

"Go home with him tonight," Eve commands.

"What?" I say, trying not to laugh.

Her eyes light up. "Enough pretending you don't want to. You've wanted to find out what he has under that kilt since the moment you laid eyes on him, and he obviously wants to see you naked, so do it already."

I shake my head. "Did you just say kilt? Is he Scottish now?"

"You know what I mean." She gives me her standard you-will-do-as-I-say glare.

But I will not be swayed by the glare. I'm a grown woman; I don't have to kowtow to glares. "What I do know is that I'm not letting him take me home."

"You're right. It's the twenty-first century; you should take him home." Her eyes sparkle like when she talks about a new artist and how she is going to make them a star.

My body hums at the thought of Ben in my bed, and I clench my palms. "That's not a good idea."

"No, it's not. It's a fabulous idea." She places both hands on my shoulders and gently shakes me. "Stop thinking and start doing."

"Eve, I love you, but…"

"If you say he doesn't fit into your plan, I'm going to smack you right here and now in front of all of these people. Your 'plan,'"—she uses air quotes. Why is she using air quotes? It's a real plan—"is ridiculous." She continues, "You can date people with the sole purpose of having fun. Everything doesn't have to be perfect or lead toward marriage, or a promotion, or your perfect life. Life isn't perfect, no matter how hard you try to make it so."

Ben walks up to us with a questioning look on his face. Please tell me he didn't hear that.

"Ladies, you look like you could use a drink. What can I get you?"

"Actually Ben, I need you to do me a favor and take Lauren home tonight." Eve lays on her best southern accent. I close my eyes so as not to roll them.

"Um. Okay. Sure." He looks to me and gives me a once-over. I'm obviously not drunk.

"Great, now that all that is settled, I need to go mingle." She glares at me as she walks past. "Have fun."

"How much have you had to drink?" he asks as she walks away.

"Not enough that you need to drive me home. Eve's just…" I try to downplay her words.

"I don't mind," his voice dips low.

"Seriously, she's annoying." I can't look at him. Taking him home is a bad idea even if the idea pops in my head every time I see him. A bad idea.

"Well, Eve said I need to take you home, and she's kind of scary, so I better do what she says." His voice is deep and full of playfulness.

Damn, he's cute and sweet and funny. What's the worst that can happen? We have sex. It's awkward after and I have to mail him the ideas for the bar instead of meet with him? That he hates me when this is all over and I never see him again? That I become a cheater even though I haven't met my husband yet?

I shake the thoughts from my head. "Ben, you don't have to do this."

"I told you, I don't mind." He tilts his head to the side and catches my eye. "It's only a ride home."

I bite the inside of my lip. What's the harm in a ride home if it will keep Eve off my back?

"You're right. It's just a ride home. I would appreciate it."

His back straightens and his head jerks a bit to the side. I think I surprised him by agreeing. "Let me know when you're ready," he says.

"Is now too soon? I don't think I can handle Eve glaring at me the rest of the night."

"Nope." He sets his drink down and grabs my hand. He waves to Eve with the other hand, and I give her my best stern glance which makes her laugh.

We walk through the street toward the parking lot a block away, my hand still wrapped in his. My hand fits perfectly in his, like they were a matched set. But we aren't; we're just two people passing through each other's lives.

"What time do you work tomorrow?" I ask, breaking the awkward silence.

"Seven, why?"

"There's a bar I want you to check out. They have a layout I like, and I thought maybe we could run over there before you start work. It's the last place I wanted to show you and then I can have all my final recommendations ready."

Ben looks off toward the parking lot and squeezes my hand. "Sure."

"Good, I'll meet you at Grayson's around five."

I spot my car as we near it. Driving myself home makes more sense. I don't want to leave my car here all night. And having him drop me off seems silly. Plus the feel of his hand in mine is too comfortable, too tempting to not want to touch other parts of him. Eve will just have to get over it.

"Hey, my car is right there. I should just drive myself home."

"But I promised Eve." He looks confused.

"She'll survive." I remove my hand from Ben's and pull the keys out of my purse, taking a few steps to get ahead of him.

I open the door of the car and turn back to Ben who's standing directly behind me. He looks down at me. His jaw is clenched.

"We can't start anything," I blurt out.

"I think it might be too late." His eyes search mine, and I can't look away. I'm swimming deep in the stormy ocean, and right now I don't know if I want to find a life jacket to save me.

"Ben..." I breathe out.

"You know I'm right. We've already started something, and we might as well see where it goes."

He steps closer. His shirt brushes my arm, sending a shiver down me. "Ben..."

"Give me a good reason why not." He gently lifts my chin with his finger. "A good reason." The storm rages on in his eyes. I don't want to get his hopes up this can be more than it is. I have a deadline. I have a plan. I have...

"Well?" he asks.

"I don't want to hurt you."

"Then don't."

"I can't do serious right now."

"Then we'll keep it casual." He has an answer for everything.

"You don't do one-night stands."

"Casual doesn't mean one night."

With each word, he is breaking down my resolve. His hand wraps around my back as he draws me toward him. His eyes search mine as if he's trying to read my mind. Screw it. My hands wrap around his neck, and I pull his lips to mine. They are soft and demanding. His tongue touches my lip, and I part them allowing our tongues to meet and tangle. I breathe him in and take my time exploring him as well, until I need air. I lean back, breaking the connection at our lips while still connected everywhere else. I tilt my head back.

"Are you really okay with no strings, no labels, no expectations?" I rattle off fast through my ragged breath.

He takes a deep breath and stands up straight. "Anything you need." His words are right, but his eyes seem conflicted.

I should say no. I should walk away, but instead I launch myself at him and kiss him again.

9

LAUREN

I arrive at Grayson's exactly nineteen hours after I reluctantly got in my car and drove myself home, alone. Things are going to be awkward. Do I kiss him? Do I pretend it didn't happen? Why did it have to be so amazing? Why did my dreams have to be so vivid and show last night not ending in just a kiss? Ugh.

The parking lot is jam-packed. I don't see Ben's truck in its usual spot, so I park across the street and head in to find him.

Are things picking up already? We haven't made any real changes yet.

There are people everywhere. Three-quarters of the tables are full as are all the seats at the bar.

Ben and Dex are making drinks as fast as they can. His eyes go wide as he sees me, and he nods to me with a smile.

"Hey, what's going on tonight? You giving away drinks?" I ask. He'd better not be.

"No, The Home Run down the street shut down unexpectedly, and the softball teams that usually go there came here," Ben answers.

"That's awesome. How do we keep them coming back?" An early evening rush would go a long way to helping the bottom line.

"Well, right now my only goal is to get them served. We weren't staffed for this many people tonight. I've called in everyone I could. I'm gonna have to bail on you." Ben mixes two margaritas while he talks to me. He steps away and hands them to a waitress and grabs two more glasses and starts mixing martinis.

"No problem. What can I do to help?"

"What?" He stops midpour.

"You need help. I'm here, so let me help." I take off my jacket and fold it over my arm.

He seems conflicted. He knows he needs help but probably isn't sure that my spreadsheet skills are going to be of use in this situation. "You don't need to do that."

I ignore his denial of help and walk behind the bar. I remember he had aprons stacked in the small room behind the bar and make my way back there. I emerge from the door, and Ben smiles and his eyes move to my lips. I see pretending it didn't happen isn't an option. He wants to kiss me, but there's a room full of patrons and customers so now isn't the time. I chuckle to myself.

"What are you doing?" He rolls his eyes, but I can see how thankful he is I'm offering to stay.

"There is no way I'm leaving here knowing you and your team are shorthanded. I can take a few orders and help get you caught up."

"Ummm… Do you have any waitressing experience?" I glare at him, and he raises his hands in defeat.

"I need a name tag."

"What?" The confusion on his face is adorable, and the fact that he can carry on a conversation with me while he makes two drinks at a time is impressive.

"I need a name tag, so they know I work here."

"Oh, um..." He nods to a box under the bar to his right. The one on top says "Roxie." I attach it to my apron.

"Hell, yeah, tonight I'm Roxie the waitress." I shoot Ben my best devilish grin.

BEN

IT'S AFTER MIDNIGHT, and Lauren has been working all night even though I've told her several times she can head out. She's halfway across the room, filling her tray with dirty glasses and chatting with Sue, one of the waitresses. We officially closed ten minutes ago; Lauren's done more than enough to help us tonight.

"Hey, Roxie, time to clock out," I yell. She refused to answer to anything but Roxie all night, and I have to admit it was cute as hell.

Her head whips my way, and a smile fills her face. Damn that smile. Damn that woman behind the smile. What is she doing to me?

"Coming, boss."

She lifts the tray and weaves her way through the tables like a pro. She out hustled everyone in here tonight and all the while smiling back at me. I felt her watching me. She can deny it, but I know.

"Here's your tips." I lay them on the bar between us.

"Can you split them between the staff tonight?" she asks.

"You worked hard; you deserve these."

"They need it more than I do. And besides, I had fun."

Her face lights up like it's been doing all night whenever I caught her looking my way.

How can one woman be so smart, beautiful, and kind?

"Fun, huh?" She's right. My team worked hard, but we had fun, and having Lauren around smiling with excitement didn't hurt.

She nods.

"Yeah, fine, I'll see they get them. Now time for you to go home. Let me walk you to your car."

"But the place is a disaster." She looks around the room, and she's right. The tables are still full of glasses, and the floor is littered with napkins and dirt from the softball teams' cleats. It's going to be a long night.

"Yes, and the staff and I can clean up. Right, guys?" I yell.

"We got this. Thanks for helping tonight," Sue calls out from a few tables over.

"Yeah, we got this, Ben. You both need to go home." Dex sets a load of glasses next to the sink.

"You sure?" I ask.

"Yeah, thank you both for helping out tonight." He looks over at Lauren and chuckles. "Most people run from a burning building, not into it. We can handle the cleanup." Dex gives me a nod of approval.

"I guess we've been dismissed." I finish wiping off the last glass and stack it on the shelf before following Lauren toward the exit.

The light in the parking lot casts deep shadows on the gravel as we walk toward her car. Lauren pauses before opening the door and turns to me.

"I really did have fun tonight. We're going to make Grayson's busy like that every night."

"If that's true we're going to need another waitress. You

interested?" I take a step toward her, and she holds her ground.

She looks at me from under her bangs. "Maybe." Damn, I love when she does that. Her head tilts up to mine. "But I could make better tips if we served food too."

She won't stop until she gets what she wants. Determined.

"I'll take that under consideration." My eyes narrow and all I can see are her lips. They part slightly as she smiles, and my instincts take over. Kissing her makes any thoughts of the crazy day disappear.

My hands wrap around her back, and I walk her two steps until she's leaning against the car. She moans into my mouth and I push closer. My hands are on a mission of their own and cup her ass. It's firm and round and exactly how I imagined it in my dreams. I wonder if everything else is as I imagined. My hand moves up her side toward her breast.

I jerk back. Shit. I'm trying to get to second base with Lauren in a parking lot like some idiot college kid who can't control himself. She deserves better than this.

Her face is flushed, and she leans her forehead on my chest so I can't see her eyes.

"I'm sorry," I whisper to the top of her head. I pull her chin up with my hand until our eyes meet. Her usual brazen stare is gone. Instead she fights to keep her eyes on mine and not look away. Damn, I want this girl. I want to know every inch and every thought.

"What are you thinking?" I ask.

Her eyes look to the left.

"That I should probably get going." Her voice trails off at the end.

"And?"

"And that I don't want to." Her words come out almost as a sigh before asking, "What were you thinking?"

I scan the quiet road as a lone car passes by before my gaze returns to her beautiful eyes.

"I was thinking how I would like to continue this...somewhere not so public."

"Oh." Her eyes widen. Oh, she wants that too.

But she just spent her night running around waiting on tables to help me. I imagine she's exhausted and looking for a hot bath and bed. Those thoughts lead to images of Lauren emerging from a bath and walking toward me as I wait for her on my bed. Shit.

"But another night," I reluctantly say. "You have to be tired."

"I'm not...that tired." Her eyelashes flutter and I kiss her again.

LAUREN

After several minutes of kissing like teenagers, again Ben takes the keys from my hand and walks me to the passenger door of my car. He slides into the driver seat and starts the engine. Oh shit. This is really happening. I'm going home with sexy-as-hell bartender Ben.

I snap my seatbelt on. It's fine. He's an adult, I'm an adult.

The fact is, I haven't had sex with anyone but Matthew in the last ten years, and well, we...Wait, when was the last time I had sex? Hmm. Old me—maybe two months. Current me—umm. Who did I date before Matthew? I can't remember; must have been awhile.

My hands unclasp as we take a left turn out of the

parking lot. "Where are we going?"

His voice is deep and gravelly. "My place."

"Oh."

"We can go to your place if you want," he quickly adds. Always the gentleman trying to make sure I'm comfortable.

"No, your place is fine." My heart goes into overdrive. His place. A glimpse into who Ben is outside of Grayson's. I shouldn't be surprised he's not afraid to show it to me. He never misses a chance to be honest.

His profile is lit by the street lamps as we pass by. I bite my lip thinking about the kiss we shared, and my whole body vibrates thinking of sharing other parts with him.

I set my hand on his thigh, needing contact with him before I lose my nerve. His body tightens. He's as anxious as I am. It's nice to know I'm not alone in my feelings. My hand runs up his thigh. He lets out a low hum, and I chuckle.

His eyes don't leave the road. "A little more to the left."

I follow his directions and feel how excited he is. His low growl fills the car, and his hand grabs mine, forcing my hand back to my lap.

"I'm kidding. I need to concentrate on the road, and if you keep doing that I'm going to have to pull into an alley and finish what you're starting." He glances my way, and I see the flash of hunger in his eyes.

I tilt my head back on the seat, letting the thoughts of Ben and me in an alley wash over me. I've never had sex in a car, but I would rather not get arrested for public indecency, so I sit on my hands.

Ben drives us through an old neighborhood filled with bungalows and beautiful houses. The car slows as Ben turns into the driveway of an older two-story craftsman house. It's a medium-size house—well, by today's McMansion standards.

We enter through the back door and Ben ushers me into the kitchen, guiding me with his hand on my back. My eyes can't focus on the kitchen as all my attention is on the heat coming from where he's touching me. His hand moves from my back, and his fingers link with mine as he pulls me through the kitchen and into the living room.

I guess we don't have time for a tour. I chuckle a little at his haste, which matches my desire to touch him.

His living room is dark except for the light filtering in from the kitchen. He twirls me into him like he did that night on the dance floor. The cells in my body ignite one by one as his fingers caress my arm. I can feel him against my stomach, and my need to touch him grows.

Oh hell.

With his shirt untucked, I reach under and make contact with his abs. My touch causes him to lean back a fraction of an inch, unlocking our bodies from each other. His chest heaves as he attempts to catch his breath alongside me.

What're we doing? This might be a bad idea.

"I don't think..." I breathe out.

"Don't think. Be here with me right now. Nothing else matters."

His fingers trace down my cheek and neck. His eyes change from soft and dreamy to intense as they lock with mine. My body screams for more.

I'm paralyzed. I need air.

I need his touch.

I need him.

Our bodies being separated is brief, like he's giving me a chance to run, and since I didn't, he can resume his survey. I part my lips as his reach mine and his tongue slides inside. His hands glide under my ass as he lifts me up. I would be impressed by the ease in which he lifts me, but all I can think of is how to get his clothes off faster.

He stops walking and kissing and releases his vise grip on my legs as he gently sets me upright at the foot of his bed. He takes a step back, and the look on his face reminds me of someone trying to decide if they should lick or bite the ice cream cone.

Both, please.

The room is full of dark shadows and small pockets of light that slip through the gaps in the curtains.

I turn around and motion for him to unzip my dress. He slides the zipper down my back causing my body to shake. I turn around to face him and let it drop to the floor. His hands are in fists at his side. Knowing he's hanging on to his control by a thread, I give him a wicked smile.

I take my own moment to appreciate the man in front of me in a dark blue T-shirt and worn-out jeans...but it would be better if the clothes were gone. He doesn't move. My fingers fist his shirt and I pull it over his head to reveal the tight stomach I felt earlier and the dark chest hair I imagined he would have. My breath catches as he removes his pants and boxers to reveal all of himself to me.

Damn.

I reach behind my back and unclasp my bra, freeing my breasts. A low growl surrounds me as well as Ben's hands on my back pulling me into his body.

Ben's face comes into focus, and his lips turn up into a sexy predatory grin.

"Not wasting time, I see." A nervous laugh escapes me.

"Since we are all about honesty, I've been thinking about doing that since the first time I met you." His head bends, and his lips land on my collarbone. The heat from his breath sends a tidal wave of molten lava down my body. His feet move forward, and I step backward until my calves hit the bed. Ben lowers me to my back, and with one swift motion pulls my panties down my legs and throws them to the floor. I gasp as the cool air in the room hits me. I start to kick off my shoes, and he wraps his hand around my ankle. "Leave the shoes this time. We'll be quick."

This time? I don't have time to register what that means when his fingers touch my overly sensitive center. As much as I love his fingers, I want him.

"I need you."

He reaches over me and into the nightstand. He returns with a condom which he promptly tears open. The next few minutes are a blur of Ben above me and the feel of him inside me, so good neither of us lasts long. My cry of pleasure is loud enough to wake the neighbors.

Ben pauses above me before unlinking us, scorching part of my soul with his gaze. The storm clouds in his eyes whirl like a tornado, and I feel as though I'm being sucked into the vortex. My heart beats faster. I move my attention to his shoulders. He pulls back, and suddenly I feel empty and alone. A tear runs down my cheek. What the hell is that? Feelings are not a part of this arrangement. I wipe it away while Ben has his back turned.

He returns to the bed and scoops me up in his arms. I let my shoes fall to the ground before he lowers me back at the head of the bed and on the right side. He slides in next to me, and I curl into him as if I've done it a thousand times.

"Thanks," I breathe out.

His chest jumps as he chuckles. "No, thank you."

I join in his laughter.

"That was pretty nice," I add, twisting a piece of hair on his chest.

"I'm not sure nice is the word I would use." I can hear

the smile in his voice.

I pull my head up and place my hands on his chest before laying my head back down and watching his lazy grin fill his face. Damn, he does that well. The need to kiss him races through my body, but instead I turn my head away.

After a year of silence, or maybe five minutes, I catch my breath. Now, what do I do? If this were a one-night stand, I would grab my clothes and go home, but Ben is not a one-night stand, he's a...I don't know...a friend, and I don't know what the protocol is in this situation.

"I feel your brain working. I told it to take the night off."

I pop my head up and look up at him. "Obviously, I already did that, or I wouldn't be naked in your bed."

His smile returns.

"Can I have my keys back?"

"Nope."

I should be mad; they're my keys and I can leave whenever I want, but him not wanting to give them back means he isn't ready for me to leave either.

"Then I need a shower."

"That can be arranged."

Prying myself off of him, I roll to the side of the bed, taking the sheet with me and leaving Ben lying in the middle of his bed naked. He doesn't move to steal the covers back; instead he lies still as my eyes work their way from his long legs to his beautiful eyes.

A smile spreads across his face as he meets my gaze head-on.

I divert my gaze to the floor. This is sex, no longing glances. Stop it.

"Go on in. I'll bring you a towel."

I nod and attempt to wrap the sheet around me only to

tangle my legs. Screw it. He's seen me naked and orgasming; no need to be shy now. I drop the sheet to the floor. I could be nice and give it to him, but if I'm going to be naked then so is he.

I make my way to the bathroom without looking back at him. I'm sure he's watching me, and I hope my ass lives up to his expectations cause I know he's been thinking about it since that day on the stairs. I chuckle to myself as I enter the bathroom and turn on the water.

BEN

As the water turns on in the shower I lie back in the bed, allowing myself a moment to relive this night. One night is not enough. Not enough of Lauren's smiles or her sweet voice or her body wrapped around mine.

I run my hands through my hair. Now what? How do I do casual with her? Hell, I don't want to let her leave this house without me. I'm so screwed.

How do I get her to stay the night with me? The minute she starts analyzing everything, she's going to bolt. And dammit, I need to keep my distance. I need to let her leave, so I don't get too close. The last thing I need is a woman who wants to settle down and live a normal life.

"Hey, Ben," I hear her yell from the bathroom. "Mind washing my back?"

Screwed. I slide off the bed and walk into the steam-filled bathroom.

"Need a little help?" I ask.

She slides open the shower door and holds the soap up for me.

So screwed.

10

LAUREN

The bed next to me is empty when I wake. I suppose no strings means no sleeping in. I sit up and pull the sheet around my chest. Where are my clothes? The wood floor is empty, no sign of my dress or shoes or underwear.

Where are my clothes?

I can't leave without my clothes, and I can't find Ben without something to cover my ass. His closet doors are wide open. He won't mind if I borrow a T-shirt while I search for him. I wrap the sheet around me and walk to the closet.

There are about twenty T-shirts, a handful of flannel shirts, and an assortment of long-sleeve Henleys lined up on the left side of the closet. The red flannel shirt is longer than anything else in the closet. I button it up and make my way to the bathroom.

I find a washcloth in the linen closet behind the door and wash off the makeup from last night and borrow Ben's brush to tame my hair that is currently going in fifty different directions. One last thing—I push some toothpaste on my finger and "brush" my teeth.

My reflection resembles a human being again. Sort of.

Ben walks in behind me with only blue-and-grey-checked pajama pants on. Where is his shirt? How am I supposed to concentrate with his naked torso on display like that?

"I see you're up." Ben slides his hand around my waist and fits himself behind me. Oh my.

I pat my hair down. "You scared me." I turn around to face him, but his arms don't release me. My hands land on his chest, and I raise my head to find him studying me. Why does that look leave me wishing this could be more? But it can't be.

I want to reach up and kiss him, but the sun is up, and our night together has come to an end. Back to business. Too bad. He's a great kisser.

As if reading my mind, Ben's lips touch mine in a sweet and gentle kiss.

His eyes crinkle in the corners when he smiles. "Good morning," he says with enough Tennessee twang to make my belly do a flip.

"Morning," I repeat, caught in the haze of his kiss and the smell of him that now surrounds me.

"Hungry? I made breakfast. I figured we both worked up an appetite last night."

Embarrassment floods me.

I'm acting like a teenage girl who's had sex for the first time. I'm a thirty-five-year-old woman for crying out loud.

He lifts my chin with his finger. "Don't get all shy on me now."

How does he do that? Read my mind before I've even

figured out what I'm thinking. Act your age, I manage to only yell in my head. "I am hungry. But first can you tell me where my clothes are?"

"I rinsed out your dress, and it's hanging in the laundry room. I wasn't sure if it could go in the dryer." He touches his shirt at the base of my neck. "You can wear that to breakfast. We're casual around here." His hand wraps around mine, and he leads me into the kitchen.

He sets a plate stacked high with food on the counter in front of me. He's been hard at work; there are scrambled eggs with some kinds of vegetable and cheese in them, bacon, and fresh orange wedges arranged neatly on a plate.

The cold leather of the barstool hits my legs, and I decide leaning against the stool might be a better option.

Ben returns from the stove with a pan of cinnamon rolls.

Exactly how many people is he expecting for breakfast? I look behind me to see if anyone else is coming in the back door.

Ben sets the rolls down and pulls up a barstool next to me.

"You can sit," he says.

"I'll stand," I say.

I follow Ben's lead and dig in. The first bite of eggs is heavenly. No one has made me breakfast since...well...since I was a kid, I guess.

Stay in the present. Stay in the present.

"Mmm, these are great," I say, my mouth still full.

"Glad you like them. Oh, I forgot drinks." He stands and walks to the refrigerator. "Juice or milk?"

I hesitate. I want milk, but I only drink milk from my own fridge. And juice is not my favorite, but better than water. I twist my mouth as I try and decide.

"Which one do you want?" He chuckles at the dilemma that is surely being broadcast on my face.

"Juice is fine," I say, putting a piece of salty, crispy bacon in my mouth.

"Want more?"

"Maybe. Let me finish this first."

The juice glass slides in front of me. Ben picks up his fork and dives in. The juice from the orange slices runs down my fingers as I eat it, but I can't find a napkin and lick it before it runs down my arm. I hear Ben let out a small grunt and look over to see his attention on me instead of his bacon. His warm fingers leisurely run up the back of my thigh.

What am I doing? I'm standing in Ben's kitchen in a shirt and no underwear, licking juice off my fingers like some X-rated movie star. What has gotten into me? The thought really should cause me to run into the other room, but instead I'm rooted to the floor as my whole body heats. His hand stops when it reaches my ass. My bare ass. A wide grin comes across his face as he must now be remembering where he put my underwear. The fork clinks on the plate, and he turns his body to me, pulling me toward him for a long and steady good morning kiss.

The kiss slows and his hands move to my back. My brain begins to work again.

It's morning. I need to go. I can't do this. I step back out of his arms. "Ben, can you tell me where the laundry room is?"

"No." His voice is playful as he reaches for me, but I back up.

"It's a little chilly in here, and as you know, I'm not wearing anything under this shirt."

"I did notice, and I like it...a lot." He stands and covers

the distance between us with one step. His head swivels around the room before he lifts me and carries me to the empty dining room table behind me. My legs are pushed apart, and the void is filled with his body. I gasp and pull his neck down in order to kiss him. His hands run up my inner thighs, and my body shivers at the anticipation. When his fingers reach their goal, I involuntarily arch my back and moan. I lean back on my arms as his fingers stroke and swirl and his mouth sucks my breast through the shirt. I've never had anyone touch me like this on a table.

Oh hell.

"Yes," I scream.

He doesn't stop; the rush of pleasure fills me. His lips come to my ear. "Let go, Lauren."

The words send me over the edge. My body feels like it's going to explode. I scream his name and give in to the beautiful rolling ecstasy.

My eyes open to find Ben grinning like a Cheshire cat. I reach for his pants and snap the band to get his attention.

"Take off your pants," I order.

"Anything you say, ma'am."

His pants fall to the floor. The view of him ready for action causes me to lick my lips and stare. Guess I'm not the only one going commando today.

So hot.

He pulls me off the table and carries me in his arms.

"Where are we going?"

"Condoms are in the bedroom."

"I would have waited."

He stumbles a bit at my words, no doubt picturing me sitting half naked on his table waiting. I chuckle into his chest.

"Next time, I'll let you wait."

He sets me down on the edge of the bed and grabs a condom from the drawer. The sight of him ripping it with his teeth is one of the top-ten sexiest things I've ever seen. He lifts my ass up and dives right in. Obviously, there is no need to wonder if I'm primed and ready. I push my hips toward him, driving more of him into me.

The orgasm builds fast. I hear his breath start to hitch. "Look at me," I command. He obeys, and I watch as the hurricane in his eyes swirls faster and faster until he bends his head and kisses me gently. Two orgasms in ten minutes is a new record for me. Damn. And I thought having sex twice last night counted as amazing.

I lie motionless on the bed, lost in thoughts of the last twenty-four hours. Ben climbs in behind me and wraps his arms around me. He sweeps the hair from my shoulder and rests his head in the base of my neck. I never want to leave this bed, and my body sinks farther into him. The clock to my left says nine. I'll rest my eyes for a second and then grab my dress and call Eve to tell her I'll be late.

THE FAINT SOUND of a phone going off in the distance wakes me, and at first, I ignore it—it's warm and cozy wrapped in Ben's arms. Oh shit. What time is it? I look at the clock and it's one. Shit. Eve is probably ready to call the cops. I'm never late. I slide out from under Ben's arm and grab my shirt from earlier. He stirs but doesn't wake. I follow the sound to my phone.

Shit, thirteen missed calls.

I hit redial as I close the bedroom and tiptoe into the living room before tripping over a plastic bin. I start speaking the second the phone picks up before she can start yelling. "I'm fine. Don't call the cops."

"Thank God. You had me worried. You're never late," she sounds relieved.

"I've been a little busy."

"Busy? Busy doing what?" Her voice drips with suspicion.

"Um...taking your advice," I whisper.

"You mean you've been at Ben's place since Thursday?" She can't hide the surprise in her voice.

"No, but I'm here now. I'm sorry, I should have texted you when I woke up, but..."

"But you were tired from your wild night of sex. I totally forgive you for missing brunch. As long as you give details tomorrow." Her giddy excitement leaps through the phone. I turn down the volume so as not to wake the neighborhood.

"No, I'll meet you in thirty minutes. His place is close by."

"You don't have to do that. Stay, enjoy!"

"I'll meet you in thirty minutes," I whisper.

"Fine. How..."

The door to the bedroom opens, and Ben leans against the doorframe in nothing but what he came into this world with and a sheet.

What did Eve say? "Excuse me?"

Eve giggles. "I asked how it was?"

"Later."

"Oh, he's standing right there, isn't he? How about you tell me you love me if it was fantastic and bye if it was merely good."

"Love you, I'll see you soon," I answer, my eyes never leaving Ben's.

I hang up on her as she laughs.

BEN

"And exactly who do you love?" I keep my face as emotionless as possible, trying to hide my disappointment.

Her lips mash together as she holds in a grin. So not some other man.

"Eve says hi."

I hold my position, shifting the sheet slightly with my left hand to keep it from slipping off. Her eyes follow my hand, and I'd be lying if I said I'm not happy she likes what she saw last night and this morning.

I could drop the sheet now and see what she thinks of that, but I think I'll hold off.

"Nice of her to check on you."

"Yeah, we had plans for brunch...I fell asleep."

"We were tired." The best kind of tired in the world if you ask me.

Her face shifts from dreamy to all business. Damn, I want the dreamy face back.

"I need to get going. I'm late."

"I think she knows you aren't going to make it. Spend the day with me?" I don't move. Everything in me wants to close the distance and pull her back to bed, but Lauren needs to make that call.

"I'm not sure my body can handle all day in that bed with you." Her voice sounds as though she's considering giving it a try.

I laugh and it earns me a smile.

"And here I thought you were trying to kill me." But what a way to die.

She rolls her eyes.

"Well, since you need to recover, how about another activity. I have a plan."

She cocks her head and takes a step toward me. "What kind of plan?"

"It's a good one."

"Since when do you make plans?" I knew me making a plan would get her attention.

"Let me clarify. I've been working on 'Operation: Save Lauren from Work Overload.'"

She crosses her arms trying to look unhappy, but I see the curiosity as she looks at me. "You don't have to do that."

"Already done. I made a list and everything."

"You made a list? I gotta see this." Her eyes sparkle when she's excited.

"Nope, you will just have to come with me and find out."

"Ben..."

"Don't do that. Don't get all 'Ben' on me." I'm not done with her yet. This is not some one-night stand. I need more time.

"But...we said casual." The apprehension in her voice is thick. I don't buy for a second she doesn't want to do this again, but she also needs a minute to regroup. Lauren needs time to work out a plan. I need to give her a little space to maneuver.

"Yes, and we said friends, and friends help friends get out of a rut."

She bites her nail before crossing her arms.

"True. But we're clear. This can't be more than friends... and sex. And the sex part has a short shelf life."

"I'll take what you can give me." Five days, five weeks, five months... My heart sinks. For the first time I would like to think about a future with someone beyond a few weeks. But she's right. Enjoy the moment; who knows when it will be our last.

"My life isn't really set up for long term either."

It might be wishful thinking, but I swear her face falls at my last words. Does she really think we could have a future?

"I have to go. I promised Eve, and I'm not breaking promises this time around. Can you get my dress for me?"

This time around? What promises did she break before?

She walks toward the bedroom door before stopping and turning back to me. "Oh, do you need a ride back to your truck?"

Always taking care of others.

"No, I'll get someone to swing by and pick me up." I drop the sheet to the floor as I walk to the laundry room and hear a gasp escape her lips.

We both may only be capable of short term, but that doesn't mean I can't make her regret that decision a little.

LAUREN

AFTER SPENDING a late lunch deflecting all of Eve's questions and Sunday avoiding Ben's calls, it's a welcome relief to go back to work on Monday, even if it's the most boring place on the planet right now. My boss gave me a new account, and I finished the bulk of the project before the end of the day. Now I have a few weeks to kill before I can present it to the client. I'm not sure I can redo every account I worked on for the next ten years. At least right now I have Grayson's to work on.

If I stay in this time, I'm going to need to take on more side projects. If I stay and if I can get through this one first. I'm not sure how happy Ben will be with my suggestions, but if he wants to save the place, he's going to have to make some decisions.

Ben... My mind keeps going back to this weekend. I've

never had a night like that, one where I couldn't get enough of a man. Sex with Matthew has always been good, but... Stop comparing them. Ben is short term; Matthew is my future or past or, well, both.

Matthew is my long-term plan. Maybe seeing him will bring things back into focus. I wonder if his calendar password is still the same... Oh, it is. Bingo. Drinks with the boys Tuesday night. "See you then."

Izzy is waiting in front of The Sports Score when I walk up. The smell of fried food and beer permeates the air. Matthew and I never went to sports bars, not even early in our relationship. Is this normal for him before me? He loved...loves sports and we would go to games in skyboxes with clients and watch at home, but never at a bar over beer and wings.

"What are we doing here?" Izzy asks, looking confused as I've never suggested a sports bar for drinks before.

"This is a no questions asked kind of night," I point out, and she nods.

"Well, that explains Eve's absence."

"'No questions' is not her thing." Eve wouldn't let me get in the door without forcing me to tell her everything.

"That's for sure," she chuckles.

"We're going to get a drink and hang out at the table for a bit. I just need to find the right table to overhear a conversation."

And maybe see his face.

And accidentally brush into him.

No.

No touching; touching might change things.

"Sounds easy," Izzy says, as she pulls open the door.

"And then you pick the place. Drinks on me."

The room is wide open with tables and TVs every ten feet. I scan the room for any sign of Matthew.

"Who are we looking for?" Izzy asks. I give her the side-eye. She nods in understanding—no questions. I should tell her what's going on. But each time I think of saying it out loud, I get the image of a padded room with me sitting in the middle. Plus, I don't want her asking questions about her dead-end future. I'd rather help her make it better without her ever knowing where it could have led.

"I'll know him when I see him."

Her eyebrows waggle and she tips her head in approval. This is why I called Izzy. She knows when to keep her mouth shut, at least until she's had three or four drinks. We need to leave before that happens.

As we weave our way through the tables, I spot him about five rows back from the bar. There are two tables near him that are empty, but the one directly behind him would be better for listening and not being seen.

Not that he knows who I am...but still.

We double back so we can sit at the table without Matthew ever seeing us sit down. He's focused on the TV, so I can see his back but he can't see me. He and his two buddies seem to have already had a few and are talking over the chatter of the other patrons. I tilt my ears in their direction.

Once our waitress takes our order, I focus all my attention on Matthew.

"Man, you have to join us. You already know about investing and you can get anyone to do anything. I swear you could sell ice to an..."

"I know, I know...I need a few more weeks to think about it," Matthew says.

"What's there to think about? You hate your job. You love

sports. We already have the start-up money lined up. All we need is your yes."

"I got it, but I need a little more time."

"All we can give you is six weeks. We need your answer before we sign the paperwork." I think that guy's name is Tre. We met him a few times. He and—oh, what's the other guy's name—Carter started their own sports agency and made a ton of money. Whenever Matthew saw them, his mood changed. I didn't realize they wanted him to be a partner; I thought they'd offered him a job managing the clients' money.

"I understand. Now how about I get us another round of drinks and we watch the game."

Matthew hates his job? He never told me that. He never stopped talking about work. Even when we met that first night and he asked my opinion on two job offers. He never said he hated investing. Did he? No, if he didn't like his job, he would have told me. We spent hours talking about our futures and what we wanted. I would know.

He returns with drinks, and they cheer and try to coach the team from their table.

Izzy nudges my foot with hers and whispers, "How long are we going to be here?"

"Another thirty minutes?"

"Sounds good. I'm ordering us some food and more drinks." She waves at our waitress.

I nod my head, refocusing on the table behind me.

"That guy is going to be the first person I sign. His agent's an idiot, and his contract is up with him in three months. I already started talking to him about our new venture. He's excited. I think he could bring along a few of his buddies if we take good care of him," Carter says.

Matthew shakes his head. "He would be a good start. But

you should really be looking to land his buddy. The forward. He's the one that's going to be a superstar if he stays healthy and the team is smart enough to foster his talents."

"No way, the point guard is the one to watch," Carter says.

"I agree the point guard is good, but he doesn't have the discipline of his buddy, and he's about to peak, whereas his buddy is only starting his rise." Matthew sounds like someone who has been studying these players. He always did love sports and watched game recaps like it was his second job.

Tre chuckles, "And that is why we need you. You see the future and can talk to these kids and help them make solid decisions."

Matthew is right. I look up at the screen. The forward will be one of the most well-known athletes in the world in a few years. The guy's not only the top scorer in the league, but also supports tons of charities. Matthew spent an hour talking about him last year after we met him at a charity auction. He was so nice and down to earth. Matthew couldn't talk him into changing investment companies, but they did have lunch.

"And you know more about playing sports at a higher level than we do. I know you only made it to college level baseball, but you speak these guys' language," Tre says.

Matthew's hands go up in the air. "I know. I know. Stop with the hard sell. You know I want to say yes. But it's not all about what I want. I have family obligations, and there is risk. You guys think this is going to be easy. You're talking about taking on some of the biggest sports agencies in the world. They're not going to give up their talent easily. And even though you have the money to get started, there's no guarantee anyone will sign with you or stay with you."

Matthew's worrying for nothing. In ten years' time these guys go from nothing to the third largest agency in the country. Matthew said he knew the guys that started it, but I didn't realize they had been friends. I've never heard him talk about anything with as much excitement as he is now. Maybe...maybe he would have been happier had he taken the risk.

A risk I talked him out of taking.

My stomach clenches. Did I talk him out of his dream? No, I gave him solid advice. At the time I had no way of knowing they would be a success, and Matthew has always worried about what his father would think. Being a sports agent wouldn't be highbrow enough for his father, though I'm not sure it matters since his father never seems pleased with anything Matthew does. Maybe he should have gone with his dream.

Carter doesn't give up. "We know that. Our choice in investors was very strategic. They're our connections to some of the largest retailers and owners in the country. We did our homework."

"Don't look so surprised," Tre says.

"Oh, I am...You usually need me to do your homework." Matthew chuckles.

They all laugh. When's the last time I saw Matthew hanging out with friends? It's been a while. Not that I remember him laughing much with the guys from the firm.

"So true. I wouldn't have passed Finance without you. Another reason we need you," Carter adds.

Matthew's chair scrapes as he pushes back from the table. I turn my head in the opposite direction so there is no chance he sees my face. "Enough shop talk for tonight. I'm going to head to the bathroom. When I get back, we watch the game."

His cologne wafts my way as he leaves the table. My lips curl up, and my eyes fill with tears. He always did smell good. But now isn't the right time. Another month. I need to wait until the right time.

"Are you going to eat any of those fries?" Izzy asks.

I shake my head, and she pulls them toward her. For a small girl she sure can eat when she's hungry.

Who is this Matthew? My Matthew's always serious and always about appearances. He would never come to a sports bar or sit around laughing with the guys over beers. What changed him? Me?

I can't think about this now. Drinks with Izzy now. I'll fix this later. "We can head out when you're done."

She drops the fry in her hand and picks up her whiskey sour and downs it. "Ready."

"You hate this place that much?"

"No, it's fine, but I'm looking forward to the expensive drinks you're going to buy me tonight." Her eyes light up like Christmas. I roll my eyes and chuckle. This is going to cost me.

I RELAX on the couch as Izzy makes me one of her blueberry whiskey drinks. She said drinks at home in her comfy clothes sounded better than going to another bar.

"So, who's the guy?" She hands me a drink and sits beside me. Oh, now I get the real reason to come home. She wants to ask questions. I should have figured that out.

"No questions asked, remember?"

"He looks like the guy you saw on the street the other day." I ignore her and she continues. "I was quiet while we sat there and you listened in on his conversation, but now it's time for you to spill. Tell me."

Her glare could melt steel. I swear.

"He's just an old friend. I wanted to make sure he was doing okay."

"Old friend? I know all your friends, and I would have recognized that hottie," she says, piling her long curly hair on top of her head and securing it with a hair stick.

"You don't know him, yet." But you will and you will like him—not that we all spend that much time together *before*, but we will this time.

"How do you have a secret friend? Were you out with him all those times you said you had to 'work late'?"

I roll my eyes. "No."

She sets her drink on the table. "Then why haven't I heard of him?"

"That's a long story," I breathe out. I'm sure full of a lot of those lately.

She watches me for a moment before her head lands on my shoulder. I lean into her, and we sit in silence for a few minutes.

In the quiet, my mind races with all the decisions I need to make, the weight of them pushing me down. The thoughts I've been keeping hidden suddenly spill out in whispered fragments that make no sense. "I don't know anymore. Everything is so different. I thought I could make things better for all of us, but now I'm not sure what to think. It's been almost a month and what have I accomplished?" I sit up and place my head in my hands. "I had sex with Ben and I'm not sure if I should feel guilty or elated. Hell, Matthew doesn't even know I exist and yet I'm banking on our meeting going as planned to bring us together again." I down the rest of my drink before setting the glass down on the table again.

Izzy's arm wraps around my shoulders. "What's going on? What have you been trying to accomplish this last month?"

What did I say? I rerun my last comments. No time travel nonsense specifically, thank goodness. "Nothing. I just realized that I'd been working so much, and I was losing touch with my friends, so I've been trying to figure out a better work life balance."

"Really? Well, you've been more available and even made our lunch date, so why are you feeling like it's not working?"

"I'm just tired. It's harder to balance than I thought, and throw Grayson's into the mix and things get even more overwhelming. But I'm fine."

"So how was sex with Ben?" Izzy pipes in.

I chuckle and lean toward the other end of the couch. Of course, I should've known to always deflect my crazy with talk of sex.

"Amazing," I say, reluctantly.

"And that's a problem, because you like this Matthew guy?" She squishes her face in confusion, but apparently, she didn't miss my words.

"You could say that," I almost groan. What kind of soap opera drama am I creating for myself?

"So, Matthew really isn't an old friend. But you want to make him a new friend?" Her voice trails off as she continues to question me.

"Technically, yes."

"But he doesn't know you exist?" Izzy asks.

I breathe out. "Not currently"

Izzy kicks my foot with hers. "Then why should you feel guilty?"

Because somewhere in time, he's my husband, and a decent one at that. And I'm hardwired for feeling guilty. "Because someday he's going to be important to me."

"But right now, he isn't. You have to stop planning out the future and actually live in the present."

If only it were that easy.

11

LAUREN

Professional.

We need to keep things professional. I repeat those words to myself as I walk up the stairs to Ben's office for our meeting. The sex was good, but we need to focus on work. We probably shouldn't have sex again. Things don't need to get more complicated. As I turn the door handle I whisper, "I can do this."

Ben smiles as I walk in. A half grin, half full smile that reminds me he knows me intimately and has my insides twisting in knots as he walks toward me. I take a deep breath as I turn and shut the door behind me. I will not let his smile sway me, I promise myself. But when I turn back around Ben is standing in front of me. His hands go straight to my face, and he pulls me into a deep kiss. The papers in my hand fall to the ground as I clutch his shirt and lean into him.

After a few moments, he pulls back, and my pounding heart sends blood rushing to everywhere but my head. My body wins this battle. Tomorrow we will stop thinking about Ben. I smile. Yeah, tomorrow.

"Hey," my voice comes out breathy and weak.

"Hey, I've missed you." His fingers stroke the back of my neck, and I fight the urge to moan. I need to move away.

"It's only been a few days," I say as I squat down to pick up the papers I dropped. My hands shake. I missed him too. But I can't say that. We're just friends. Friends who had sex.

That's it.

It's just sex.

No missing yous.

There have been a few texts volleyed back and forth the last few days, but they were light and fun or about work, not about feelings.

"A very long few days," Ben says. His eyes follow me as I stand. I feel a little lightheaded; I must have stood up too quickly. I take a deep breath. I'm here for work.

Work now. Sex later. Yes, later.

I move to his desk. After setting the papers down, I start to reorganize them. "Ben, I'm here for work, not for...the other. We need to keep those things separate."

"Does that mean no sex on the desk?" he says, sitting in his chair opposite me.

Normally, I would be happy to have a large desk separating us, but now I'm left wondering how fast we could clear it off and...ugh. Stop it. "Probably not a good idea."

"Probably." He tilts his head to the side as if trying to figure out the odds. "I'll take that as a maybe."

"Ben, work. I'm here for work. Do you have last week's sales numbers?"

"Yes, ma'am."

For the next forty-five minutes we review sales numbers,

check off a few things on the easy-to-fix list, and I ask a few more questions.

"I'll have the final plans ready next week. Then we can get to the things that will make those numbers we were reviewing move in the right direction."

Ben stands and walks toward the wall of postcards. "It's nice to see the numbers are less negative than the prior weeks, but... I can't keep it up much longer." The defeat in his voice knocks me in the gut. "Maybe I should sell. I'm not sure I'm cut out for this. Working every day in the same place doing the same thing. My buddy called, and I don't know. It...."

"It would be easier, but you need to be okay with them turning it into a Subshop." Did he know that before? Did he ever come back to Nashville after he sold the business?

"A Subshop? The guy who offered to buy it said he wanted to turn it into a juice bar and health food store."

"Subshop ," I say under my breath.

"How do you know?" His eyebrows furrow together, and he studies me.

"I just do. I know a lot of random things." I smile. "But if we add food options and get the softball teams to come back each week, you won't have to worry about that." I hope. I think. No. My plan is solid. If he follows it, it will work. Exactly like all my other plans.

He turns and gives me a nod.

I lean back in my chair and enjoy the moment. He's starting to see it can work.

"Don't get too cocky. I haven't agreed yet." His deep voice is saying he's not sure, but I can see his shoulders relaxing a bit. He'll see it my way.

I stand and walk toward him. My body is humming. My

mind has unwound all the info I needed to share with him, and now I can relax.

"You lived in Seattle?" The photo is of Mt. Rainier. I've never been there, but I hear the view from the plane when you land in Seattle is incredible. Maybe someday.

"Yeah." His finger lingers on the postcard, and for a moment he's not in the room with me. He's obviously remembering something important.

"I take it you had a good time there?"

"I spent almost four months there. I made a few friends. I worked at a coffee shop, if you can believe it." His chuckle rumbles through his chest, deep and mesmerizing, like rolling thunder during a summer afternoon storm.

"Well, if you're going to be in Seattle it seems fitting."

"Yeah, I loved the city, but really I went for the hiking. Tennessee isn't short on trees, but the ones out there are...I don't know...it seems like they reach the clouds."

His appreciation of his experiences is evident, but how can he move and meet new people every few months? I hated moving. Trying to make new friends, hell, most of the time I didn't even try. I threw myself into schoolwork. I knew even then that my way out of the constant struggle meant I needed a solid education. Then I could make my own plans and stick to them.

"How can you enjoy it? Living out of a few bags? Meeting new people? Never knowing if you will find a job?" The question is more to myself than Ben, but he pauses his inspection of the postcards and looks at me.

"I didn't leave Tennessee until after I turned eighteen. Hell, I don't think I went more than a hundred miles from Nashville until I was twelve. But I liked to read, and my mom used to get this travel magazine with stories and photos from all over the world. We would spend hours talking about all the places we would go one day. Then she got sick."

He shuffles his feet as he walks to the desk and sits. I knew his mom had passed, but I didn't know how. I can't imagine not having a mom. My mom is my safe place. She worked tirelessly to make sure I had food and a place to sleep, and I worked hard to make her proud and to make sure I never had to struggle the way she had.

"How old were you when she got sick?"

"She got sick when I was ten. She fought the cancer for two years, but ultimately, she ran out of fight. It's tough to watch, but when we went through the magazines she would brighten up. We'd make up stories about the people who lived there. I had a journal where I would sketch our adventures and make lists of places we would visit."

I slide back into my chair. "So, you travel for your mom?"

He stares at the postcards as he speaks. "Yes and no. I think she'd be happy to know that I'm getting to see the world like I always wanted. Life is short, and she would be glad I didn't chain myself to this bar like my dad did. I know he thought he was taking care of us—me, my mom, and my uncle—by running the bar, but after my mom died it's all he cared about. He basically lived here. And then he died like everyone else in my family, having never lived life outside of their little bubble."

His attention returns to me. He gives me a small smile as he cocks his head. He's trying to make me believe that wound has healed. But I know it hasn't. "I knew then I couldn't stay."

"If that's how you feel, why not sell the place?"

"I don't know. Part of me wants to sell it and move on, but at this point...it's the only family I have left. Plus, Nashville is still my home and always will be. But I still want to have a life beyond this bar, beyond this town."

Unstable.

Unpredictable.

The kind of life I had as a kid. The opposite of the life I've made for myself. The opposite of what I need. I don't want to go with the flow. I need to know where my next meal is coming from. Where I'm going to live. Who I can count on.

"Starting a new life every few months is exhausting," I say, without thinking.

"That a question or a statement?"

"Both," I sigh.

"Meaning you moved a lot?" Ben asks.

I sit up straight as my stomach tightens. "Been there, done that."

"Really? What happened?"

My hands clasp together to keep me from biting my nails. "Yeah, I think I mentioned my dad. He got fired or quit a lot and that meant we had to move to wherever his next great idea took him. So, for about six or seven years we moved a lot. It only took me ten minutes to pack my stuff for the last move. I never even unpacked." I laugh to myself. "I just lived out of boxes."

"It's crazy to think of how little you really need, right?" Ben's enthusiasm for travel shines through his voice.

I look over at the wall of postcards. This is a life he loves. No material things holding him back. His living room contained several bins labeled: Kitchen, Bedroom, Clothes, and Outdoor. Four bins to contain everything you need in life.

"Yeah, but I kinda like having more than what can fit in three boxes. Hell, I have more than three boxes of shoes."

Enough about the past. It's time to concentrate on the future. "I need to get home. I have work tomorrow."

"Have dinner with me."

What? Dinner? "Like a date?"

"Yes. A proper date."

"We aren't dating. Friends. Sex. Nothing more," I remind him.

"No, we said casual which means while we're seeing each other we should make the most of it."

"Ben..."

"It's dinner. I'm not proposing to you. Calm down. Tomorrow night. I'll pick you up at seven."

I should say no, but it's just a date. I've been on lots of dates. None in the last ten years—or in the next ten years, I mean—but a date doesn't mean we're a couple or we want more than to enjoy each other's company.

"Okay."

Dinner. No strings attached.

"How did you find this place?" I ask as we are seated in the back-corner table at what Ben declared the best Cuban restaurant in town. "Wait, let me guess. You spent some time in Cuba rolling cigars and this is one of your new friend's cousin's place?"

He bites his lip to keep from laughing. His whole body vibrates with life when he laughs. It's contagious. I feel lighter when I'm around him, like life isn't weighing me down. But life is meant to weigh you down, keep you rooted. Being weightless is for vacation. For temporary. Like us.

"Close. I spent a winter in Miami working at one of the hottest bars, and one of my friends came to Nashville to open a restaurant. He even stayed in my house for a few months while he got settled."

"Wow. You really are a nice guy."

He shakes his head and leans back in his seat. "There was doubt?"

I tilt my head and smile coyly. "Ummm...what should I get? I don't know much about Cuban food."

"Can't go wrong with empanadas or boliche—it's like a stuffed pot roast. Oh, you have to try the red beans and rice, and my favorite, the ropa vieja." My confusion must show on my face as he sets the menus down. "How about we order a few things and share?"

"That would be great."

As Ben speaks to the waitress about our order, I look around the room. It's a large open space filled with dark wooden tables and chairs. Near the back of the room is a small stage with a four-piece band playing. A few people dance in front of the stage as the singer serenades them. The food must be good since almost every table is brimming with smiling and laughing people. Ben really must know the owner in order to get us a table.

"Like it?"

"Yes, it smells wonderful, and the music sets the mood."

He rises from his seat and extends his hand. "Care to dance while we wait for our food?"

Dance? Is he crazy? The place has the right ambiance with the low lighting and candles at each table, but dancing in front of people eating? I'm not sure I'm that type of girl. "I don't think..."

"Please, for tonight, don't overthink it." His voice pleads for me to let go and stop being square-peg me.

I take his hand and follow him to the dance floor. Temporary.

BEN

Surprisingly, Lauren lets me lead. Part of me expected her to take over and keep control of this situation. Instead, once I pulled her to me and wrapped my arms around her, she followed my every move. Rigid at first, trying to figure out the steps, but once she got the rhythm, she just danced. She's so beautiful when she lets her guard down; she shines as bright as the sun. With my hand at her back I dip her down and kiss her gently before pulling her back to me. Her smile is so captivating, it draws me in closer. Damn, I could get used to that smile.

I mentally smack myself. She's been firm this isn't long-term. And who am I to even think about promising anything long-term. Graysons don't get long term. And this Grayson doesn't plan to stay put long enough for long term.

"You're a good dancer," I say, bringing us both back to the present. "I didn't get a chance to tell you last time. Did you take lessons?"

"Yes, I went to a whole eight classes." Her eyes light up. "The best eight weeks of my life," she says wistfully.

"Why only eight weeks?"

"Oh, the usual...my dad quit his job and his new one overlapped with my mom's so no one could take me to the lessons." She shrugs. "It was fine. It was just dance lessons—it's not like I could make a career out of that."

"I'm sorry something you loved got taken away from you." Why would anyone allow her to be so disappointed? She obviously loved it. I want to take the hurt look off her face.

"It's fine. I got used to never knowing how long something good would last. I think my brother joined the Army in order to get some structure in his life." She chuckles at this, but I see the pain. I pull her toward me, bringing her face to my chest, and hold her.

"Do you talk to your brother?"

"Occasionally. He likes the Army. It suits him." We sway with the music.

"And your dad?" He needs someone to knock some sense into him.

"No, he...um...I haven't spoken to him in years." A shadow passes over her eyes.

"Maybe you need to." He needs to apologize. He needs to see what he's done to her.

She grimaces. "Why? I'm sure he's still the same selfish man I last saw as we pulled out of the drive."

"Maybe he is, but I think you need to see him for yourself so you can move on." I twirl her out and back to me. She laughs, but there's hurt in her eyes.

She's clearly still hung up on the fact that he didn't care enough about her to put her first. I want to slug him. Is this why she doesn't do long term? She never wants to be like her family?

"I've moved on; no need to rehash my crappy childhood," she says.

I pull back a bit to see her face clearly. "Really? You have a wonderful life but...never mind."

It's none of my business. This is supposed to be a fun evening. I should stop talking about the past.

Lauren slows our dancing. "No, say it. I can see you want to. I can take it. My friends and I call it sharing a Hard Truth."

"Hard Truth?" What? She wants me to tell her I think her dad is an ass and she needs some therapy? I don't think that's a good idea.

"When my friends and I need to tell each other something that the other is blind to or doesn't want to see, we call it a Hard Truth. They have to listen and think about it. And we never mention it again, unless they want to talk about it. So out with it, friend." She gives me a tight smile, daring me to respond.

"Well…"

"And the receiver of the news can't hold a grudge for what is said."

I chuckle a little. Oh, I have a feeling there are still grudges. The truth is painful. But if that's what she wants.

"Well, friend… I think… that you think having a job and a place to live are the only ways to feel safe and secure, but there's more to life than work. And I'm not sure you can see past your dad changing jobs and you having to suffer the consequences of decisions you didn't get to make. But…this is your life. You get to make your own decisions. You always assume that anything risky will end badly when sometimes the reward is doing something new, even if it fails."

"What's wrong with having a plan and following that plan instead of taking risks that you don't know will pay off?"

"You really think you can plan your entire life? Things happen, you adapt. You have to enjoy the time you have."

"Or you can use the new information as it comes along and update your plan. You don't throw out a perfectly good plan because something changes. Life may be short, but without a plan you will be unprepared for what it throws at you."

"Let me guess. You know exactly what your life will look like in ten years." I can see it now—a notebook full of goals and action items.

Her body stiffens as she stops moving. "I know exactly."

There is a sadness in her words, but then she turns her

eyes up at me and gives me a playful wink. This girl...I can't quite figure her out. This should be good.

"Do tell."

"It would seem boring to someone like you who likes to live by the seat of his pants."

"Nothing about you is boring." I pull her closer, removing the space she has created between us, forcing her to look up at me as we sway to the music.

"I'll live in a five-bedroom, six-bath house in Brentwood with a three-car garage and state-of-the-art kitchen that I'll never cook in. I'll be the VP of Business Development at McNeil and I'll be married to...the head of finance at one of the top investment groups in town."

House, job, marriage. Everything she's ever wanted.

"That's very specific, and you forgot to mention if you're happy. Did you forget to plan that?"

"Of course I will be." Her words say yes. Her gaze on the floor says no.

Before I can comment further, Lauren pulls away and announces the waiter has dropped off our food.

LAUREN

The food is magnificent and washes away the awkwardness of our dance-floor conversation. Spicy and full of flavor, but not so hot you can't enjoy them, our meals pair nicely with the wine Ben picked out. I take a sip before trying another one of the dishes he's chosen.

"The food is great. Thanks for sharing this with me."

"Anytime. So, you mentioned your mom. Where is she now?" Ben tries to steer the conversation back to me.

"She's in Hendersonville. She got remarried to Charles

—he's an insurance salesman. Nice guy, takes care of my mom the way she should be." I take a drink of my wine. "But enough about me. Tell me one of your favorite memories as a kid."

Ben lifts an empanada onto his plate and cuts into the piping hot pastry. His lip twists a little as he looks off to the side, as if seeing the memory come to life.

"Every year on my parents' anniversary, we would all go to a fancy restaurant downtown—the one where my parents met. They would order a drink from the bar and I would order a beer…well, a root beer I know my dad owned a bar, but that was always work, not fun. The bartender would put my drink in a fancy beer glass, like I was an adult. It always tasted better in that glass."

I chuckle at the idea of a little Ben sitting in his dress shirt and tie, drinking his "beer" and swinging his feet on the barstool while his parents stared into each other's eyes. "They went every year?"

"Oh, yes, and it had to be the exact day and time." He chuckles to himself.

"How did they meet?" I take a bite of the ropa vieja and enjoy the flavor combination.

"My mom was sitting at the bar waiting on her very late blind date. My father's friend was a chef there, and my dad came in to pick up a to-go order and saw her sitting alone. Something about the sad look on her face made him stop in his tracks." Ben smiles and shakes his head.

"He said it was love at first sight, so he paid for his dinner and then gave it to a guy walking out the door. He sat next to her, ordered her a drink, bought her dinner, and a year later he married her."

I swallow hard. That's a little too close to how I met Matthew. Chance encounters or fate?

"Really?" Is it hot in here? Maybe the food is spicier than I thought.

"Yeah, my mom said by the end of dinner she knew he was the one. She always said fate brought them together."

"That's sweet," I manage to say.

"And each year on their anniversary, I still go to the bar and have a drink in their honor."

My face heats up, and I'm overcome by thirst. I take a long drink of my wine. Fate? Matthew's and my meeting had to be fate. He always said it happened at exactly the right time—that he had a big life decision to make and my showing up is what helped him decide. What if...what if fate got it wrong the first time and that's why I'm here?

I finish my wine and set the glass on the table, placing a smile on my face to cover the emotions raging through me. "I can't imagine knowing that fast that you had found the love of your life." Matthew and I were compatible, but not love at first sight. He checked all my boxes and I checked all of his. We found love along the way. So, it wasn't exactly the same.

"They were lucky. Some people never recognize it."

The rest of dinner, Ben and I focus on the food, both seeming to know we have pushed the boundaries of a friendly dinner banter and gotten a little deeper than we planned. We keep the conversation focused on the bar and make small talk as he drives me home.

BEN STEPS SILENTLY into my living room. Since we left the restaurant, he's been a little distant. I'm not sure if it's something I said or if he's still thinking about his parents, but he keeps looking over at me with his stormy eyes.

"What's going on?" I finally ask.

"Sorry, I just got stuck in my head."

As we sit on the couch, his hand rubs the side of my arm down to my hand. He gently lifts it to his lips and kisses it with a feather-like touch.

"Do you ever wonder if we could be more than...friends and sex?" he whispers, still holding my hand in his.

I take a sharp breath. Oh no. He can't be falling for me. Talking about his parents is making him sentimental. We aren't... He's not...

"I have plans," I blurt out.

His leans his head back on the couch and laughs. Not a happy chuckle—more like he thinks I'm crazy and he's laughing at me, not with me. His eyebrow lifts. "Aren't there a hundred quotes about life not caring about your plans?"

I sneer back at him. Bastard. "I know you don't believe in plans. You prefer to see the world and just see where life takes you."

"I do believe in plans, but I don't believe you can plan out your entire life."

"Why not?"

"Well...I doubt my mother planned to die when I was twelve, or my dad planned to die before I turned eighteen, or that my uncle planned to drive his bar into the ground and get cancer. And I sure as hell didn't plan to meet a girl who makes lists and thinks she can't deviate from her plan even if something is standing right in front of her."

I lay my head on his chest. I can't look at him. My eyes are wide, and tears are threatening to fall. He's been through so much. Why did I do this to him? I'm just adding one more name to the list of people who are no longer in his life. I'm a horrible person.

"Ben," I whisper.

"Don't." He shakes his head and stands. "I should go. I didn't mean..."

"Ben." I mirror his stance, but I don't touch him. He takes a few steps toward the door. "Don't leave." I'm not going to let our beautiful night end this way. We only have each other for these few moments. I don't want him to remember it ending like this.

He stops but doesn't turn to face me. I wrap my hand around his and pull him toward the stairs. He follows, clearly knowing my intentions. "I hear angry sex is hot." I nod up the stairs.

He doesn't move.

I bite my lip. Maybe I went too far.

And then in one swift motion he lifts me up and carries me up the stairs.

He growls, "Let's find out."

12

LAUREN

My fingers brush the grey painted bricks, testing for wet spots before I lean against the wall. The painters were here two days ago, and I assume it's dry, but I like this dress so best to verify.

A whistle sings out behind me. Turning my head, I see Dillon, an old friend from college and a sound system expert, walking across the street. His hair is a bit longer than the last time I saw him. He has it pushed back and is sporting his trademark movie-star grin.

"Well, aren't you looking lovely today," he says.

One thing Dillon is not, is subtle. He stops a few feet before he reaches me and doesn't hide his perusal of my body from head to toe. I shake my head and take a step toward him.

"Thanks, Dillon. Now remember your eyes belong up here." My hands wave over my face.

He laughs. He's a major flirt and could charm anyone into doing anything. Including getting me to help him with his final marketing project the night before it was due and playing wingman a few times while he scoped out dates at the bars. Back when life was simple.

"Let's go in and I'll show you around."

Dillon reaches for the door handle and holds it open for me. He really is a gentleman if you get past the ass act.

The bar is empty as it doesn't open for another few hours. Ben should be around somewhere. I'll get started with Dillon and then introduce them.

"I can't believe it's taken you this long to call in your favor," he says.

He has no idea. I never called it in the first time.

"I know. I've been busy, but I figured I better call it in soon or you'd forget all about me."

His business has really taken off since college. I helped him put together a business plan senior year. It only took me a few hours of work, and since then he's worked incredibly hard to put together a quality team and has become the go-to company for new sound systems in the area.

"I could never forget you."

"Please, so many girls, so little time." This time I roll my eyes to the ceiling and laugh.

He leans in and whispers, "It hasn't been that many girls."

"It's been too many and you know it. And personally, I'd like to have words with the first girl, the one who broke your heart." I feel like his big sister who needs to protect him and keep him from being alone for another decade.

"What?" His smile fades.

"You know." I give him a long stare down. "Listen, a word of advice from someone who knows a thing or two. Forget about her and move on. You deserve better."

His face is blank. His whole body tenses, and his eyes

look through me. I know it's none of my business, but when I see something that needs fixing—and he needs fixing—I can't help but nudge my friend in the right direction. I don't know where he ended up. I lost touch, like I did with so many of my old friends. Not this time.

Wherever he went, he rockets back with his trademark smirk in place. Someday, some girl is going to fall for this boy and have to bring a sledgehammer to break down that wall. She's going to have to be tough enough to keep pressing until he breaks, but it will be worth it.

"So, what's the favor? I'm guessing it's not a date to one of Eve's art shows since you told me to meet you here."

"I don't need help in the date department."

"I didn't figure you did, especially with the guy behind the bar plotting my demise." Dillon nods his head behind me.

I turn and find Ben behind the bar. He nods. And Dillon might be right. Ben is throwing off unpleasant vibes.

I chuckle. "That's Ben, the owner. I'll introduce you."

I wave Ben over and then turn back to Dillon.

"Oh, he's the owner. Nothing more?" Suspicion fills his voice, which I choose to ignore.

"Dillon, this is business, not a dating show."

Ben steps next to me, his sleeve brushing my arm.

"Ben Grayson, this is Dillon Winters. Dillon is a friend of mine from college. He installs sound systems, among other things. And he owes me a favor, so I asked him to come and see what we need to do."

"Nice to meet you." Dillon extends his hand to Ben. The boys shake and glare and then smile at each other. What the hell? Guy mind-speak? Whatever.

"I appreciate you stopping by to check out the sound

system. It works, but that's about all I can say for it," Ben says.

I point toward the stage. "We need you to check it out and let us know what it would cost to get it brought into the current century. It needs to work for both a DJ and bands."

"Can do. What are you looking to spend?" Dillon asks.

Ben stands straighter and crosses his arms. "Well..." he starts to speak.

"I got you. Actually,"—he pauses and looks around the room—"a guy had us take out a perfectly good sound system at this club over in Knoxville a few months ago. He wanted the latest and greatest even though what he had worked great." Dillon shakes his head and obviously thinks the guy's an idiot. "Let me see if the specs would fit in here, and if they do, I'll give it to you and you only need to pay for labor."

"Are you serious?" Ben asks.

"Yeah. It's taking up space in my warehouse, and I owe Lauren a favor. This would make us even."

"I think I would owe you one for all that," I say.

If he can get us a new system for the cost of labor that would be amazing and help keep our budget down. The return on investment of a sound system is hard to calculate, but without good sound, who wants to come and listen to the bands or the DJ?

Ben stiffens beside me and says, "That's more than generous."

Dillon reaches his arm around me, giving me a side squeeze. "This girl right here helped me get through college and set the course for my business. There's nothing I wouldn't do to help her. Trust me, when she's done with you, you'll feel the same."

"I think I already do." Ben glances over at me, and I roll my eyes before stepping away from Dillon's arm.

"Thanks, Dillon. We'll leave you to do the measurements and work your magic. Let me know if you need anything," I say.

Ben and I walk back toward the bar.

"Old boyfriend?" There's jealousy on the tips of his whispered words.

A laugh escapes me. "Hell, no. I love him like a little brother. One you want to strangle and protect all at the same time."

"Seems like he can take care of himself," Ben says as if I didn't know that. Of course he can, but if I'm back I should try and help, right?

Ben pauses as we reach the bar and touches my arm gently. "We okay?"

"Yeah," I say, keeping my voice even. Waking up alone was a bit unexpected, but I have no right to be upset. We're casual, so I can't assume he can stay over each time we're together.

"I didn't mean to leave the other night without saying good-bye. I..."

"It's fine. You don't have to spend the night. It's just..."

"Sex. I got it." He keeps his voice low and steady, but I hear the disappointment in it.

"Yeah." Sex. No emotional attachment or need to wake in each other's arms. I look away, away to anywhere but his eyes. He knows what we are. We can't be more.

"I'd better check on Dillon, then we can review the final plans in your office."

BEN

The final plans. I'm not sure I want to hear them. Once we make these changes she's gone. She's always had one foot out the door, but...dammit. It's not like I have anything to offer her.

The walls of this office and this town are closing in on me. I can't get stuck here forever. The email from my friend Evan is still open on my computer. His dad needs some help at his cattle ranch in Texas and offered me a spot when I'm ready. Once Grayson's is squared away, maybe I can take a vacation, but will I ever be able to go back to full-time traveling? No, but maybe I can figure something out.

I jump out of my chair and back to the present when Lauren drops a three-inch binder on my desk. When did she walk in?

"This is Grayson's holy bible. It has all your important information. You need to keep it up to date. You need to make notes of what specials you ran on which days, which bands played, and which DJ worked. This way you can track what is and isn't working." Lauren is all business. Damn her for being cute and captivating when she's bossy. How am I expected to sit here and listen and not pull her onto my lap and kiss her?

"Yes, ma'am," I force myself to say, as I cross my arms over my chest to keep from reaching for her.

She takes her normal seat on the opposite side of the desk and pulls out her notebook. We spend the next hour reviewing all of the financials and her ideas for cutting costs, some of which we've already started and are already working. We were in the black last week after her analysis showed a change in liquor distributors would save us ten percent.

"Now about food."

"I'm in."

Her head jerks up. "What?"

"You haven't steered me wrong yet. I'm willing to give it a try."

Her face lights up like I've given her the best present ever.

"I suggest a very limited menu to start. Make the things we offer the best you can get."

We? Does that mean she's more invested than... Stop it. Not now. Pay attention. "I agree."

The shock on her face is barely noticeable as she keeps talking. "The equipment all checked out, Chef Kamara will call you tomorrow and go over her ideas for the menu, and the Health Inspector is scheduled for Friday."

"Wait. How do you already have a chef and a health inspection lined up? I said yes like ten seconds ago."

She bites her lip and half grimaces, half smiles. "I knew you'd come around."

"I guess we have a plan." The smile she's fighting would have me agreeing to anything she wants. I'm not sure she realizes that.

"I've also included a list of artists to be on the lookout for and approximately when to start having them play."

My hand goes over the list. It's long. And detailed. And goes on for years. How can she know about a band that is going to be good so far out? "Some of the dates aren't for like...a decade."

"True." Her answer is quick, and she tries to move on. "Now—"

"How do you know that? You got a guy on the junior future country all-stars committee in your pocket?" I can't help but laugh. She always knows random information and...she's always vague about how. Is she some kind of psychic?

"Long story. You'll have to trust me. And concentrate on this year's list. There are a lot of good names, and these performers are going to be big, so don't waste any time. You need to book them soon. If you give them a break this early in their career, it may pay off for you later."

She's serious. She's not going to tell me how she knows about these bands.

I shake my head and ask again. "How do you know this?"

"I just do." Lauren gives me a tight smile. I know that look; I'll get nothing else from her on this subject.

I study her as she tilts her head down and scribbles in her notebook. She's hiding something. There are so many things I don't know about her, but now's not the time to figure them out. Grayson's is the priority right now.

"All this is great. But how can we actually compete with all the country music stars opening bars and all the famous tourist traps downtown?"

All the local bars spend tons of money on advertising or pull in big-name artists to partner with them. I don't have that kind of money or connections. We can't compete with that.

"We don't," she says with a smile.

"Oh, really, that hasn't worked so far." I laugh.

"Listen, we can't compete with a celebrity bar or one that's been established for a hundred years, so we don't try."

"So, we close down?" Sarcasm drips from my words and she rolls her eyes. Surely, after all her hard work, "don't try and compete" is not the plan.

"No, we don't want to cater to tourists. We're for the locals who don't want to deal with all the tourists. We're for people who still want good music, good food, and a place to have a drink with their friends. We have parking. We have local and up-and-coming bands. We don't make people wait in long lines or shun people for not looking a certain way." She pauses and waits until she sees me catch up to the ideas she's helping me shape in my mind. "We're Grayson Brothers' local bar and grill. Keeping Nashville Real."

"Huh..." She might be on to something. "That might work."

"It will work. You're already a local bar, and once we get the word out to more of the locals that you are offering them entertainment and food, they will come."

A bubble of hope springs. We might actually be able to save this old place. My dad and uncle would have loved Lauren with her never-say-die attitude. They might have even agreed to her new ideas if it meant more people in the door. I look to the ceiling and send a little prayer up that she's right. When I open my eyes, I find Lauren watching me. Her face is hard to read, but she looks happy. I go to her without realizing what I'm doing and pull her from the chair into my arms and kiss her. This crazy, smart, beautiful woman. Every day she changes me, and every day I love her more.

Damn.

I love her.

How did that happen? No, it can't be love. I'm confusing my excitement for saving this place and her part in it. That's all. This is just casual.

I kiss her before I say anything stupid. "Let's go. I need to show you how much I like your ideas." I wink, and she rolls her eyes before placing her hand in mine and letting me lead her out the door.

If this is love, how will I be strong enough to walk away when it's time?

LAUREN

Is it a walk of shame if you're showered and dressed?

All week I've worked my day job and spent my evenings with Ben, putting all our plans in place before finding our way back to his bed. It's been fun being a part of executing my plan instead of just submitting a proposal and hoping they implement it correctly. But it's time to get back to my routine and not lose sight of my friends.

I set a cup of coffee in front of Eve with her name in big black letters. The perky barista at Eve's favorite coffee house added a big heart with fireworks all on her own. The place is a few miles out of the way, but since I was MIA last week, I figure a little coffee love might buy me back into her good graces.

"Oh, you do remember my name. I thought maybe you forgot. Or wait, did you have so many orgasms you forgot your own name?"

I roll my eyes and drop into my usual chair, leaning back and waiting for her to finish. "Or did he tie you up all week and only allow you to text, so we knew you weren't dead? Or were you actually having such a good time you forgot your to-do list?"

Eve pulls the coffee cup toward her.

"You done?"

She cocks her head to the side with a smile, and I know that means she's only done for now.

"So, I don't follow your advice and you lecture me, and then I follow your advice and you give me grief. I'm not sure I know which is better."

"Oh yes, you do."

We both laugh. Oh yes, I do. This week has been the best

I've had in a long time. Ben is easy to talk to, amazing in bed, and our work at Grayson Brothers' is starting to take shape.

"So, your texts have been a little vague. Spill."

"It's been…good," I say casually.

Eve peers over her coffee. "Good?"

"Fine. Better than good." I keep my voice as flat as I can, while my body and mind scream "liar." It really has been better than good, but…it can't last. I bite my lip as a jolt of pain runs through my chest, reminding me that time is almost up on this little tryst.

Eve leans back in her chair, and if this were a spy movie, she would be petting a cat or knocking her fingers together and creepily smiling at her handiwork. "Define better than good."

My body warms as I think of being wrapped in Ben's arms again this morning, and I can't fight the grin that fills my face. This morning, I purposely set an early alarm to make sure I had time to get Eve's coffee. My good intentions were almost foiled when Ben groaned and begged me not to leave. I resisted the temptation; I promised Eve I would meet her and I'm keeping my promises this time around.

"We've made progress on the bar. I spoke to Gabby earlier this week, and she's sending over the new logo and some marketing ideas tomorrow. I'm not sure Ben's excited about marketing, but he needs it and it's free, so he didn't complain. Oh, but the best thing is he hired a new DJ."

"Thank the Lord." Eve raises her hands in praise.

"He was so horrible. The new one is great; he starts a week from Saturday," I say.

She looks over her laptop at me. "Who's covering this Saturday?"

"Not sure yet. We're looking for someone. Ollie's got

some calls in for me. If not, we'll try and get a band to cover." I reach into my bag and pull out my notebook.

"What about Ollie?"

I look up at her. "He already has a gig."

She runs her fingers through her hair. "I should probably know that, but I've given up. I only ask a day or two in advance now."

Maybe that's part of the problem; never knowing where the other is makes it hard to connect. I need to focus on figuring out where things went wrong, but right now things are fine. Hmmm.

"Maybe you need a shared calendar. I can set it up for you."

Eve shakes her head. "No, thanks."

If one of their problems is not knowing where the other is or when they have free time together then I can fix that. I stick out my tongue. "Some people appreciate my help."

"Like Ben. I bet he's been showing you exactly how much he appreciates you." She crosses her arms in complete smugness.

I would like to say I didn't blush—that I'm too old for that—but I did. My face feels like I've been in the sun for hours. He has been showing me lots of appreciation.

"Did you think you could get away with changing the subject and not telling me the good stuff?" Eve always finds a way back to her original question.

"No, but a girl can hope," I say.

She watches me closely. "I feel like you're glossing over the good parts."

"Oh, I am. And Ben has some very good parts." I bite my lip and close my eyes for effect.

She grumbles, "That's all I'm getting, isn't it?"

"Yep."

She concedes defeat for now. "What's next on the list?"

"Dillon is installing the sound system this week, and we're planning the soft opening of the new food offerings a few days before the grand opening. Thanks again for asking your friend Chef Kamara to get us started and for helping to find a chef willing to work with us on such short notice. Chef Allen is great, and Ben already trusts him with the menu."

"You look happy." Her tone is serious.

"I am. I told you it's been a good week."

Eve crosses her arms and sighs. "You can thank me anytime now."

I should have known she needs to gloat one more time about being right. Sex with Ben has been incredible and allowed me to get out of my head about this whole time-travel magical crap. I twist the bracelet on my arm. I haven't thought about it all week. I lived my life in this timeline without thinking about what's next. My stomach clenches. I also didn't think about Matthew. What does that say about me?

"Fine, you were right. Ben has been good with casual and I'm happy. But that time is going to come to an end." Soon. But I will think about that later. I sip my coffee, and we spend the next hour catching up. Austin is headed on a trip to Washington to scout out a new hotel, Gabriella is reading her 450th book of the year instead of going out and meeting people, and Izzy is upset about something but won't tell me what. Sigh. How do I help? How do I make their lives better this time? Am I allowed to? Nothing I've said to them so far seems to be working. After Grayson's is finished, I'll get to work on the girls.

I pick up my coffee and it's cold. Crap. "What time is it?"

"Eight thirty. Why?"

"I gotta go. I have a meeting with my boss at ten." I grab my coat and drop my coffee in the trash.

Eve stands and walks with me toward the door. "You still work at McNeil?"

"Funny."

"Seriously, you should think about quitting and starting your own company. You light up when you talk about the work for Grayson's but not about your day job."

"McNeil is great; it's just the last few jobs have been a little repetitive." The understatement of the year. "And you know I could never start my own company. I've seen how that ends."

Eve touches my arm lightly. "You're not your dad."

"Why does everyone keep bringing him up?"

"Maybe because you need to deal with your unresolved feelings about him?"

I want to smack the false smile off her face, but I'm late. "How cliché to assume I have Daddy issues."

13

LAUREN

Knock Knock Knock.

Regret hits me with each knock on the door. I shouldn't have come. We need some time apart. We need to keep it casual. I've spent too many nights with Ben and yet I'm back again. He won't be around long; I need to remember that. I can't depend on him.

I turn my head to the car. Maybe he didn't hear me.

The door opens with a creak.

Luck is not my friend.

"Lauren? What's wrong?" His eyes do a quick sweep up and down my body, and he places his hand on my shoulder. "You said you weren't coming over tonight."

Tears well in my eyes. What's wrong? That's a loaded question. I'm somehow a time traveler, which should be ideal for a control freak like me, but it's not. My future husband has a girlfriend and apparently is the kind of guy who laughs and goes to sports bars or was that kind of guy before he met me. And now all of my goals are within reach, but for some reason I can't seem to reach out for them.

"Yeah," I say standing up straight, pushing down my emotions with a sledgehammer. I shouldn't be here. Everything is according to plan. Everything is right on track. Everything is the same, except him. He's new and warm and sweet. He's...

Ben takes a step back into the house, catching my attention. He looks comfortable in his grey T-shirt and black-and-red pajama bottoms. His night was probably nice and quiet until I came to ruin it.

"Lauren, do you want to come in?" He speaks low and slow like he's afraid to make a sudden move or I'll bolt like a little mouse and scramble back into my hole in the wall.

Obviously, he knows I'm not fine.

Instead of answering, I nod and walk past him into the hallway. He motions to the right, toward the living room. The room is dark except for the light by the chair where a pile of books sits. Ben loves books about far-off places. He's all about new experiences, and I suppose a book is a new experience you can get without leaving home. But it's not enough for him to read about it. He needs to breathe the air, smell the smells, live in the life.

I, on the other hand, do everything I can to avoid new experiences, to stay on the path, and to never allow myself to wish for more.

He kisses my forehead and brushes his hand down my cheek. "Can I get you a drink?"

"Do you have any Scotch?"

His deep chuckle is barely audible, but the grin on his face is in full force. "That kind of day, eh?"

I nod.

"How do you want it?" he asks, as he walks to the kitchen.

"Neat. And a double," I yell.

"Make yourself at home. I'll be right back."

The fireplace light fills the room with a soft glow. The mantel is filled with picture frames in which Ben is the star of many of them, but also his uncle whom I've seen pictures of at the bar. There is a picture of a dark-haired man with his arms wrapped around a beautiful blonde woman holding a baby. Ben's parents. He has his mother's eyes and his father's dark hair and chin.

Must be hard, being all alone in the world. At least I have my mom and grandparents to lean on. Well, maybe not lean on. I can take care of myself, but having people around that love you is important.

My hand falls from the picture frame as I hear Ben's footsteps on the hardwood floors.

"Your drink, ma'am." His voice is playful, but I see him sizing up the situation. I'm such an idiot lately. I shouldn't have come here. I should've gone home. I should just...deal with this myself. I told him casual and then I show up here an emotional wreck. I'll just take a few sips and then go. Or take a few sips and tell him to take me to bed and let all my troubles wash away for a time.

"Thanks."

Ben waves his hand toward the couch and seats himself at one end. I follow suit, placing myself at the opposite end, turning toward him as I pull one knee up on the couch before letting my other leg dangle. He smiles and raises his glass to his lips.

The glass in my hand is almost identical, though mine seems to have a touch more than his. Ben's eyes grow wide as I tip the glass up and drink it all in one swallow. It burns, but who cares.

"Do you...need another one?"

"That would be great." I sigh.

He stands and leaves the room, returning moments later with the bottle. "I think you may need more than one more drink."

"No wonder you're such a good bartender. You read your customers so well."

"Normally, but I can't figure out what's going on with you tonight."

Always straightforward—it's one of the things I love about him. Wait...not love...definitely not love...like...I like about him. My face warms and I take a sip from the newly poured drink. "Nothing. I just needed a drink."

Ben sits next to me and turns to give me his full attention. "Really? I don't think you came here for a drink. What's wrong? Tell your friendly bartender. I'm a good listener."

Wouldn't it be nice to just lay all my troubles out and let someone else sort them out? I suppose that's what going to therapy might be like. But talking about something doesn't fix it. Action does, so what's the point?

"Nothing's wrong. Actually, I got a promotion today." I try and make it sound like a triumph.

"Con...gratulations?"

"Thanks." My eyes burn with tears. I blink them back. Not here. Not ever.

His foot nudges mine. "Why does that make you sad?"

"I'm not sad. I came over to celebrate."

He scoots closer to me and pulls me into his arms. I lean against his chest and let him take the weight from me, just for a minute. He doesn't speak; he pulls me tight and brushes his hand down my arm.

"Talk to me," Ben whispers to the top of my head, his voice almost pleading for insight that I don't wish to give him.

"I'm fine. I just needed a drink. I should go," I say weakly. Ben pulls the glass from my hand and sets it on the table.

"You keep saying that, but yet here you are, so talk to me." He pulls us back toward the opposite end of the couch, and I sink into him even more. Everything feels right. I breathe him in. Absorb his warmth.

He whispers in my ear, "It's my turn to be here for you, Lauren. You've done so much to help me; let me do the same for you."

When was the last time I let someone truly help me? When was the last time someone offered? Tears fall along with my ability to keep the seal on my emotions intact.

"I'm just so…tired. I can't do it again. I can't work twelve-hour days again. My body might be willing, but my heart isn't in it anymore, which makes no sense. I've spent my whole life trying to make my life predictable, and now that I literally know exactly what is going to happen, I…" Stop talking. What am I saying?

His fingers pull through my hair.

"What happened?"

"I got the job. Just like last time. And tomorrow I'll get the Monroe account and I'll spend four months going through all their financials and speaking to their employees and then tell them they need new sales data management and additional customer service reps, and they will double their business over the next three years. And then after that I'll work on the Bernstein account and after that the Fields. And I won't go out with my friends or have dinner with M…" Stop. Stop. Stop. I try and sit up, but he pulls me tighter. "I don't know what I'm saying."

"It's okay. I got you. Say whatever you need to say."

I don't need to say any more. I've already said too much. I pull out of his arms and sit up. "I really need to go. You didn't sign on for this."

"Why'd you come to my house tonight?" His thumb strokes the top of my hand.

"I don't know. I needed a drink, and I knew you had the night off."

"No, why did you come to me?"

His dark eyebrows furrow in response to my silence.

My eyes sting, and I tip my head down to avoid looking at him. Instead I concentrate on the fire he's built and the way the red-and-yellow flames dance around the logs. Everything is a dance, and someone always gets burnt in the process. I don't want to burn him.

"You know how you said that you don't want to waste your life only working and not living?"

He nods slightly.

"Today, I realized you were right. And...I don't know what to do with that."

How do I, Lauren Mitchel, proclaimed planner queen, not want a perfectly outlined life?

"You still haven't answered my question." His fingers intertwine with mine. His voice is gentle. "Why did you come to my house and not one of your friends'?"

"I had a bit of a rough day, and I didn't want to be alone and...the only person I wanted to see was you." The look on his face when I'm finally able to look up is priceless. Joy fills his eyes, and the corners of his mouth pull up slightly in a sexy grin. And all I want to do is kiss him and forget everything. Forget my plans, forget the next ten years, forget everything except him.

But I can't.

I have promises to keep.

"I should probably go. I keep muddying the water between us," I say.

"There is no way you're driving yourself home. Stay with me. Please." His eyes are soft, and he pulls me in so that all thoughts of leaving disappear. He brings me back against him and strokes my hair as I lie with my head on his chest.

"What are your five favorite things?" he asks.

"What?" What's he talking about? How much has he had to drink? My favorite things?

"I read this book once, and it said you should know what your five favorite things are."

Lying here is pretty nice, but I can't say that. "I don't know."

"I'll go first. One of my favorite things is that moment when I'm on a hike, and I realize I'm all alone in nature. The only sounds are my breath and the birds and the wind. It's peaceful."

"Sounds scary."

He laughs. "Scary?"

"Being alone in the woods with no one around to hear you scream for help."

His whole body shakes, causing my head to bob up and down on his chest. "I really don't think you get the point of a hike. It's on my Lauren list and I think we need to move it up."

I glare up at him. I'm not kidding. Why would you walk alone in the woods? But I keep my opinions to myself since he seems so adamant about it.

"Your turn."

My mind is blank. What do I do the most? Work. Can't say that. "I don't know."

"When do you feel at peace? When do you close your eyes and think, yes, this feels nice?"

When am I ever at peace? He's not going to take never as an answer. I close my eyes and say the first thing that pops into my head. "I love getting my hair blown out."

"Really?"

"Not in a high maintenance way, but...never mind." Why am I playing this game? Knowing my favorite things isn't going to help me build the best life for myself.

"No, tell me." His voice pulls me in. He really does want to know.

"It's relaxing. Someone is playing with my hair, which I love, and the hairdryer drowns out all the other noise. I close my eyes and feel the brush on my scalp and my hair whipping all around me. It's...relaxing." I never thought of it before, but it really is something I look forward to.

"What else?" Ben asks.

Isn't one enough? "I think it's your turn."

"Easy. The first day I pull into a new town, I always go to the coffee house closest to my new place, and I ask the waiter what their favorite place to eat in town is. I always go for dinner, and nine times out of ten it ends up being my favorite place while I'm there. Sometimes it's an upscale steak house and sometimes it's a crazy food truck. I love trying everything."

"Sounds fun," I say.

"Did you just say...not having a plan and being spontaneous could be fun?" Ben bends to the side to look at me.

I attempt a glare, but he isn't buying it. "I change my mind."

"Too late. I heard you. Lauren Mitchel can be spontaneous." He tickles my sides, and we are both laughing.

It's been a long time since someone tickled me or made

me laugh as much as Ben does. I'm not sure just having fun has ever been a priority for me.

"Occasionally." Like being here with you. This is not in the plan, not even close. Old me would never have allowed herself to be here, but old me missed out.

His fingers stroke my hair as I come down off my laughing high.

"You're up," he says.

"Oh...I know. I love going out with my friends, but my favorite part of the night is the first drink. We always toast. And it's the same toast we've said for years. 'To friendship and lives well lived.'"

His voice is slow and deliberate, mimicking the feel of his fingers dragging up my back. "Why is that moment so special?"

"I don't know, I just feel...loved. I feel our friendship is being reforged each time we say it. We only do it when all five of us are together. If someone is missing, we toast to something else. We never talked about it; it's just the way it's always been."

"It's a little secret bond you have."

My heart feels full, and I smile into the darkness of the room. "I guess so. It feels special."

"That's..."

"Lame?" I groan.

Ben tips my head up toward him with his finger so I can see his eyes. "No, it's beautiful."

My body temp rises with each touch and sweet comment.

"Don't ask me any more. That's all I can think of tonight."

He pulls me in tight to his chest, and his lips graze my ear.

"That's fine. There will be other nights. I'll get all five out of you. And tomorrow you are going to practice your newfound spontaneity and call in sick so I can take you on a hike and show you another one of mine."

At this rate, his lips whispering in my ear might become one of them.

BEN

As the sun peeks over the horizon, I glance at the passenger seat where Lauren is sleeping soundly. Her hair is pulled back in a ponytail, and there's no makeup, just Lauren. She's as beautiful as the sunrise in front of us. I hope she thinks the hike is worth getting up so early, but after last night, I know I need to help her find another outlet for her energy instead of work. She was so lost, she wasn't making any sense. How could she possibly know all that? I chuckle to myself. She's a mystery, always speaking in some kind of riddle I can't seem to unravel.

The sign for the park pulls me back to the present. She needs a vacation, but the best I can do right now is a day of hiking. So here we go.

"Wake up. We're here." I run my finger along her cheek in hopes of waking her without startling her.

"Hmm…one more minute."

"No more minutes or you'll miss the beautiful sunrise."

"Fine." She sits up in her seat and opens her eyes. "It's beautiful, but I could have seen the same one at my house… so not sure that's worth getting up at the crack of dawn or calling in sick for." She yawns and stretches in the seat next to me. "And I'm not sure why I let you talk me into going on a hike."

I laugh. It's not that she's not a morning person, just not an O-dark-thirty morning person. I practically had to carry her to the truck.

I park in the lot at the entrance to the trail. Lauren puts on her jacket as I grab the backpack with our food and extra water.

"Ready?" I say, extending my hand to her. She laces her fingers in mine and nods.

The first thirty minutes we don't speak. Lauren wasn't too keen on hiking so I figured she would feel the need to fill the silence, but she seems to be stuck in her head—or maybe she's still half-asleep. We stop to eat our breakfast on a log overlooking a valley of trees before continuing our quiet trek.

The terrain is uneven, and several places have been washed out by the rain from earlier this week, but Lauren follows my lead, no questions asked. The birds chirp a song in the trees as the morning light fills the sky. Beautiful. The tension in the air lessens as we walk, and the crease between her brows is almost gone. The cute crease—the one I want to kiss each time she gets worked up about something not going according to plan.

"You doing okay?" I ask, breaking the silence when I see her face fall.

She smiles at me. It's not a real smile; it's a fake reassuring smile.

"Yeah, it's so quiet. It took me a few minutes, but I can feel all my thoughts slowing down. It's like I have time to think about things and not just...push them to the side. But I don't really want to think about them either." She straightens her shoulders and puts on another fake smile. "Have you always enjoyed hiking?"

Nice redirect. I squeeze her hand. What has her thinking

so hard? I want to know everything, but I won't push, for now. "I've loved it as long as I can remember. And no matter where I live, I always find a favorite place. Nature is always changing, so even if you go on the same hike you see something new."

"How do you decide where to go next?"

"I have a list of places I'd like to see and sometimes I just decide on a whim. One time I met a guy who had a job lined up in Wyoming working at Yellowstone. So, I followed him out there, and he helped set me up with a job as a trail worker. I helped fix trails, build erosion control structures, anything they needed. It was hard work, but the views...it's hard to explain how big the sky feels and how a sunrise can paint a whole valley. It was an amazing experience."

It's been two years since I was there. I can almost smell the buffalo who decided to wander too close to where I was working or sense the wolves who would watch me from the underbrush. And I can't help but think that it may be two years until I get to see anything new. I'm not sure I can wait that long.

"Sounds like it, but..." She stops and looks at the large tree that has fallen over the path.

"But what?" I jump on the log and hold my hand out to her. She clutches my shoulders when she reaches the top, trying to keep her balance. She doesn't look at me, but looks toward my chest.

"But isn't it lonely? Do you ever see yourself settling in one place?" She releases my shoulders and drops to the other side of the log. "What happens when you finally fall for one of the girls you leave in every port?" She laughs at her words and reaches her hand up to me, helping me jump down.

"I don't know."

"Very noncommittal." I hear the strain in her voice even though she's attempting to sound casual. Does she actually want me to stick around? Every time I get close, she pushes me away. But could I stay for her? Even if what I feel really is love, could I stay in one place the rest of my life?

"I learned from the best." I nudge her arm. "Shall we? Only a little farther, and we'll be at my favorite spot. We can stop for lunch."

"Excellent. I'm starving. I hope you brought something good, not just another granola bar," she says, teasing me.

"Trust me, you'll be astounded by what's in this pack."

The sound of the waterfall greets us more loudly with each step, and the path begins to clear out. She's going to love it. The sun is just high enough in the sky that the mist should be full of rainbows.

"One more turn," I say.

I walk a few feet ahead as I want to see her face when she sees all the beauty the falls have to offer.

As we turn the corner her face turns pale, and she freezes in place. She whispers, "No, not here."

LAUREN

I PLASTER a fake smile on my face to reassure Ben I'm fine and he won't need to carry me out of the woods or call for help.

"It's...it's just so pretty. I just need a minute to take it all in," I manage.

He sees through my facade like always and pulls me to his side and walks me to a small flat area close to the pond at the base of the waterfall. I keep an eye on the plummeting water as we walk. My heart pounds as I wait for something or someone to emerge from the water and pull me back to my life. But nothing happens. Ben releases me, and I stare at the spot where all of this started.

Nothing from our hike seemed familiar...wait...Ben must have started us from the opposite end of the trail so the waterfall would be last. The girls and I never made it on the trail. We stopped to throw in our rocks and never finished the hike. Well, I didn't make it. Is there another me still with the girls? Did this whole thing create another multiverse or whatever they call it? Is there another me still living my old life? No. That can't be right; the woman said I could go back.

I shake my head. *This is not funny*, I scream in my head to the waterfall gods. *Not funny.*

Ben spreads a blanket and starts to unpack lunch, which pulls my attention back to him. The granola bar we had for breakfast a few hours ago is long gone. I can do this. We'll eat, pack up, and get the hell out of this place.

Ben leans back on his hands and watches me walk toward him.

"Impressive," I say, gesturing to the food and presentation. No sandwiches and chips for this guy. He has laid out a charcuterie tray, without the heavy wood tray of course, with meat, cheese, fruit, and crackers, all nicely arranged, as well as a small bottle of wine and plastic cups. I've never had anyone do something like this for me—take a day off to spend with me and make me lunch.

"I promised you lunch, and I figured I'd better up my game."

I lower myself to the blanket with the food separating us and the view of the waterfall cascading in front of us, watching us. Judging me. Waiting to turn my life upside down again.

If this wasn't THE waterfall and I didn't have a husband

—future husband—I would say this was romantic. And perfect. But it can't be romantic. Even if Ben's eyes are clear today, there is a storm on the horizon. I can't trust myself to sail those seas without one or both of us falling overboard.

"Thanks, this has been a really nice day. It's been a crazy few weeks," I say, giving the waterfall a glare just in case the gods who sent me back are watching, "and I needed a chance to clear my head."

"I owe you a lot more than a hike. I couldn't have done any of this without you. Before you came along..." Ben pauses and looks up at the sky before returning his attention to me. "I didn't think much about the future, just my next step. But with your help, I think I can see what the future might hold."

His gaze catches mine, and I feel the words fall on me like little drops of hope. Hope for a future I can't give him. "Glad I could help," I say with as bright a smile as I can manage while trying to hold in my tears.

His face falls slightly, and he picks up his drink.

I grab a plate and fill it with a piece of everything. Ben hands me a glass of wine, and I force myself not to down it in one gulp. We eat in silence, both studying the rainbows as they start and stop in the mist. I feel him watching me several times, and my instincts cause me to turn and smile.

"So, what's your third favorite thing?" he asks.

"It's your turn."

He doesn't answer. He waves his hand at the waterfall.

"This? This is your third favorite thing?"

"Yeah, this waterfall never disappoints. The flow is always steady, there are usually rainbows, and it's a great place to just sit and listen. Whenever I need help making a decision, I come here and somehow always feel like I find my answer."

This place? The place that turned my life upside down. My fingers twirl the bracelet on my wrist around and around and around. The sunlight catches the beads, and sparkles dance on the ground. It's been over a month since I came back. It feels like years. Time is weird.

"Lauren?"

"What? Sorry, I was listening to the water." I only have a few weeks left to decide. Stay or go. "You don't throw anything into the water, do you? When you ask for help?"

"Ummm, no."

"Good. Don't. Don't ever throw in a rock."

"Noted. So it's your turn."

"Oh. Um…I really should make a list, so I'm prepared."

Ben's laughter echoes around me. "No list. What's the first thing that comes into your mind?"

"Um…I love writing in a journal. I haven't done it in years. As a kid I would just write down all my thoughts, or stories, sometimes poems. Really bad poems." I chuckle. Back then I thought all poems had to rhyme. So bad.

"Why don't you do that anymore? I know you have a notebook handy."

My eye roll makes him smile. He has a good smile, the kind of genuine smile you can't help but mirror. Everything about Ben is genuine—no BS, no hype, no lies.

"I don't know. No time, I guess." No time for things that don't keep the plan moving forward. My dad always said he had a plan, but the moment his attention shifted, he threw the plan out the window.

I stand and walk to the waterfall. I'm doing what my dad did. I'm deviating from the plan. Ben is not the plan. He isn't stable. He isn't going to stay in one place and help me build a life. He needs freedom to roam. I can't hold him back.

Ben stands and steps over the food in order to come face to face with me.

"Lauren, are you going to tell me what's going on?" His voice is low and thick.

"I..." I swallow hard, unable to answer his question. It's not like I can tell him that in ten years I'm going to throw a rock into this waterfall and end up here with him.

He places his hands on the sides of my head, blocking out everything but his face. His eyes move to my lips a second before his head dips to mine for a kiss. And not just any kiss. The kind of kiss that happens at the end of a romantic movie when the fountain shoots water high into the sky or the fireworks explode in the background. It's that kind of off-the-charts kiss. My hands wrap around his back, and I pull him closer, letting myself get lost in the moment until my bracelet catches on his shirt, knocking me back to reality like a blow to the gut. In this reality, I shouldn't be kissing him like that, giving him false hope that I can love him. I can't have these feelings. I made a commitment to Matthew. I don't take that lightly. Though technically I haven't made a commitment, and he doesn't know who I am, but still. I know.

Ben senses my change as he pulls back, moving his hands from my hair to my waist. I drop my arms and step back out of his embrace. The loss of his touch feels like I left a part of me with him. I walk closer to the edge of the waterfall, focusing all my effort on it. The bracelet twists off easily. One flick of my wrist and I could be back home, back to my old life, back with Matthew. Matthew who never kissed me like that. Matthew who helped me build a steady life—one without surprises. I lock my fingers tighter around the bracelet.

Ben pulls me close, but he doesn't speak. I lean into him and try to breathe.

"I felt it too," he whispers.

Felt what? The merry-go-round we're on spinning faster and faster, leaving us no choice but to jump and hope we land on our feet. I need it to stop. I need to know where I will land.

I loosen my fingers and dangle the bracelet.

If I let go, it will all be over.

BEN

She's leaving soon. I can feel it. Tonight at dinner, she didn't say it with words, but every mention of the future was met with a vague response. I can't hear the words. The words will make it real.

We said short term, and I thought that's what I wanted, but I need more than a few weeks or months. Hell, I'm not sure a few hundred years would quench the thirst I have for her.

This isn't enough.

"Ben."

I finish hanging my jacket in the closet and turn around to find her standing at the bathroom door in nothing but her slip, watching me.

How long have I been standing here?

She steps to me and dismantles the knot of my tie before slowly pulling one end until it falls to the floor, taking with it the last of my resolve not to love her, not that I had much left. I lift her chin with my finger and search her eyes for any chance she feels the same. Her dark green eyes are like a dense forest, keeping all her secrets hidden inside.

The speed of her breathing increases, and I drag my finger down her neck and to the strap of her black slip. My eyes follow the path as I trace a line to her breast. Her nipples peak through the silk, and I lift my gaze to meet hers. She gives me a playful smile, but I'm not interested in playing tonight. Tonight, I want to make love to her, not the hot, fast sex of our first night or the playful sex from the last few weeks. Tonight, I'm going to take my time and memorize every inch, every reaction, everything that is Lauren. Tonight, I'll let her know I'm not giving up without a fight.

I RETURN TO BED, and Lauren lays her head on my chest. I close my eyes and soak in the perfect moment. I stroke her hair lightly until her breathing slows.

"What do you want?" she whispers.

You.

This.

Always.

But I can't say that, and that's not what she's asking.

"To save the bar," I answer automatically.

"What if the bar wasn't a factor? Then what would you want?"

"Is this like that 'what would you do if you had all the money in the world' question?"

She shifts her weight before answering. "Yeah, if you had unlimited money and time, what would you do?"

"What would you do?"

She pauses, like she always does when I ask a personal question. "I don't have an answer."

I shouldn't ask, but I want to know. "Get married?"

"Someday," her voice is quiet, and I feel tears on my chest. I don't comment. Tonight's not the night for that discussion. I know if we have the discussion then she'll leave. Not yet.

"But this isn't about me. This is about what you would do."

"I'd keep traveling. I wouldn't have to work, so I could spend more time seeing the world. Maybe find a way to give back. I really liked my work at the national parks. Maybe I could build houses or help build clean water systems. Maybe even..." Find someone to share my life with. But I shouldn't say that. I can't tell her that I love her.

Three words. Would she stay if I said them?

"What?" she whispers, trying to get my full answer.

"If money and time were not an issue, then I'd want to find someone to share my life with, someone to start a family with...but that's not something Graysons are good at." Though I wish I could find someone and break the cycle of dying before living a full life.

"Why do you think you need to keep people at a distance?" she asks.

"Less chance of hurting them when I'm gone."

"You mean when you leave for another town?"

"No, when I'm dead."

"Are you dying?" She sits up in the bed and searches my body as if there is a physical wound she can fix. I pull her back to my chest and chuckle at her concern.

"Not at the moment, but Graysons have a track record of short lives and so I've tried to avoid causing anyone heartache over me."

"Why do you think you're going to die young? Because your parents did?"

"Not just them. Two of my grandparents, my great-aunt, and my great-great-grandfather died before they hit sixty and a great-uncle and first cousin before they were forty. Seems bad genes or bad luck run in my family."

She lifts off my chest and gives me one of her earnest glares.

"But that shouldn't stop you from getting what you want. You talk about living your life to the fullest. Without those things, are you?"

"Maybe not, but who would want a man who doesn't want to settle down or may not be around long enough to raise our children? Who could love me like I love them knowing that?"

Her head lowers to my chest before she answers.

"I don't think it would be hard to find someone."

Someone.

But not you.

My hand absentmindedly strokes her hair as I settle my mind. The only one I want is her. I'm not sure what's happened to me, because a few weeks ago I never would have considered saying these words.

"I've spent the last few years searching for something. I thought I'd find it along my travels. I never stayed in one place too long, never letting myself get close enough to anyone to feel I had to stay. I don't just want someone. I want..." I pause, not ready to say it straight on. "Love is not something I ever planned on allowing myself to find. But with you...the moment I saw you I found myself knee-deep in quicksand, and I've stopped trying to find my way out."

I wait in the quiet of the night for her to respond, to challenge my not-so-subtle test of the "I love you" waters.

Lauren always has a plan.

Always knows what to do next.

But tonight is different. Tonight, she's quiet. Tonight, I told her what I want, and she knows she can't help me get it.

14

LAUREN

Matthew really should change the password on his calendar, though if I'd have known he was meeting his dad today for lunch I could have guessed the location. The Capitol Grille is one of his father's favorite places to eat and be seen as the restaurant is located on the top floor of one of the nicest hotels in town. When I arrive, I slip the host a twenty to seat me directly behind Matthew and his father.

After ordering, I set my notebook on the table and pretend to work while listening to the two men. Matthew's father is on a roll today, pressuring him into joining his firm and working his way to the top.

"I'm not going to give you my company; you have to work your way up. You need to know everything about the place."

"I understand that, Father, but I don't see why I need to start at the bottom when I've already worked my way up at Warner," Matthew counters as he sits up straighter and takes a sip of water. I'm sure he's wishing for something a little stronger.

"Yes, and I understand your need to work at another firm and prove yourself, but now you've done that, and it's time for you to come and work for me."

"You mean with you?" Matthew is keeping his anger in check. I can hear it in his voice, not that his father would notice.

"No, *for* me. You'll be like any other employee, learning the ropes and moving up," his father says.

Matthew pauses. I can only see his side profile, but his jaw is set tight.

"What if I don't want to work for you?" His voice is calm and even, but his father doesn't miss the challenge in it.

"Excuse me?" The indignation in his father's voice almost makes me laugh. Mr. Spencer is a first-class snob. How dare anyone not fall at his feet? His son included. We always had to put on a show and impress them when we went to their house. It could never just be dinner, instead it felt like being on a perpetual job interview. We knew it was a means to an end—keep his father happy so that he would allow Matthew to someday take control of the company.

"I don't mean to offend you, Father, but there are other opportunities out there for me. Warner wants to promote me to Assistant Director, and I have an opportunity to get in on the ground floor of a new business."

"That nonsense about the sports agency with your fraternity brothers is not an opportunity. It's a chance to lose all your money. And of course Warner wants to promote you. They want to make sure you don't leave and go where you belong."

"My friends have a sound idea and already have clients and investors lined up. It's not some whim." Though

Matthew is doing his best to remain composed, I hear the passion rising. The waiter arrives with the check, and they are forced to pause their discussion. His father pulls out his wallet and hands his card to the waiter. Matthew turns his head to the wall of windows, and I see his shoulders slump.

"I need to get back to work. You have until your mother's party at the end of the month to decide. This is the last time I will make this offer. After this you are on your own, and you will never run the company. Understand?"

"I understand." Matthew stands, shakes his father's hand, and watches as his father walks toward the exit.

Matthew always said we met at the right place and the right time and that meeting me was the sign he needed to make his decision. He never fully explained, but a final ultimatum from his father is pretty massive, and at the time, I was happy to provide a big bright sign for him. I remember his face was full of relief when I gave him my opinion that he should join his father's company and work his way up. It was the most logical decision and the one that would make him the most money and secure his future.

Was it the right advice? Matthew doesn't really like working with his father. He's drowning in work to prove he's better than anyone else there, which leaves little time for us, even if I wasn't also working the same crazy hours. The question Eve posed to me the night I arrived at the cabin echoes in my mind. Were we really happy? When's the last time we shared a meal together for pleasure and not work? When's the last time we spent the day together just talking and laughing? When's the last time I asked him what made him happy?

Never.

He deserves better. I deserve better.

Maybe this is why I'm back. To fix this mistake.

BEN

Ding Dong...

Shit. My back screams as I sit up. It might be time for a new couch. This one has to be older than I am.

Knock, knock, knock.

I'm in no mood for visitors. I'll just stay here until they leave. Maybe I'll just stay here until I become one with the couch.

Knock, knock, knock.

"Ben?"

Lauren. Dammit. I'm not ready to face her.

I pick my phone up from the floor—five missed calls and six texts from Lauren since I fell asleep. I don't want to do this right now. I can't believe...I thought maybe, maybe we had a shot, that if she just gave me more time, I could prove to her that I could be responsible, maybe even dependable. But apparently, I really am the short-term guy, just keeping the seat warm when Birthday Boy isn't available.

My stomach clenches as I think about him.

Maybe this is for the best. I don't want to be tied down to anywhere or anyone.

The knocking continues. "Ben, I know you're home. Open up."

"Shit."

With the effort of a turtle fighting to get across the sand, I walk to the door. Might as well get this over with.

Lauren stands in front of me in the same clothes from earlier. Up close, the light blue shirt makes her eyes appear even greener. Why can't she look like the bulldozer she is? Why does she have to look hopeful and worried?

"Hey," I manage.

"They said you called in sick and that you never call in sick. Are you okay?" She looks me up and down, obviously looking for what ails me. I'm sick all right—sick of wanting what I can't have.

"I brought soup." She holds up a bag and watches my reaction. She doesn't miss much, so she knows something is up.

"I'm fine. I just needed some extra rest. I had a few things to...do today."

"Oh, I'm glad to hear that." Her voice sounds relieved, but her feet shuffle on the porch and she looks over my shoulder into the house, waiting to be invited in.

I pause, prolonging having to say the words, but it's time.

The end was coming anyway.

And this way I'm in charge of when and not her.

I take a step back and open the door wide. "Come in. We have a few things to talk about."

"What things?" she says as she steps over the threshold.

I'll make it quick and easy on her. Something she hasn't done for me.

"I went over everything in the manual, and I wanted to thank you for all your help, but I think we can take it from here. You can go back to your life and focus on your plans."

"Ben...what's going on? What happened?" Her face turns pale. I guess I surprised her for once.

"Nothing." *Don't make me say it. Just leave and put me out of my misery*, I beg her in my head.

"Bullshit." She sets the soup down on the side table and squares up to me in the hallway.

Why is she fighting me? I'm making it easy on her.

"We've got it. All the pieces are falling into place, and it's time for the shelf life on this relationship to expire. I know you have a life to get back to."

"Ben? I...don't understand. Yesterday, you were saying..." —she closes her eyes and takes a deep breath—"yesterday, things were fine and today you're telling me to leave. What happened?"

"Don't pretend you were planning to stay with me. We both know you've had one foot out the door this whole time. You were always going to leave. I seem to remember the words 'short term' and 'just casual' being mentioned several times." The agitation in my voice builds, and I look anywhere but at her.

"Leave? Where am I going?" she asks slowly.

She doesn't get to be coy any longer. She knows exactly what she's doing; pretending she doesn't know is beneath her.

"Back to Birthday Boy." I keep my eyes locked tight to her. She takes a step back as if I've slapped her across the face with my words.

"What?" she breathes out.

I keep my voice as steady as possible. "Let's be honest. Wait...what was it? Oh yeah, it's time for a Hard Truth. Maybe you should have shared one with me. The one where we never had a chance and that I'm just a way to pass the time before you could return to him."

"Ben, what..." Confusion and hurt cross her face. She places her hand on my arm and latches on as if I'm about to disappear.

The pain in her eyes catches me off guard. I fight with everything I have not to scoop her in my arms and tell her not to go, to love me, to stay with me. But it wouldn't last, and it would hurt even more than this slow removal of a sticky bandage.

"I saw you with him today," I state flatly, pulling her hand off my arm.

"With whom?"

Like she doesn't know. How many whoms are there for us to discuss?

"Him." The contempt in my voice leaves no room for confusion as to what *him* we are discussing.

She swallows hard and shuffles her feet. Oh, now she knows.

"You were leaving the Hermitage Hotel with him this afternoon. I saw you walk out of the building, and I started to call your name but stopped when I saw him a few yards ahead of you. What, is he married? Is that why you have to pretend not to know him? Are you using me to make him jealous, so he'll leave his wife?" I list off a few of the options I've envisioned this afternoon.

"You saw Matthew." Her face falls as she realizes that I know her secret. Her shoulders hunch down as she puts her hands in her pockets and looks away.

"So, you do know his name." The sarcasm drips from my voice as the anger at her not telling me the truth builds from a stick fire to a bonfire inside my gut.

She pushes her shoulders back and takes a step toward me. "Yes, I told you I knew his name…he's an old friend. I'm not having an affair with him. I just had lunch at the hotel."

"So, you didn't see him there?"

"I did, but I didn't have lunch with him, and I didn't even speak to him," she says as if arguing a case in front of the Supreme Court.

"Are you stalking him?"

She pauses. "No."

For someone who has been lying to me all this time, she is a terrible liar.

I rub my temple. "Please stop lying to me."

She reaches out to touch my arm again, but I take a step back.

Her arm falls to her side, and her fists tighten into balls. "Ben, it's a long story, but I promise I didn't have lunch with him. I wouldn't do that to you. We may have agreed on casual, but I'm not sleeping with anyone but you." Her eyes come back to mine and she holds them firm.

Oh, that's not going to work this time. I cross my arms over my chest and study her for a moment. There's something I'm missing. The woman standing before me is giving me her best false bravado, but I can tell she is uncomfortable and trying to calculate her next move. I'm done with this game. We need to end this now while I can still duct tape my heart back together.

"You know what? We both seem to have some extra time right now, so let's finally hear one of your long stories." I lock eyes with her, daring her to argue the point before turning and walking to the kitchen.

I pull out a chair and sit, bouncing my leg up and down and listening for any movement in the hallway. I let out a breath as I hear the clip of heels on the floor growing louder. Lauren appears in the doorway and stops. She glances around the kitchen, then slowly walks to the chair across from mine and sits.

I wait. She lowers her head toward her lap and starts to bite her nails, but catching herself, she pulls her hands down to her lap before looking up at me.

"I'm not sure where to start."

"Why don't you start with Matthew?"

"We were friends a long time ago, but he's...forgotten. I just haven't had the guts to go up and speak to him yet."

I study her for a minute. There's some truth in there, but not the whole story.

"I want the long version," I say, leaning back in my seat and folding my arms over my chest.

She bites her top lip and looks out the window. There is some internal debate going on, but I'll wait, if it means I might get the truth. After a few moments she takes a long deep breath and leans forward.

"Fine. You want the truth." She shakes her head a little, and her voice is low as if she doesn't want to be overheard. "You're not going to believe me."

"Let me be the judge of that."

She takes a deep breath, letting the air out through her lips like she can feel every air molecule leaving her body. "Actually, it will be nice to finally tell someone. It's been harder than you would think to keep my secret." Relief fills her last words. She pulls out her journal and sets it on the table between us. She taps it. "The truth is..." She shakes her head and rubs her face. "I can't believe I'm saying this out loud. The truth is that six weeks ago, the girls and I went to the mountains to celebrate Austin's thirty-fifth birthday."

She pauses, letting her words sink into my brain. Did she say thirty-fifth? I thought they all went to college together? Austin doesn't look thirty-five. I hold my reaction as best I can, keeping my eyes on her as she continues.

"The weekend didn't start off great. I...um...arrived late the night before because I had a client meeting that I thought was more important than keeping my promise to my friends. And of course, everyone was mad at me."

She wipes a tear but doesn't stop. "Eve was especially mad at me, and when we went for our hike the next morning, she would barely speak to me. Anyway...before we could start the hike to the waterfall, an old woman was selling jewelry and I bought this bracelet and one for each of the girls, trying to buy my way back into their good graces. The woman was so happy to make a sale that she gave each of us a stone and told us to make an offering to the gods at the base of the waterfall."

Wait. The sign at my favorite falls says to make an offering. It can't be the same one. Can it?

She twirls the bracelet on her wrist like she always does when she gets lost in her head. "I made a wish to fix things, and when I opened my eyes, I was twenty-five again and in my old apartment."

"What?" My body betrays me as I speak without meaning to, and my face contorts to what I can only assume looks like a confused mime.

She puts her hands on the table and shrugs. "You wanted the truth so I'm telling you."

"Continue," I say, managing to push down all of the questions in my mind—most of which revolve around her mental status.

"I came back or whatever this is on the night I met you at the bar. I thought I was dreaming, which is why I flirted with you and why I agreed to help you when Ollie asked. The whole night felt like this weird mash-up of memory and dream. Ollie'd asked me to help you the first time around, and didn't because I was too busy building my career." Her voice dips a bit at the end, and she gives me a weak smile.

She tilts her head and waves her hand over the Grayson how-to bible she made me like a game show host presenting a new prize. Her attempt at lightening the mood isn't working.

"Which is how I know if you sell the bar it will become a SubShop and why I got distracted at the waterfall on the hike." Her hands ball into fists. "It was the same waterfall."

What is she saying?

She continues before I can ask questions. "Anyway, the next morning I realized I wasn't dreaming, and since then I've been trying to figure out what to do. Having to relive your life is a lot harder than you would think."

Her gaze moves to the window, and she touches her knuckle to the side of her eye trying to mask the tear streaming down her face.

All I can do is stare at her.

Time travel?

There's no way. I mean it would explain a lot—the list of bands for the next ten years, the stock she keeps hinting I buy, the...but it's ridiculous.

Her voice pulls me from my thoughts. "Sorry I didn't actually answer your question. Am I stalking Matthew? I suppose some people would call it that, but really I'm just occasionally checking in on him."

I narrow my eyes and grab my chair so as not to hit the table with my fists. Keep quiet. Let her finish.

"Matthew isn't some random guy, and technically in this timeline it is a lie to say he's an old friend because we've never met. He doesn't even know I exist." She smiles and looks away from me as if she needs to convince not only me, but herself that it's okay.

The look on her face has me starting to rise from my seat to comfort her, but I can't do that. How can I comfort someone when she's telling me she's a time traveler and stalking some guy?

"Which is a bit hard for me when in my old timeline he's...my husband, and in this timeline, we meet for the first time in about two weeks. So, now I have to decide if I want to throw my bracelet into the waterfall and go back to my old life or keep this new one. I have two more weeks to make that decision."

I sit up straight and place my hands on the table. My head is throbbing from her crazy story, and my back is aching from lying on the couch. Why is she saying all this? I try to control my tone and frustration as much as I can as I ask, "So, now instead of old friends, you're married, or I'm sorry, going to be married to this guy?"

"Yes." She looks me straight in the eye.

Normally, I'd say she's telling the truth, but there is no way she's traveled back in time. "Now it's my turn to call bullshit."

She opens the journal sitting on the table in front of her. "This is where I write anything I remember about the future—big world events, personal things, whatever I remember." She sets the book in front of me. I pick it up without thinking and flip through the pages. It's full. I pause near the end when I see a section titled Bands. It's the same list she gave me. I flip back and land on a list of Presidents.

"This doesn't prove anything except you have a good imagination." The words come out harsh like my feelings, but Lauren isn't the fantasy type. Lauren believes in what she can see and what she knows. Where is this coming from?

The book is pulled across the table, and she flips a few pages before pausing and ripping a page from the book.

"You asked why I had a bookie." She shrugs and slides the page in front of me. "When you know who's going to win, why not make some money to start a nest egg?"

Her bravado deflates in front of me like a balloon with a slow leak as she scrutinizes my reaction. "I understand if you don't believe me; I wouldn't if you were telling me."

"How can I?"

She taps the journal, picks it up, and puts it back in her

bag. Lauren turns to me, back straight, shoulders back, and all business.

"I think you're right. Our time is up. You're going to Texas in a month. Back to your nomadic life all alone. And I need to get back to...my life." Lauren bats her eyes a few times but keeps her business armor in place.

"How did you..."

"Texas? It's not a time travel mystery. I saw it on your calendar. So, did I do all this work for nothing?" She pats the Grayson bible sitting open on the table.

How could she think that?

"No! I'm not abandoning the place. I'm just going to Texas for a few weeks to help out a friend. Everything will be in place before I go. And you were planning on leaving me before then anyway." My voice comes out strained as there is a dull ache forming in my chest. "You have a husband to meet in...what was it...two weeks, right?"

She bows her head and stands.

"Right. I should go. I don't want to waste any more of your time. I just hope I didn't...ruin anything for you."

She lifts her bag and turns to me, her bracelet twisting around as she moves. Her voice softens. "I really thought helping you might be part of the reason I came back. I didn't mean for things to get...complicated. Good luck, Ben."

The weight of her words keeps me rooted to my seat. She really believes she's come back in time. Twenty minutes ago, I would have said Lauren is the most logical-minded person I've ever met. She doesn't have big lofty dreams of castles and unicorns. She wants stability and safety. She wants someone to hold on tight to her, someone to be there if she falls. How can she be asking me to believe she's traveled in time?

And now...now she's going to leave. And I'll never see her again.

She was right all along; we shouldn't have done this. But if we hadn't, Grayson's would be gone, and I never would have met her and never realized how much I've missed out on having someone to care for.

"So, that's it? You tell me you've time traveled, have a husband, wish me luck, and that's it? We're done? I'm just supposed to accept that. Maybe it's for the best. I don't fit into your perfect little idea of what life should be anyway." My heart races as I walk toward her. "You know, being blinded by your plan is just as bad as your dad being blinded by his search for the next best thing. Both are selfish."

Why am I saying these mean things? Why can't I just let her leave? Why can't I stop the anger from boiling inside me?

Her eyes well with tears, but she pulls her shoulders back and squares up to me.

Dammit. I'm making her cry. I need to stop being an asshole. I want to beg her to stay but can't find the words.

She takes a look around the room as if it's the last time she will see it. "I've already stayed too long."

I know she's not just talking about today.

"I really do hope you have a long and happy life. I hope you find someone to share it with—you deserve it."

And with that she leaves.

I knew it was coming. I planned to end it today. I said things to make sure it ended today, so why does everything in me feel like it's breaking? I should follow her, tell her to stay, that we can work through whatever breakdown she's having. Hell, I never should have let myself think she might stay, that somehow fate had thrown us together, and that a

Grayson might finally be catching a break. But I should've known fate doesn't give me people to love, it only takes those I love away.

LAUREN

The keys hit the bowl and echo through the hall.

My purse drops to the floor next to the table.

Not yet, I repeat to myself for the millionth time since leaving Ben's house.

Not yet.

I lock the door, remove my shoes, and walk to my room.

As I sit on the bed, the tears stream down my face.

How is it that your body knows the exact moment to let go? To let the emotions that have been building behind the dam flow over, down, and through you?

Now.

Now I can let go.

It feels like a minute ago I was going seventy down the interstate, making good time, and then BAM someone hits me, pushing me off course. Now I'm a broken-down pile of twisted metal in the middle of the road, and all the semi trucks keep colliding into me, knocking me farther and farther away from where I should be headed.

I curl up on my bed and let the pain take me. I broke it. I hurt Ben. I saw it in his eyes. I deserve to feel the pain. I deserve the weight of the pain pushing down on my chest.

All the memories of us flood back. His hands pushing the drink to me the first night, the glint in his eye the night he kissed me, him twirling me on the dance floor. I'm going to miss sitting in his office, seeing the pieces fall into place for Grayson's, and seeing Ben's face light up when he talks about all the places he's been. But would I have ever really fit into his life? Could I be free and not chained to a job? Could Ben stay in one place longer than three months? I see his eyes and the storm of curiosity brewing in them. Who am I to decide anyone's fate? The thoughts keep rolling through me like the waves crashing on the rocky shore. My last mental picture before sleep is of Ben sitting at a bar smiling at me as if it's the first time he's ever seen me.

THE MORNING LIGHT bathes my room in bright yellow as I pry my eyes apart. I stare up at the ceiling. Sometime in the night I managed to take off my clothes and throw on a T-shirt. The ceiling fan goes round and round and round. I watch it while I figure out my next move.

Wallowing all day is not in my nature. I need a plan. But what do I do? First, I should probably decide what I want. I chuckle to myself, sounding a bit like a person who has stopped taking their meds. When's the last time I asked that? I made a plan when I was fifteen, and I haven't deviated from it since.

I reach for the pen and paper I keep by my nightstand and start to write. Just words. No organized list, just words, all the thoughts caught in my head. All the ones that I've pushed out of the way. All the pain. All the things I loved but chose to ignore as they didn't suit my plan.

Thoughts of my mom and how hard she worked and how happy I am she has someone to help take care of her for a change.

Thoughts of my brother, out there fighting for our country and loving every minute of it.

The truth about my life with Matthew, the good and the

bad. It wasn't perfect. We were partners, not soul mates, but we had a good life.

How I wish I could snap my fingers and make all my friends' dreams come true.

My feelings for Ben, the real ones. The ones I didn't want to fully admit even to myself. I love him. I didn't mean for it to happen. I shouldn't have let it happen, but I did, and now we both have to pay the price.

How much I've truly loved being hands-on in helping his business come back to life instead of just typing up a report and letting someone else do all the heavy lifting.

My dad. How I let his failings influence my life. How the pain I've been carrying has tainted everything. How in five years he'll be gone, and I'll have never spoken to him again.

Everything comes pouring out.

Hours later I run out of ink in my pen and words in my heart. I feel like a mop being wrung out after scrubbing a floor.

After falling back to sleep and waking up again as the moon fills the sky, I make my way to the kitchen. I feel better. Not whole. Not even close, but not gulping for air under my emotions.

After some food, I sit on the couch with my phone. I send a text to Eve letting her know I'm alive and that Ben and I are done. A response comes immediately, but I ignore it.

In order to move forward, I need to go back. I take a deep breath and dial a number I swore I never would.

"Dad?"

15

BEN

Everywhere I look today I see echoes of Lauren. How did I let this happen? We said casual, but I'm not sure I ever truly believed that. The moment I laid eyes on her, I gave away a piece of me, and now she's gone, and I'm left here remembering every damn moment we shared.

The door swings open and Ollie walks through. I know why he's here.

I'm at the bar early, waiting on the sound system contractors to arrive and install the new system so we are ready for the grand reopening party next week. Once the party is over then I can get out of this memory-infested town for a few days and try and clear my head.

"How's it going?" Ollie calls.

"Fine," I answer with all the energy I can muster after another sleepless night.

He doesn't say a word, just makes his way to the bar.

He knows Lauren and I are finished. It's been forty hours; I'm sure she's spoken to Eve by now.

"Have you been sent here to check on me?" Lauren wouldn't send Ollie, would she? She made it clear we were over when she left.

"Maybe."

"By whom?"

"I'm not at liberty to say," he says, as he parks himself on the barstool in front of me.

"Well, you can tell whomever it is, I'm fine." I'm not fine. But it's probably better I got out now. Who knows what other crazy she's been hiding from me?

"Your message will be conveyed. Now, tell me what happened."

I stop what I'm doing and turn to him. "What do you mean? She didn't tell you?"

"She told me that she has fulfilled my request to help you with the bar and now her services are no longer needed."

I guess she didn't want to tell them the same tall tale she told me. These are her real friends, and she wouldn't want to lie to them. "That sounds about right."

Ollie shakes his head. "And she mentioned that you were no longer seeing each other. When my wife asked for more details, she was told, and I quote, 'Ben has his own life to get back to and I will not mess it up further.' So, I ask. What the hell happened?" His tone is serious; he really doesn't know.

I don't want to get into this. I need to focus on work and getting this place to make money so I can get some Lauren-free air.

Ollie doesn't move from the seat; he just leans back like

he has all day to wait. He's obviously not leaving without an answer.

"She was seeing some other guy. I called her on it. She made up some bullshit story and when I didn't believe her... she left." Simple and sad as that. My heart constricts, but I shake it off. Damn, I need a drink.

The thing about owning a bar is that there is plenty of liquor available to drown your sorrows in, but you're too busy pouring them for everyone else to have one yourself. But since we aren't open yet, I grab two glasses and reach for a bottle of whiskey. I tilt my head to Ollie, and he nods. Two whiskeys coming up.

"Who else was Lauren seeing?" The confusion at my statement is written all over his face. He didn't know either.

"Some guy named Matthew. Know him?" I take the shot and pour myself another one. One more won't hurt.

"No, I don't know anyone named Matthew that Lauren would know. What kind of bullshit story? Lauren isn't really known for bullshit. She doesn't really know how." He chuckles like it's the most insane idea he's ever heard. But he has no idea how crazy she can get.

"She does now," I say, shaking my head and reaching down to grab a stack of napkins to refill the station.

"What kind of story?" Ollie sounds concerned.

She's made her choice, and I should let her live her life and stay out of it.

"Nothing."

"Listen, I appreciate you not wanting to spill dirt on her, and I would appreciate you continuing to do that, but as one of her oldest friends, I really need to know what happened." Ollie leans his arms on the bar and waits. His eyebrows are drawn in tight, creating a giant crease in the middle of his head. He's her friend, so maybe he can get her some help.

I lean on the bar next to him and keep my voice low, even though we are the only ones in the room.

"Okay...she told me—and I can't believe I'm saying this—that she's traveled back in time. That a few weeks ago she was thirty-five, and after she made a wish at a waterfall, she woke up and was twenty-five again."

The shocked look on his face tells me she has not shared this fantasy with him. "Hold up. Time travel? I did not expect that." He sits up and crosses his arms.

"You and me both. She even has a journal where she keeps all the information she remembers about the future." I pull the page from my pocket and unfold it. "Part of me wants to believe her, but it's...insane." Ollie reads the page and his eyes grow wide when he sees the entry about last night's Bobcats game. Not only did she get the score right, but she also noted that the catcher got hurt when the other team's second baseman slid into home and his cleat got caught on his face mask.

His hand rubs his forehead a few times before he rereads the page. "When did she give you this?"

I meet his eyes. "Two days ago."

"Shit." He falls back to his seat and grips the whiskey glass tight before downing it in one gulp.

"Yeah, makes me wonder about all those odd things she's said and the list of bands she gave me that goes on for the next ten years. I could almost believe her if it wasn't so—"

"When did she say all this started?" Ollie cuts me off and slides his glass back toward me.

"That first night I met her. The night your band was playing."

I pour another drink and slide it back as he runs his hands through his hair and stands up.

"Ollie, what's up?"

He doesn't answer my question and instead starts pacing back and forth. Finally, he stops and walks back to the bar. "She's been different since that night. I knew right away something was off. I wouldn't have guessed time travel. But honestly something big had to have happened to change her this much. What else did she say?"

Does he believe her?

"She said she's married to this Matthew guy. The other night she mentioned something about her new promotion leading to the next promotion and her finally landing the VP job she's been working toward. Lots of crazy things." But are they? Could she be telling the truth? Am I a jackass for not believing her? No, it's crazy. I pour myself another drink before turning my attention back to Ollie. Things like that don't happen.

"Listen. I don't know if it's time travel, but something has been different about her since that night. Lauren before that night only cared about work. She lived and breathed it, she rarely came out with us and only then when guilted. She regularly canceled plans because she had to work late. Over the last few weeks she hasn't said no to anything. I never in a million years thought she would make time to help you, but I asked anyway. Hell, I thought if I was lucky, she would help by giving you a few ideas about how to cut costs and increase your revenue, but instead she's invested time in this place. Spent her nights and weekends helping you. Hell, she hasn't talked about work or her plan for her life since then either."

"You're saying you believe her?"

He looks to the floor as if the answer might be there among the cracks before sighing and looking back up at me. "I'm saying...the Lauren you know and the Lauren from two months ago are very different people. I'm not sure what to believe yet, but I'm gonna talk to her about this because clearly something has changed in her life. I thought it was you."

"Me?"

"I thought you were a good influence on her. Getting her to see there is a life outside of work."

"I'm not sure I did that." My eyes prickle, and memories of Lauren flood my mind.

"You did. I've never seen her so in the moment than with you. So, what now?"

"What do you mean? She's been clear she's done with this job and me and ready to move on to...whomever." Birthday Boy in his suit and tie and perfect job and perfect life that fits in her perfect image of her future.

"But you made her happy."

Ollie stands in front of me like being happy is all that should matter. That I should forget her lying, or she should give up on the life she's been dreaming about.

"I'm not so sure about that. Anyway, the bar's grand reopening party is coming up and there's a lot of work to do. We're closing for three days starting Monday and then planning a soft opening of the food until the Grand Opening party. Is the band ready to draw a crowd?" He glares at me, letting me know that he knows I'm changing the subject.

"Yeah, and the Bobcats are playing in town, so Austin's bringing a few players over. If they like the place, they agreed to snap a few pics and put them up on social media."

"Really? I figured they would cancel since Lauren won't be here."

Ollie shakes his head as if I'm the one who's lost my mind. "Lauren would never do that, plus Austin says this is the kind of place Tommy and his friends will love. They don't go for fancy nightclubs. They like the local places where people will let them have a good time and just hang out."

I figured Lauren would have called all her friends and told them to stop helping me. Shit. That's not true. That's not Lauren.

"I don't know what to say. That could be huge." Maybe this place really can be saved.

Ollie's hand slaps the back of my shoulder hard enough to make me stagger.

"Be prepared. This place is going to be fine. The improvements you and Lauren made are just what this place needed. And the new sound system is going to blow people away."

"Guess I should go ahead and hire a few more waitresses."

"I would do that. And get your head out of your ass and talk to Lauren."

LAUREN

I LOOK at the address on my phone one last time. The house is small, but nicer than the last one we lived in. The yard is fenced in with a hammock off to the side under a large oak tree. The perfect place to take a nap. Oh, a nap would be nice; it's been a long couple of days—actually a long month and a half.

It's been forty-four days to be exact. Forty-four days since I landed back in my old life, and what have I accomplished? I'm no closer to figuring out why Eve and Ollie split, the girls are still not listening to my advice, and my perfect job has now become the least exciting thing about my day. Plus,

Matthew is different, not the same man I knew. Did I change him? Was it the choice he made? Did I push him into that choice? And Ben knows the truth and thinks I'm crazy. Of course, I don't blame him. Hell, I'm starting to think he's right.

Look where I am? A place I swore I'd never go.

Do the hardest thing first. "Eat the frog" as the leadership book says. "Screw you, frog," I mutter, as I exit my vehicle and stretch my legs. My dad has lived three hours from me for the last I don't know how many years and I never bothered to ask. He used to send cards on my birthday and Christmas and even a few in between, but I guess when he didn't get replies he finally got the hint. I'm a rotten daughter. I never opened them, never sent him a graduation invitation, wedding announcement, or well, anything. I blamed him for everything wrong in our lives, and the moment we left, I refused to think about him. My mother tried to make us see him, but we were old enough to have a say and I chose not to.

Just keep putting one foot in front of the other. He's not some monster. He's a man. One who wasn't around much, but before he lost his business, we had some good times.

Knock, knock, knock

After the initial shock of me calling wore off, he said he would be home today. He didn't push for details about my visit. I could tell he didn't want to say anything to change my mind.

"Lauren?" I hear my father's voice crack as he opens the door.

"Hi." My heart goes to my throat. He looks the same—a few wrinkles and his hair is a little greyer, but still my dad.

He steps onto the porch and starts to lean in for a hug, pulling back at the last second. A flood of emotions hits me as I realize I would like a hug, but I'm also not ready for a hug. My father waits for me to respond. I guess he's going to follow my lead, so I need to take charge.

I pull my shoulders back and keep my eyes level with his. I'm an adult. I can do this. I can talk to my own father. "Thanks for seeing me on such short notice."

He ushers me into the house with a sweep of his hand.

The house is minimally furnished. Not in a minimalist style, just that there's not a lot of it. A sofa and a chair in front of the TV with a small table in between. Off to the side is a small table and chairs leading into a galley style kitchen. It's clean, but the curtains are drawn, so even though it's afternooon, the room has the feel of being closed up for the night.

My heart constricts and I bite my nails. This isn't the man I knew. He would have the curtains wide open. He'd be sitting on the front porch talking to the neighbors as they walk by. What happened to him?

"Sorry for the mess," he says, his voice a little wobbly.

"Everything looks fine. How are you?" For lack of a better starter question.

He points to a chair in the dining room.

"I'm good. Can I get you a drink?" he mumbles as he walks to the refrigerator.

"Water would be good." Three hours of driving and I really should know what I want to say, but my mind is blank. Where is the man I'm mad at? I can't be mad at this sad man. Where's my dad? The larger-than-life man who couldn't sit still or take care of his family properly?

"Thanks."

The water glass slides in front of me, and he takes a chair across from me. His dark hair is still intact but thinning a bit in the back.

"Is everything okay?" His brow goes up, causing wrinkles to form across his forehead.

"Yeah, I...I just thought it was time."

He lets out a breath and wipes his head with his hand before giving me a small smile. Did he think I might be dying? In my other life, it would've taken me dying to come and see him. Ben's right; I really am selfish.

"Time for what?" he asks quietly.

The truth? It's not like I can make our relationship worse.

Be strong. Just say it.

I look at the table. "Time to tell you how mad I am at you."

When I muster the courage to look up, he nods.

"I figured. I just didn't know exactly why. Your mom didn't seem to know either. Is it because your mom and I broke up?"

"No, it's because..." My throat tightens, and I swallow as hard as I can to keep the emotions in check. I need to say it. I came all this way. All these years I've tried to push thoughts of him aside, not wanting to waste one more minute on him, and here he is right in front of me, and I can't form a proper sentence.

"Take your time. It sounds like you've been holding this in for a long time."

I sit up straight and look him in the eye. "Because you were selfish. Because what you wanted always seemed more important than what we needed. Because..." The words come rushing out, and I mash my hands together to keep from crying.

"Keep going."

"Because you didn't listen. If you would have sold the business when everyone, including Mom, told you to then we would have had the money to keep our house. If you had cared more about us than finding the next exciting thing then we wouldn't have had to move so many times. We would still be a family." The tears fall as my voice rises.

My father walks to the living room and returns with a box of tissues. He gives me a moment to get the tears under control before answering my charges.

"You're right. I can't disagree with anything you just said. Of course, I didn't realize at the time I was being selfish. I thought each of those opportunities would be a winner—that they would put us on a path to a good life, but they never did."

He knows I'm right? Never in a million years did I think he would say that. I close my open mouth as he continues.

"It took me a long time to realize this. I met my girlfriend, Trish, about two years ago. She called me on all my bullshit, and I realized how much I screwed up. I've spent the last few years trying to get my life straightened out. I even got a real job. It's eight to five in an office and everything." He smiles, but in no way do I believe he likes this new life of his.

"Are you happier now? You used to hate offices."

"I still do, but I have a steady paycheck, and I haven't had to move in two years. So, that's been nice. And honestly, the work isn't bad, plus I get nights and weekends off which I've never had before."

Looking at him now, I realize the life in him has died out. My dad had this energy that almost surrounded him, but now he seems smaller than I remember. In my memory he's larger than life. "What if I was wrong too?"

"About what?"

"Maybe I should've tried to understand why you were

doing the things you were instead of assuming you were selfish. I wanted everything to be perfect."

His hand lands on mine, and the rift between us doesn't seem insurmountable. Maybe we can find a way to build a bridge between our lives.

"Princess, none of that was on you. I should have been home more and found a way to take care of you all first. I kept thinking the next thing would make enough money to get us back on track. Looking back, I came up with some crazy ideas." His eyes roll to the ceiling as he shakes his head.

I can't help the laugh that bubbles out of me when I think about some of his crazy schemes.

"The bowling alley you managed? What about the great deal you got on those cell phones you were going to resell at double the cost? And..."

His hand leaves mine and he throws them both in the air. "Oh stop. Listing them out is worse."

We both let the laughter die out, and I take a drink of water.

"Dad, if you could go back and do it all again, what would you do differently?"

"I thought about that a lot after your mother left. And for a while I blamed her for all the issues in our marriage. If I could go back, I'd get help. Maybe even a real job. But most importantly, I'd talk to your mom instead of shutting her out. But you can't go back. You can only move forward no matter how much you wish you could change things. At least that's what Trish and my therapist keep telling me." His smile fills his whole face, and I know he means it.

"Maybe. Or maybe you would have settled down and hated every minute and driven us away in a different way?"

He chuckles. "Probably."

. . .

THE AC IS BLASTING in my face as the two-hour mark on my drive home approaches. Anything to keep myself awake. My dad and I talked for almost two hours. There were a lot of awkward pauses, but we managed to get through it. It's been two long emotional days, and my eyelids are heavy. My dad offered to let me stay at his place for the night, but I'm not quite ready for that. Baby steps. We took a big step today, but we have a lot of things to work through before we can truly be father and daughter again.

My phone rings, pulling me from my thoughts.

"I heard you broke up with Ben. Are you okay?" Izzy says, before even saying hello.

"I'm..." I'm not fine. No more hiding. "I'm a bit of a mess, but I'll be okay."

"Do I need to call the girls to cancel plans for the grand opening weekend?"

"No, please don't cancel. And call Austin and make sure she and Tommy are going to bring some other players. We... Grayson's needs all the free media it can get."

Not we, only Ben. His eyes fill my thoughts, but I push them away and focus on the road.

"Are you sure?"

"Yes, thanks for looking out for me, but Ben's a good guy. This is all me. The bar is great, and you'll have a great time. Ben doesn't deserve to pay for my mistakes."

"Lauren, are you sure you're okay?" Izzy's concern is real.

As it should be. I'm not the same Lauren from a few weeks ago and I'm sure the change seems rather abrupt. It was abrupt for me too.

"It's been a long day. I'll tell you all about it soon, but

right now...I need to concentrate on getting myself safely home and into bed. I'm wiped."

"Where've you been?"

Should I come clean? Keep another secret? No. I'm tired of keeping secrets.

"I went to see my dad."

I hear her gasp. I never talk about my dad, so I'm sure this is a big surprise.

"What? Are you serious? That's...great."

"Yeah."

It was better than I expected and something I should have done the first time.

"Where does he live?"

"Up near Lexington. I'm just passing Bowling Green now. I'll be home soon."

And then I can crawl into bed. After this week I feel like I need to sleep for a thousand years.

"Do you want to talk about it?"

"Not right now, but we had a good conversation. I promise I'll tell you about it soon." I don't have anything left in me to give, not even to Izzy right now.

"Okay...but call me tomorrow. Drive safe."

Now I just need to decide what to do with the rest of my life. Working at Grayson's has been the most fun I've had in a long time. If only I could have helped my dad all those years ago. If I only could have traveled back to that time.

I laugh hard as I imagine my twelve-year-old self waking up with the mind of thirty-five-year-old me. I was independent enough then—what would they have thought of me telling them how to manage their business and how to invest their money? And going through junior high and high school again would have been a nightmare.

The miles tick by as my mind whirls around like a leaf

caught in a breeze. Every new idea or thought twists and turns me in a new direction until the answers hit me in the chest.

I know what I need to do. Now the question is, am I strong enough to do it?

16

LAUREN

An hour later I pull into my drive and find Ollie sitting on the front porch drinking a beer.

"Hey, Ollie. What's up?" The words come out slowly and dripping with suspicion.

He knows about Ben and me, but I told Eve I needed a minute before discussing it. Did Izzy call him about my dad?

"You've had a rough couple of days, so I thought I should check on you."

I flop into the chair next to him as he reaches in his cooler and hands me a beer. An ice-cold beer is exactly what I need after the day I've had.

"You could say that." I lean back and take a long drink. "Who sent you?"

"No one. I'm your friend too. Can't I be concerned?" He cuts his eyes to me and looks all innocent. He doesn't want to be one of the girls, but we've been friends for long enough to share a few secrets.

"I'm okay."

Ollie lets out a low grunt. I ignore him and take another drink from the life-giving beverage. The water in the car did not quench my thirst. This is much better.

"If you went to see your dad, you're not okay." Damn, he doesn't miss anything. I can only chuckle at how fast information travels.

"Izzy called you, not Eve. I wondered who she would call first. I really thought it would be Eve."

"No, she called Eve, but she's stuck at work. I volunteered."

"Works for me. You brought beer. And you don't talk as much. I've talked enough today."

"Well, you're not done yet." Ollie's voice is quiet, but firm. It's going to be another long night. It's not like I was going to get any restful sleep anyway.

I finish my beer and place the empty bottle on the table between us.

He laughs and hands me another bottle from the cooler. "What happened with your dad?"

"I finally said what I've been holding in for years. He got to give his side, which wasn't quite what I thought and... we...we made progress toward moving forward."

Ollie tips his head back and lets out a belly laugh that most likely woke the neighbors two streets over. I glare at him and tell him to shush.

"You made progress toward moving forward? You really did love business school. Can't you just say it in English?"

"I could. But it doesn't sound as fancy." I smile. Ollie always calls me on my business phrases and he's right, they are sometimes ridiculous, but it's a habit now.

His laughter dies down. "What about Ben? You gonna forgive him?"

Ben. My stomach churns as my mind fills with his face

the moment before I walked out the door, the confusion and the sadness written all over it. Maybe I should have let him believe I cheated on him instead of burdening him with my truth.

"Nothing to forgive." And there isn't. We were casual even if sometimes it felt like it could be more. He needs to resume his life, not get bogged down by my fears. My face burns as tears begin to form. I shake them away.

"I'm the one that screwed up," I add. "I know better than to mix business and pleasure."

Ollie pauses and finishes his drink. He obviously has more to say, and I'm not going to like it.

"Just say it. I'm tired and need to go to bed. You've never held back before; please don't start now."

Ollie takes his time as he opens the cooler, gets out another beer, and unscrews the cap. This can't be good.

I pause midsip as he asks, "When were you going to tell me about the time travel thing?"

Every fiber in my body freezes and then goes into overdrive.

Ben told him? I didn't think about that. I didn't ask him not to tell anyone. Oh shit. How do I explain so he doesn't haul me to the psych ward? "I..."

"I believe you."

My head twists so hard and fast in his direction my neck muscles burn. How can he believe that? "What?"

"Don't get me wrong. It's crazy, but I also know it would take something as big and complicated as time travel or a brain injury to get you to change. I've been watching you the last few weeks and you're different. So much so I almost asked you several times if you had forgotten to tell me you had an identical twin and had decided to play a trick on us and switch places."

He believes me? I don't even believe me most days. I twist the bracelet and count the colored stones. Five stones, one for me and each of my best friends. I need to have a sixth one added for Ollie. He's always been the open-minded friend. The one who doesn't lock into one way of doing things or seeing things.

"Why didn't you tell me?" If I didn't know better, I would say he sounded hurt.

"I didn't know how. It's all been so unbelievable. I was afraid if I said it out loud, someone would come and lock me up." And I didn't want him to ask questions about his future. A future where his marriage is over, and I have no idea why because work was more important than being there for my friends. So, now I don't know how to fix it because I didn't see it fall apart.

"No one is locking you up. Give me the details."

We move the conversation inside to the living room, and I tell him everything that's happened since I returned. He listens, asks questions, and doesn't ever waver from making me feel like he believes I've actually time traveled, or mind traveled or whatever the hell this is.

Eve calls as I tell him about seeing my dad. He tells her I'm fine and he'll be home soon. But he doesn't move.

"You've told me everything that's happened except what happens in the next ten years to all of us." The dreaded question. The real reason I never told him.

"Spoilers," I say, in a ridiculous British accent.

"Don't *Dr. Who* me? You've only seen like two episodes."

"Actually, I've seen them all now. I thought maybe a Time Lord might give me some idea of what's going on. But it turns out the Doctor is only helpful if aliens are attacking the planet."

He crosses his arms. "You're really not going to tell me?"

I shake my head. "I don't want to mess things up."

"That bad?"

I roll my eyes. "Not going to work."

"I'll get it out of you."

I smile big, but he's right. He'll figure it out. I may be the one who is always attempting to fix things, but Ollie is the real mechanic here—he likes to take things apart and see how they function. He knows how my mind works and will take it apart until I reveal my secrets.

"What's next?" he asks.

"Well, I haven't figured that all out yet, but I will."

He stands and reaches for his cooler and walks to the door whistling the intro to *Dr. Who*.

"So, was the old me the good twin or the evil twin?" I call as he walks out the door.

"I'll never tell."

LAUREN

I HAVEN'T SEEN Ben since I told him my secret. Maybe in time he can forgive me, and we can be friends. Maybe. But for now, I will keep my distance and let him keep his focus on the bar.

Grayson's reopened last week to a packed house and rave reviews. Not that I'm surprised. Gabby outdid herself with the marketing plan, and from the pictures she sent they drew in a large crowd. Austin and Tommy came through in a big way, and half the Bobcats team showed up and blew up social media with how much fun they had.

I didn't attend, but I may have sent a few extra tweets to help the cause #graysonsbarandgrill. And I may or may not have driven by a dozen times that night to look through the windows.

One good thing complete.

Now to my next.

First things first. Find the right seat.

In my mind, I remember this place being bigger. The wall filled with stained glass separating the bar from the restaurant is as bright and colorful as I remember. The bar area itself has a dozen or so high-top tables and chairs, mostly filled with businessmen and women out for a drink after work. It's crowded. Like it was that night...I shake my head.

Not that night.

Tonight.

The same night.

Will this ever not be confusing?

Matthew and I never came back. Our lives started here, and some might feel the desire to revisit the spot and commemorate the moment they met, but Matthew and I were never sentimental. Anniversaries were met with flowers and a shared meal the first few years. Last year, I don't think we ever made it to dinner. Matthew had a client meeting and I had a project due the next day. I bought him another watch, and he remembered to send me flowers the next day.

We never were about romance or passion. Even in the beginning, we didn't take long walks and talk about our lives. We had long dining-room discussions with flowcharts and goal lists. We were about making each other better, reaching our goals, and being a team. And we were damn good at it. My eyes fill with tears, and I bat them away as I turn to where he's standing on the other side of the room chatting up some friends.

It's not time yet, I remind myself as I look at my watch. The reservation is at seven p.m. I made my reservation weeks ago, not wanting Eve to ask why I needed a reservation and didn't want her to come. She knows about the time travel now and has kept her questions to a minimum, but I know it's killing her. I will talk to her more once this is done.

Focus. I need to focus. I need to get this right.

Last time, Eve texted me about six thirty to say she'd be late, then again a few minutes before seven to say she wasn't going to make it. Why can't I clearly remember what happened in between? I spoke to the sports reporter, but what else? I guess meeting Matthew overshadowed everything else.

I'm doing the right thing. I take a deep breath and sip my drink. Be patient; don't look his way. I stare at the football game on the TV. I'm more of a baseball fan, but football will give me something to pretend to watch.

"Is this seat taken?" a woman asks as she sets her purse on the stool to my left.

"No." I keep my smile in check as the sports reporter is right on time. I don't remember what she wore last time, but tonight she's in a light-grey silk top that pulls and dips in to highlight her figure and dark denim jeans.

"Thanks. This place is busy." She sets her phone on the bar and gives me a bright smile.

"It's the new chef. Everyone says the food is next level." I don't remember our conversation from before. I'll just have to wing it.

"Well, as long as he can cook a steak medium rare, I'll be happy."

I smile back at her. She leans toward me, squinting toward the TV.

"Sorry." She straightening up. "Can you see the score?"

"Oh,"—I look over at the screen—"it's seven to zero, Falcons are winning."

"Dammit."

I'm about to ask who her team is as a man in a dark suit with overly styled hair sits beside her. Oh, this guy. I remember him.

I lean into her.

"Listen, don't turn around." She leans in as I give the guy a slight head shake to let him know that it's never going to happen. He grimaces and picks up his drink and walks to the end of the bar.

As he leaves, she turns her head for another quick look. Her eyes go wide when she turns back to me. "Thanks. I guess you're my guardian angel."

You're welcome, again. Who could forget him and his smelly cologne?

"Well, new friend, I'm Kelsey." She extends her hand.

"Lauren," I reply and take her hand.

"What do you do, Lauren?" she asks as she flags down the bartender and orders a drink.

"I help failing businesses get back on their feet," I answer with a little pride filling my voice.

"Who do you work for?"

"Actually...I'm starting my own company." Saying it out loud makes me smile. Me, an entrepreneur. I haven't told anyone yet, and my friends and family will be more surprised than anyone.

"Congratulations. I'm a freelance writer, so basically, I run my own small business. It's not for the faint of heart, but if you love what you do it makes all of it worth it."

"Do you love what you do? I imagine you've seen a lot of the country."

"Yeah, I get to meet new people, travel, and watch sports without guilt." Her eyes go back to the TV.

I almost changed places with her last time so she could see the game. What would have happened if I'd done that?

"Sounds like the perfect job for you. Where are you from?" I can't help but push for more information.

"I'm based out of Atlanta. I'm up here for a writers' conference. Most people think they're boring, but I love learning about the latest ways to get information to people and about writing." Her face lights up as she talks.

I see the truth in her words. She really loves her job.

She shifts off the stool. "Hey, will you do me a favor and hold my seat for me while I run to the bathroom?"

"Sure."

She jumps down from the stool, and instead of setting my purse on her seat like I did last time, I stand and take her seat. My heart is beating so fast, like I'm sprinting across the football field on TV. But this is right. She should meet Matthew. She should be the one that gives him advice. Be his sign. She can advise him to find a job that makes him happy, to live his life, and not hide behind the safety of a steady job.

I close my eyes and set my head on my hands. Please make him happy. Please help him become his own man and not get caught in his father's shadow. I chance a glance Matthew's way. He's absorbed in a story his friend is telling, and I watch as he smiles and laughs.

Goodbye.

I love you.

Maybe someday we'll find a way to be friends. I think we would be good at that, but for now, I have to let you go.

"Is anyone sitting here?" A deep gravelly voice pulls me

from my thoughts, and my head snaps up as I realize I know that voice.

"Ben?" What's he doing here? Not now. Oh no. Not now. I don't want to hurt him again.

"Lauren? What are you doing here?" He obviously didn't come here to find me as confusion fills his face.

"I...I came in for a drink," I manage. "What are you doing here?"

Ben's face falls. "I come here every year for a drink on my parents' anniversary."

"You come...here...every year on your parents' anniversary?" I repeat slowly as I feel the impact of all of my worlds crashing into each other.

"I told you about it, remember?" There is a melancholy in his tone that keeps my attention on his words and not my turbo-charged heart rate threatening to launch my heart out of my chest.

"I remember...you said every year, but you never said when and where. I didn't know...you meant...here." I swallow hard and a flash of memory hits me. A pair of stormy eyes sitting a few seats over telling me he just got back in town a few hours ago and this was his first stop before going home.

I gasp. I spoke to Ben last time. Ben was here. The undertow of emotions flows through my body with the intent to pull me under. How many times did the universe throw us together and I ignored it?

He was here.

My head falls into my hands again. "You were here last time. I missed it again." I'm not sure if I say it out loud or in my head.

"Lauren? Are you okay?" Ben's stormy eyes watch me as I lift my head and try and recover my words.

Ben and I crossed paths here and I missed it. I missed him. Is this why I'm back? The world and all my memories swirl around me. I reach for the bar to steady myself. Ben sat right where he's sitting now. We talked. I thought he was cute, but we couldn't have a future, so I introduced him to the sports reporter.

Everything stops spinning as a hand touches my shoulder and a voice says, "I'm back." Kelsey arches her eyebrow to which I can only nod. Yes, I stole your seat and yes, he's cute.

"This is...Ben. Ben, this is....my new friend."

"Kelsey." She gives Ben a once-over and extends her hand with a big smile.

My heart plummets to the floor like an elevator that's just had the cables snapped. I mentally run over my plan. Come to the bar, let Matthew spill his drink on me, let him take me to dinner, tell him to follow his heart, and then never see him again.

But then Kelsey showed up and I remembered I almost changed seats last time, and her job and enthusiasm are exactly what Matthew needs to hear. So, now the plan is for Matthew to spill his drink on her and take her to dinner and she can tell him to follow his dreams.

But I didn't remember Ben being here. What if she's meant to be with Ben? My gut clenches. But the universe keeps throwing Ben and me together, so that means he can't be happy with her, right?

The two chat over me about all the places they've lived, but all the while Ben sneaks looks at me. I can only nod and smile as I try and figure out my next move. There are only a few more minutes before Matthew is going to spill his drink on the person sitting in Kelsey's seat. It can't be me—not in front of Ben. I can't do that to him. But if it's Kelsey, am I changing Ben's life more? Is he meant to meet her? No, that can't be. He keeps ending up in my path. He's here to forgive me. He has to be.

Ben touches my arm, bringing me back to the conversation. "Lauren, I..." His eyes dart up, and I turn my head to see Matthew walking toward the bar. Ben looks back at me for a brief second, enough I can see the disbelief and betrayal filling his eyes.

"No, it's not like that." I grab Ben's arm and pull him off his stool and toward the opposite end of the bar. His eyes don't leave Matthew.

"Watch. Trust me one more time. He's going to spill a drink on Kelsey. That's how we met. Right here. Right now. Last time you were sitting there, and I didn't switch seats with her." The manic tone in my whispered voice is barely suppressed as I try and get all the words out. "I let you leave with her. I thought you were cute, but your lifestyle scared me, so I let you leave with her." My heart wrenches at the thought of him leaving with her. "Just watch." I keep him in place with my hand wrapped around his arm.

Ben's eyes move to Kelsey who has turned her attention to the TV, and right on cue, Matthew trips and spills his drink. Kelsey jumps from her stool and glares at him. Matthew grabs napkins and hands them to her to dry off, apologizing all the while. She grabs her phone and walks past us as she heads for the bathroom.

Ben's eyes find mine. They are churning like a hurricane with all his thoughts.

"He...you...you were right."

"Yeah." I turn back to the bar and watch Matthew dry off Kelsey's stool and order her another drink before sitting down in her seat. "I have to do one more thing. Please wait. Please trust me."

He doesn't respond, nor does he move.

I walk over to Matthew. "Hi, I see you had an accident with my new friend. I have to leave, but I have a reservation for two in five minutes."

Matthew stops and looks at me a bit like I've lost my marbles. I keep going. "It might be a nice gesture to offer to buy her dinner since you ruined her dress. She likes her steak medium-rare."

He looks at me stunned as if I'm speaking to him, but he can't understand. It's a far cry from the glimmer of attraction I saw in them last time. I smile bright to hide the tears that threaten to emerge.

"You know her?" he asks, looking toward the bathroom.

"Yeah, listen, the reservation is under Mitchel. Take it."

"Thanks." He seems confused, but I hope he listens.

"And good luck, Matthew. I hope you have a great... dinner," I say before turning and walking away. The weight of my decision falls from my shoulders as there is no going back now.

Ben hasn't moved, and every muscle in his body looks tense.

"He really doesn't know you, does he?" he says as he stares at Matthew.

"Nope." It's done. I can't keep the sadness out of my voice. Even though I know I'm doing the right thing, I will miss Matthew. He was my husband, my partner, my friend. But in my heart, I feel like we will find our way back to each other in the way we were meant to be.

Kelsey walks by and stops short when she sees Matthew sitting in her seat with a fresh drink. He smiles apologetically and speaks to her. No doubt offering to take her to dinner.

I force a small smile.

"Do you love him?" Ben whispers.

I nod. "Yes."

He closes his eyes.

I scramble to explain. "He was my husband. Of course I loved him, just not..." I shouldn't say it. He doesn't need to hear my heartache.

"Not what?"

"Nothing." I should have said it before, but it's not fair to say it now.

Half pleading, half commanding, he asks again, "What?"

I square up to him, looking past the pain in his eyes. I say what my heart has known and my head has blocked. "Just not the way I love you."

He takes a step back like I've burned him with my words. Too much, too soon. He hasn't forgiven me; he doesn't really believe me. Maybe he doesn't even love me.

"So, we met before? All this time you knew we would be here together?" Ben says, with a touch of agitation.

"No, I didn't remember meeting you until a few minutes ago." Looking around at all the strangers and not sure I want to have this conversation in the middle of a bar, I ask, "Can we go somewhere and talk?"

He looks down at me as if I were the stranger. "I haven't finished my drink yet."

"Oh, I'm sorry. Do you...um...could I join you?"

"I'm not sure that's a good idea." His words are slow, and his attention moves to the bar where Kelsey and Matthew are chatting.

If a heart can crack, I think mine split in two. My hand touches my chest, but I manage not to gasp at the pain.

"Oh, yeah...I get it," I say as casually as I can. As if my last shred of hope wasn't being ripped from my body. I can't blame him. Just because he now knows I'm not a cheater doesn't mean he's going to forgive me for lying. Maybe I'm screwing it all up again. Maybe I should have followed my first instincts. The bracelet tightens like a handcuff on my wrist. Did I screw it all up? Matthew, Kelsey, Ben, my friends?

The crack in my chest feels wider, like I'm being pulled apart from the inside. Is Ben supposed to be with Kelsey? Is his business supposed to fail so he can be free?

Can your heart actually break twice in the same moment? I twist off my bracelet and squeeze it in my hand.

Tears stream down my face as I touch Ben's chest with my hand. "I'm sorry. I messed it up again. I thought it would be better if Matthew met Kelsey instead of me. But...maybe you and Kelsey were meant to meet. I'll fix it. I promise." I reach up and put my hand on his cheek and kiss him quickly on the lips. "Enjoy your drink. I'll take care of it. It will all be okay soon."

Ben tries to grab my hand, but I step out of his reach. "Lauren, what are you going to do?"

"What I always do. I'm going to fix it." Before he can protest, I turn and run out of the restaurant, praying I still have time.

BEN

My truck idles as I sit in Lauren's driveway staring at her dark house. Where can she have gone? It's been over an hour since she left me standing at the bar. I really screwed up by not following her immediately. No. I really screwed up by saying I didn't want her to stay and have a drink with me. I did. But...Birthday Boy was there, and she predicted the future right in front of me. And the restaurant my parents met at was the same one she met him at. I just needed one minute to ground myself, but she took off before I got the chance.

"Dammit." My hand hits the steering wheel.

I check my phone for the millionth time for any reply to my repeated calls and texts.

Nothing.

Please call me. Let me apologize for being an ass.

The look in that guy's eyes when she spoke to him was complete and utter confusion. He had no idea who she was. And what was she spouting about meeting Kelsey? I let out the breath I've been holding. I need a drink.

The parking lot at Grayson's is almost full. Two months ago, we would have been lucky to have had four cars in the lot, but that was before Lauren. Before she waltzed in with her notebook full of brilliant ideas and her beautiful smile and turned my world inside out.

How many ways can I keep screwing this up?

A wave of sound hits me as I walk in the door. Good crowd. I make my way to the bar.

Dex flags me down to the waitress station. "Hey, man. Thought you might come in tonight."

"Why? Do you need help?" I look around. I don't see any of the customers looking for assistance or not being helped.

"No, we're good. The new girl is getting better—only spilled two drinks tonight." He laughs. "Lauren left this for you."

What?

He hands me her notebook. It's tied with a ribbon.

I slide onto a stool close to the wall and as far away from the next person as I can.

Lauren's notebook. Shit. I pull on the sheet of paper sticking out of the middle.

Ben,

I'm sorry about tonight. I had a plan. Meet Matthew, help him find his way to a happier future, and then try and find my own happy ending, but the look in your eyes told me that I'd already ruined any chance for that.

I'm sorry about all the pain I've caused. If you don't believe anything I've said, please believe that.

Before I go and before you forget you even knew me, I wanted to tell you my fourth favorite thing.

Waking up in your arms. I've been looking for a place to feel secure all my life. I thought security meant having a lucrative career and a home I didn't have to leave. Turns out what I needed was you. You make me feel safe and secure no matter where we are.

Thank you for everything. I thought I was helping you, but I think you may have helped me more.

I Love You.

Lauren

The ribbon falls off the notebook and I place the letter back inside.

"I'm gonna head upstairs for a minute," I yell to Dex. He nods and mixes another drink.

My own drink comes out of the bottom drawer of my desk. I pour myself a Scotch and lean back in my chair.

She's gone.

For a moment tonight I thought she and I were going to be reliving my parents' story. Then he showed up, and I couldn't get the thought of her leaving with him out of my head even after she proved again that she knows the future.

"Why couldn't you wait and tell me that instead of running away?" I whisper to myself, rereading the letter.

Why didn't I tell you I believed you? Now I don't know where you are and...

That bracelet.

I slam my drink on my desk.

"No." She said she could fix it. She's going to throw it in. The sinking feeling overwhelms me. If she throws it in and goes back, will I even remember her?

LAUREN

I walk up the steps of Ben's house. Everything looks the same as it did the last time I was here, but everything has changed. My footsteps are even, like a soldier headed for battle. One foot in front of the other with purpose and unwavering commitment to the cause.

The door swings open wide. Ben's in the same jeans and navy dress shirt from earlier, but now his shirt is untucked and half unbuttoned.

"Lauren." He steps out onto the porch and wraps me in a tight hug, releasing me quickly.

The unexpected embrace leaves me off balance. "Hi."

"I was afraid..." He pulls my arm toward him and twists the bracelet on my arm. He lets out a breath. "Still there. I thought you went to throw it in the waterfall."

"That was the plan."

"Why?"

So many answers to that question, I could fill a book. He watches me like he's trying to read my mind. And if I have any chance, I need to tell him everything.

"Because of you. Because of Ollie and Eve..." Tears threaten to escape, but I came to fight and that means no time to cry. "Because of Matthew…Because of my dad… Because of me."

"Care to explain?"

"I went to see my dad. You were right. I needed to talk to him. I'm not ready to forgive him yet, but maybe someday. And if I go back then he'll be gone, and I'll never get the chance to know him."

Ben opens the door wide and steps back inside. I follow and as the door shuts, his arm turns me around to face him.

"And Ollie and Eve?" he asks.

"They didn't make it last time, and I know I can figure out what went wrong and fix them. They're meant to be together. I know they are."

"You can't fix everyone. You can't take on everyone's burdens."

"I have to try."

"And Matthew?" I can tell saying his name is painful, but he does it almost without wincing.

"I learned so much about him that he didn't share with me the first time, which is probably my fault. He knew my position on life, and he followed my lead toward security, not happiness. It's not fair for me to take that away from him again. This time he can choose his own path."

"And you?"

"And me." I shake my head and chuckle. "Well, it turns out I'm not always right, and I kinda like life that isn't so planned out. If I go back, I don't know who I'll be, and I don't want to be the old me again."

"And me?" His voice is thick, the words coming out slowly as if he isn't sure if he wants to know.

"You're the reason I almost went back."

He takes a quick step back like I've slapped him in the face.

I rush to add, "I don't know if my coming back hurt or helped you. I handled everything wrong."

My feet and I stay firmly planted in front of him, waiting on his response.

His head dips, and he reclaims the space in front of me. "But you stayed?"

I look up into his eyes. "You were right. I am selfish. I could have gone back and saved you from all this, but then I wouldn't have met you. So, I decided to stay even though it would cause us both pain. I figured you needed to know I'm willing to risk it all for you. At some point, do you think...do you think you can forgive me?"

"I—"

"Wait, I'm not done, and I need to say it all before I lose my nerve. Maybe you can give me another chance?" He doesn't move. I'm not even sure he's breathing, so I continue. "I came here without a plan, so I have no idea how this will turn out or if you even want things to turn out. But the thing is, I'm in love with you. I had this whole plan laid out. I'd build a nest egg and find Matthew and he and I would rebuild our life faster with all the knowledge I had of the future." Ben straightens his back.

Ben's face is unreadable. Since the moment I looked up, he has stared into my eyes with his jaw locked in place.

"All that to ask, would you go out on a date with me tomorrow night?"

"No." His answer is quiet and concise. My heart may have stopped beating. The blood in my body and everything else has slowed as if time itself has stopped. No. I knew deep down the possibility existed he would just say no, but I had hoped he would at least think about it.

Tears sting my eyes, but I bat them away. "Oh. I..."

"You didn't let me finish."

Don't cry. This is your fault; he doesn't have to see your tears.

"I have to work tomorrow night. But I'm free now. What'd you have in mind?"

Time starts again as if someone has turned on the switch. The wall holding my tears in bursts along with a smile on my face. I wipe the tears away with both hands.

"Um…I don't know. I didn't make any plans." *Shit. This is why I like to think things through. I thought I had time to figure that out.*

The side of his lip curls up. "No plans, eh?"

"Nope. Thought I'd try something new." I take a step toward him, watching his eyes dip to my lips.

"And then I met you and my plan started to unravel. My hopes and dreams changed without my permission. And I fell in love with you. With you I didn't have to be anything but myself. I didn't have to have a plan for the future. With you anything could be possible. The first time around I took the wrong path." I lock my eyes on his. "You're my path. The first time, I missed it. Twice. I've been given another chance, and I almost missed it again because I still couldn't allow myself to see that there was another possibility. This time I see it, and I choose you."

"Any plans right now?" he says as he inches closer.

I swallow hard. "Nope."

Ben wraps his arms around my waist and pulls me tight against him.

"Then how about you let me make you a late dinner, and we can figure it out together?"

My arms slide around his neck and I pull him to me, answering his question with a kiss. Figuring out the rest of our lives together sounds like the best plan ever.

ACKNOWLEDGMENTS

Unlike Lauren, I'm not great at setting goals and making action item lists. Part of me never believed I would get far enough in my writing to actually publish a book, unlike all of the people I'm about to thank. Everyone listed here and a dozen more have supported my dream and encouraged me to finish the book and put it out into the world for others to read. Thank you for reading my words and allowing me to share my story.

A special thank you

To my husband and daughter for never making me feel guilty for spending time on something I love.

To My mom and dad for always supporting me.

To my best friend, Heidi Leerkamp, for listening to all my crazy story ideas.

To Brenda Lowder for reading all my words, meeting me to talk about all the writing things and for pushing me to publish the book.

To the Georgia Romance Writers for helping me navigate the learning curve of new writer to published author. Without Nicki Salcedo reading the first draft of my first book and encouraging me to keep going and for asking what what else I was working on this book wouldn't be possible. Thanks to Sia Huff, Susan Carlisle and countless others who have read my words and given me feedback, I appreciate you all.

To all my friends and family who didn't laugh when I said I wanted to be a writer, but instead asked when it would be ready to read - Thank you! It means the world to me that you support me.

To all the readers. Thanks for giving my book a chance. I hope you loved Lauren and Ben's journey as much as I did.

ABOUT THE AUTHOR

ABOUT KP TURNER

KP Turner is a midwestern girl transplanted to the south who loves strawberries, chocolate and reasons to stay home. She has one dog, one kid and one husband and she loves to watch cheesy romance with her fingers on the fast-forward button. Someday she'll learn to appreciate wine and coffee like her writer friends, but until then she'll write her stories of love with just a little touch of magic.

kpturnerauthor.com

Made in the USA
Columbia, SC
09 November 2022